THE COMPELLING ALLURE OF GIDEON GRIEVE

Book One Of The Gideon Grieve Trilogy

David Walpole

Copyright © 2024 David Walpole

All rights reserved

The characters and events portrayed in this book are fictitious. Any similarity to real persons, living or dead, is coincidental and not intended by the author.

No part of this book may be reproduced, or stored in a retrieval system, or transmitted in any form or by any means, electronic, mechanical, photocopying, recording, or otherwise, without express written permission of the publisher.

ISBN:9798883244666

CONTENTS

Title Page
Copyright
1	1
2	11
3	19
4	29
5	34
6	50
7	58
8	68
9	80
10	87
11	98
12	106
13	117
14	124
15	140
16	149
17	156
18	166
19	174

20	182
21	187
22	193
23	205
24	214
25	219
26	224
27	230
Books By This Author	243

1

The first time I saw Gideon Grieve he was wearing faded jeans, a Bob Dylan T-shirt and was caressing Margaret Thatcher's left breast. After wrestling with her for thirty seconds, he hadn't controlled her. He looked around, swaggered to the Communist Party candidate's desk. He handed over a five-pound note, then came away with a hardback copy of *Das Kapital*. He laid it, face down, on the base of the swaying, life-sized cardboard cutout of the Prime Minister.

'That's better.' He lovingly flicked some imaginary dandruff off the shoulders of Thatcher's sky-blue jacket. 'We couldn't have the Iron Lady falling around like some sozzled socialist, could we?'

A group of students, all wide-eyed first-year girls, approached the polling booth. He made a beeline for them.

'Hello girls, I'm Gideon Grieve, I take it you're here to vote for me.'

The girls bowed their heads, put hands over their mouths and giggled as they crept towards the booth.

That incident should have revealed Gideon's character to me, his politics, pragmatism, charm, but most of all, his narcissism. But the only one to register was his politics: his beauty blinded me to the rest. With his sleek sun-kissed complexion and shoulder-length bohemian hair, streaked with golden highlights, he shimmered as he moved. And when he was still, set against the grey breezeblock walls of the Lower Common Room, he shone like a tabernacle in a cathedral. But it was his eyes that would blind me to his character.

They turned to me as he'd decided I was his next target. 'Hello, can I have your vote?'

I was certain he was kidding. Surely the badge pinned to my chest, showing a florid red fist punching the sky, was an obvious indication of my political allegiance, even for a Thatcher-loving Tory. 'I've just voted for the Socialist Worker.'

'Oh, why waste your vote on a lentil-eating lesbian? We Conservatives are much more fun.'

To break away from his intense stare, I looked at Bryony. She was sitting next to Helga, her girlfriend, in front of a large black-and-white poster of Leon Trotsky. They were poring over the latest *Socialist Worker*. With their matching pink cropped haircuts bowed at Leon's chest level, they'd inadvertently given him a pair of pink, very fuzzy breasts. What made it even more odd, they'd placed Trotsky directly opposite the Thatcher cutout, so Maggie appeared to be admiring Leon's cleavage.

'Politics isn't meant to be fun,' I said.

'It is when you're in power.'

Next to Thatcher was a desk with one pile of Tory leaflets and another of photos of her staring with soulless eyes into the camera. Between them was a sheet of paper, blank, apart from the heading written in smudged blue felt tip, "MY VOTES!!!".

'Election not going so well?' I pointed at the paper.

'It's still early. I'm very hopeful.' Gideon picked up a leaflet. 'Read this... for next time.'

I didn't want to take it, but Gideon grinned and stared at me again. His deep-set eyes seemed to know more about me than I knew myself. Blue sapphires glinting in the sun. Kind, thoughtful, exquisitely, dangerously beautiful. In an instant my tranquil life, well, to be honest, my becalmed life, turned turbulent, as if I'd just stepped off a jetty onto a dinghy tossed on a roiling sea. Whilst Gideon remained on solid ground, staring implacably at me. And even though I was four feet away, I was being drawn, almost sucked towards him, as if he had his own gravitational pull.

To break free from his stare, I took the leaflet. 'Thanks.'

'Do you think this T-shirt's putting people off?' Gideon stretched the hem, making Dylan look even more miserable than usual. 'It was Dylan or Martin Luther King. Do you think a dead black martyr would've been more appealing?'

I reacted in a way I never did on first meeting someone, or with anyone, ever.

'I'll tell you what's putting people off. It's that bloody woman.' I jabbed my finger at Thatcher. 'And ...and'. The anger pent up since Thatcher had walked into Downing Street, and spouted, "Where there is discord, may we bring harmony...blah blah blah bullshit " and had spent the next two years doing the exact opposite, welled up inside me. I picked up one of the photos and ripped it in two. 'This bitch has put three million on the dole and wants to close this university.'

Even as I ripped the picture, I asked myself, "What the hell are you doing?" Did I rip it because he'd unsettled me so much with just a look and with so little effort, or because part of me sensed how much he was going to change and dominate my life, and kicked against it? Whatever the reason, it didn't work because all he said was, 'Maggie wouldn't do that.'

'She bloody would.'

'She promised Daddy she wouldn't.'

With one-half of Thatcher flapping in each hand, I tried to come up with a response. But the shock of discovering I was speaking to someone who knew the Prime Minister left me speechless.

'And I believe her.' Gideon held out his hand.

I pressed the two pieces of ripped Maggie into it and turned away.

'Actually, I was introducing myself. I'm Gideon.' He laid the two halves of the photo on the desk and held his hand out again. 'Call me Gid, or git....if you prefer.'

I was still fuming and wanted to leave. But his grin and joke drew me back.

'Mark.'

He had a firm, confident handshake. The sort I assumed they taught at Eton between lessons in superficial charm and corporate tax evasion. I don't know why I thought Gideon was an Eton boy, as I'd never met one, and the University of East Anglia wasn't somewhere Eton boys usually ended up. He exuded such an overwhelming sense of entitlement; I assumed he couldn't be anything else.

'Delighted to meet you.'

'Do people actually call you git?'

'Only those who know me really well.' He looked across the Common Room at a group of students being ushered to vote for the Labour candidate. He sighed. 'You know, you could be right. Maybe this is a lost cause.'

Bryony and Helga tossed away the *Socialist Worker*. They stood and glared at me with such intensity I could almost see the thought bubble "Class Traitor" flashing above their shaven heads.

'I'm bloody bored. Would you like to chat? Blue rosette wearing, strictly voluntary.' Gideon pointed to the two chairs behind his desk.

Bryony and Helga's fingers twitched. They had such visceral anger about everything in Thatcher's Britain. When their fingers started twitching I got nervous. I feared they were about to take out the ice picks I'd always assumed they'd secreted amongst the folds of their matching, handsewn, pink calico dungarees. Then impale them in the skull of the nearest "patriachichcal capitalist". Which at this moment, in their Trotskyist eyes, would have been me.

'I better not,' I said.

'Okay. I understand.'.

Speaking to Gideon caused my heart to thump so hard, I thought my eardrums were about to burst. I needed to get away, not only because he was a Maggie lover, but I had to get off the heaving dinghy before I plunged under the water. 'See you around.'

'I hope so,' he said.

My first year at university had been a lonely one. During the fleeting enthusiasm of Fresher's Week, I tried new things. Looking back, I realise most of the activities I attempted were ruinously macho. At archery, I struggled to even pull back the string of the bow. So many turned up at the Fencing Club. The equipment had to be rationed. After spending ten minutes sweating and wincing in a threadbare chest protector as my opponent gleefully lunged and prodded me with an épée, I put up my hands. l told him I needed the toilet, then didn't go back. When I saw the Rowing Club guys heading into the changing room, all nut-cracking biceps and thunder-clapping farts, I didn't even bother to follow.

The only club I attended more than once had been the Socialist Workers Students Group. My neat and always ironed brown cords and lumberjack shirts stood out against the sweaty denim and creased T-shirts. All the shirts had some logo, "CND", "Anti-Nazi League," or urgent exhortations to, "Reclaim The Night" or "Fuck The Tories". Facial piercings, Trotsky tattoos, and florid pink cropped hair were the preferred, almost obligatory adornments. When the group wanted to protest at a Norwich City Council meeting (Norwich was Labour-run) over a modest rent increase, I'd argued we shouldn't protest as the real enemy was Thatcher. There were moments during the argument when I was sure I spotted Helga's fingers twitching. In the interests of my skull, I relented and never returned.

After that, I spent all my time attending lectures, and seminars or studying in the library. So during my first year, whilst others partied, I lost myself in my studies. There had been times when, alone in my room, I'd cried.

For my second year, I decided things had to change. So after I'd said goodbye to Gideon, I looked at a poster advertising forthcoming concerts; Killing Joke, Q-Tips, and U2. I didn't like the first two bands, and I'd never heard of U2, but they were being supported by Altered Images, who last year had released "Happy Birthday": hands down my favourite single of 1981.

Tickets were three pounds. Pricey. But I couldn't wallow in my room for another year. I thought in a big boisterous concert crowd, I wouldn't feel self-conscious about being on my own. And there were bound to be girls, so I bought a ticket.

To boost my chances of catching girls' eyes, for the first time, I'd gone out with the top three buttons of my lumberjack shirt undone. I strode into the Common Room uncharacteristically confident I'd be leaving with a girl. But when all the girls were either wrapped around boys or giggling with friends, my confidence evaporated.

I stood at the back and sipped my beer as conversations and flirtations happened in front of me. Eventually, I decided I was wasting my time, and being invisible in a big crowd, I felt even more alone. I headed to the exit, but when I heard the opening bars of "Happy Birthday", I stopped. I forgot my sadness and moved closer to the stage. I joined in with the crowd as they sang along with Clare Grogan. For the first time in my student life, I felt part of something, part of the crowd. But when the singing stopped, and Altered Images left the stage, my elation evaporated. The crowd dispersed, and I was alone on the beer-stained floor. I'd seen what I'd come for, and nothing could beat the "Happy Birthday" moment. Tired, deflated, alone and, what was worse, appeared doomed to remain so.

As I was walking out, I saw Gideon sitting on the floor next to the spot where the Maggie cutout had been standing. He was sipping beer from a plastic beaker. It had been six days since the election, and I wondered if he'd been there all that time, drowning his sorrows (he'd received six votes, compared to the winning Labour candidate's a hundred and fifty-eight. Even Bryony had somehow managed to gather twelve votes.) I sighed as I remembered the encounter. Brief as it was, it had been the friendliest chat I'd had the whole time I'd been at university. I returned to my spot at the back and watched. Nobody joined him. Which puzzled me. He was the sort of boy I imagined would have girls all over him. When the crowd returned from the bar, I lost sight of him and decided to leave.

As I was nearing the exit, U2 bounced on stage, the crowd erupted, the drum beat...

Bono roared, "This is Gloria... TWO...THREE...FOUR."

When the guitar cut through the air, electricity zapped through my body—welding me to the spot. Every drumbeat thumped against my ribcage. Bono's voice, yearning with plaintive anger, spoke only to me. I pushed my way through the crowd. Determined to get as close to the stage as possible. The elbows to the ribs didn't stop me. Eventually, I reached it. Bono strutted so close I could have stretched and touched the hem of his jeans. Mesmerising, intense, angry. He gave me strength. As he sang the first line of "I Will Follow," he flicked his head forward. An arc of sweat from the tips of his hair curled above the audience. I needed to feel, to touch that sweat. To have it fall on my face like warm rain. So I jumped towards it, but as the sweat was about to touch my skin, my head clashed against something.

'Shit!' I rubbed my forehead. Gideon was standing next to me, doing the same.

He grinned and shouted, 'Oh hello again. It's me, the terrible Tory.'

'That bloody hurt.'

'Isn't this great?' He put his arm around my shoulder. 'If we bounce together, we won't clash.'

I put my arm around his waist, and we bounced like kids on a trampoline for the rest of the concert.

When U2 left and the lights came on, I stared at the stage. I wanted to savour every last second. It had been like the "Happy Birthday" moment stretched for ninety minutes. My arm, which had been around Gideon's waist the whole time, ached. But it didn't matter. I'd been, we'd been, somewhere else, away from the Lower Common Room, away from the campus, away from Thatcher's Britain, somewhere ruled by music, togetherness, and the power of Bono's voice.

Gideon said, 'Weren't they bloody amazing?'

'Incredible.'

'They're from Dublin.'

'Really? I only came for Altered Images. I was leaving until—'

'Until what?'

Until I saw you.

'Nothing. I've never heard anything like it.'

We stood transfixed, staring at the stage as roadies removed the equipment. When Gideon closed his eyes, I asked, 'What the hell are you doing?'

'I'm imagining going back and reliving that all over again.'

A roady shouted, 'Hey loverboys! Bugger off!'

We grinned at each other, then ran into The Square. Gideon pointed to the concrete steps. 'Can we sit here for a few minutes? My ears are buzzing.'

'Sure. How's your head?'

'Recovering.' Gideon rubbed his forehead. 'And yours?'

'No damage, I guess after centuries of being bludgeoned by your class, my family has evolved very thick skulls.'

Gideon gave a horrified look. But when he noticed my grin, he laughed. 'That's funny.'

'Sorry about the election.'

'No problem, we live to fight another day.' Gideon lowered himself onto one of the concrete flagstones, the muscles of his thighs almost bursting the hem of his jeans as he sat cross-legged. 'How the hell did your Socialist Worker comrade get twelve votes?'

'She's not my comrade,' I said.

'But I thought you were a rabid socialist.'

'I am, but I didn't campaign, just gave her my vote. They're not what I expected.'

'What do you mean?'

'They're all dad-hating middle-class fellow travellers who just want to kick against everything. Once they graduate, I'm sure they'll all become chartered accountants.'

'Even the lentil-eating lesbians?'

I laughed. 'Yes, even them.'

'You know U2 are appearing in Colchester tomorrow night. We could enjoy a repeat,' Gideon said.

'Really?' I was tempted.

'It isn't far.'

'I do know where bloody Colchester is.'

'Sorry.'

'It wouldn't be the same.'

'Why not?'

'We'll never experience a U2 concert for the first time, ever again. We'll never have the same feeling of being stunned by those first bars and blown away. It's kind of sad and wonderful, don't you think?'

'I guess. Weird name though,' he said.

'I kinda like it.'

'You know for a rabid socialist you're not bad.'

'And you're okay…for a Maggie fanatic.'

Gideon laughed. 'You live on campus?'

'Yep, in Waveney Terrace.' I looked around to get my bearings, then pointed over Gideon's shoulder.

'That awful crooked breeze-block building that looks like a derailed train,' he said.

'That's the one. And it has acres of carpet, which if you stare at it slightly squinty, you can see thousands of tiny Hitler silhouettes.'

'Jesus,' he said. 'I live in Cathedral Close.'

That was the moment I realised I was speaking with someone far richer than anyone I'd spoken to before. The houses on The Close were all at least two hundred years old, expensive, with neat rose-filled gardens.

'Look, it's too late to go for a drink. Politically, we're chalk and cheese. But a rabid Socialist who gets blown away by U2 must have some redeeming features.'

'Wow! Thanks!'

'So would you like to meet for lunch or a drink?'

It had been so long since anyone had invited me anywhere for anything. Maybe the buzzing from the concert had affected my hearing.

'So? Do you want to break bread with the enemy?'

'Yes, sure.'

'Excellent. Come round for tea tomorrow? Around three, three-thirty?'

'Thank you, that's nice of you.' I was angry at making such a feeble middle-class comment, so compensated by saying, 'Should I wear my Tory blue cummerbund?'

'What?' Gideon frowned. 'Oh, I see. Joke. Very good. All my cummerbunds are at the cleaners. So come as you are, or put on your very best Chairman Mao jacket.'

I sniggered.

Gideon jumped up. 'Okay, I've recovered. So until tomorrow. You can't miss my house. It's the garden full of blue rose bushes.'

'Of course it is. Did Maggie plant them herself?'

'Absolutely.' He bowed slow and deep like an actor taking a curtain call. When he disappeared around a corner my world became empty, silent, and dark. All I wanted to do was follow.

2

One of the few pleasures I'd had during my first year at UEA happened on fine days, during the spring and summer terms. I'd take a book to Chapelfield Gardens, where I'd lie on the grass studying, soothed by the sweet aroma of melted caramel, toffee and chocolate drifting from the Rowntree Macintosh factory. When I got off the bus on my way to Gideon's the smell made me wonder whether I should take something. He hadn't said anything, but I wanted to make a good impression. So I popped into Tesco.

I wandered up and down the aisles. But couldn't decide what to buy. Chocolates were for Valentine's Day, Christmas or kids. Flowers were girly. Wine, as well as being pricey, was also risky. Gideon was undoubtedly a connoisseur who'd sneer at whatever I bought. Eventually, I went to the biscuit section. I picked up a packet of Jaffa Cakes, but decided the combination of Genoise sponge, chocolate and orange jam was a bit much, a bit showy, a bit, well, bourgeois. I put it back and went to the other extreme, the *Rich Tea.* Dry, crunchy, also dunkable. Do Tories dunk? Probably not. I decided the Rich Tea was too spartan. I didn't want Gideon to think I was some sort of crazy Puritan. In the end, I settled for the Switzerland of the biscuit aisle, the Mcvitie's Chocolate Digestive. Dunkable yet chocolaty, without the decadent overindulgence of Jaffa Cake jam.

I wanted to make a good impression because I needed a friend. The long days and nights spent on my own were bringing me down. My studies were thriving, but there were times I wanted to chat with someone. But why Gideon? He was a rich Tory. I should despise him, but the way we'd bonded at the U2 concert, so quickly, so easily, it was as if we'd known each other for years. I sensed there was more to him than good looks, blue rosettes and an alarming devotion to the Blessed Maggie. I wasn't sure what, whatever it was, it was drawing me to him.

As I approached Cathedral Close, my chest tightened. My heartbeat became faster. Similar to when I was waiting for my A-Level results. It was puzzling because the contents of that envelope were going to determine the rest of my life, this was just a cup of tea with a bumptious Tory. I ambled through The Close, panicking, as all the gardens looked similar. But then I saw a garden full of neatly trimmed blue roses. It had to be his. It was a two-storey flint-fronted house with sash windows: the sort of place the BBC uses in lavish costume dramas. I took a deep breath, pushed open the gate, then shuffled up the cobblestone path. I hesitated before pulling the doorbell. When I did, a few seconds later, there were clumping footsteps.

Gideon dragged open the heavy wooden door. 'You came!'

'Of course I came.'

'So often people make promises, then break them.'

'Not me.' I wasn't aware that I had made a promise, but I didn't want to argue.

'Come in, come in.' Gideon motioned me inside.

The floor creaked. The walls of the dark and narrow corridor were hung with watercolours of the Norfolk Broads. Fearing I might knock one, I scrunched my shoulders and bent forward. Every piece of furniture and picture seemed to have been in the house since the eighteenth century.

'Come on through.' Gideon showed me into the front room. 'Mind your head.'

I ducked to avoid the oak beam that ran the width of the lounge.

'I thought it was getting a bit nippy, so I started a fire. I hope that's okay.' Gideon pointed to a hearth where a log fire was burning.

'It's fine. This place is so cosy.'
'It is, isn't it?'
'It must be expensive.'
'Not really.'

Expensive clearly meant something very different to Gideon. I was dying to ask how much rent he was paying or how much the house cost. I was sure the rent on the place must be at least as much a month as I spent on everything. But I didn't want to give him the impression I was obsessed with money.

Below a heavy blue brocade curtain was a table with a three-tiered cake stand crammed with sandwiches, scones, and pastries. Next to it was a plate with the richest-looking fruitcake I'd ever seen. I was relieved I'd kept the Mcvitie's biscuits in my rucksack. They'd look so cheap. 'You didn't have to go to so much trouble.'

'It's no trouble. Mummy maintains they don't have proper food in Norfolk, so every week she airlifts me a hamper from Fortnums.'

'Airlifts?'

'Well, Royal Mail.' Gideon pulled a walnut chair from under the table. 'Please, make yourself comfortable.'

I slid my rucksack under my chair and lowered myself onto the embroidered cushion.

'Sorry, I should've offered to take that, and your jacket.' Gideon reached out.

'It's okay. I can hang it over the chair.'

'You will not. It probably contravenes some Church of England by law.' Gideon took my jacket into the hallway. When he came back he said, 'Darjeeling, Lapsang Souchong, or good old Earl Grey?'

'What?'

'What tea would you like to imbibe?'

I felt like saying, "Whichever tastes most like Tetley."

'Or would you like some bubbly?'

'Champagne? For tea!'

'It came with the hamper, so why not?'

'Thanks, but no thanks.'

I regretted coming. I didn't want to touch anything in case I broke it. And I pictured Helga and Bryony sharpening their ice picks. I'd known there was a huge wealth gap, and a massive social gulf between us. But at the U2 concert and in The Square it hadn't mattered, I hadn't noticed it. But the house, the furniture, the food, everything was screaming "Get out you don't belong here!" And Gideon rattling off those teas, teas I'd never heard of, as if they were common knowledge, just underlined I could never fit into Gideon's world. If I hadn't been so lonely, I would never have kidded myself into believing we could be friends. I thought about making excuses and leaving, or coming over all Marxist and haranguing Gideon for living in such luxury when there were three million on the dole. I'd make him so angry he'd kick me out.

The awkward silence was broken when a log in the fire split and fell into the embers.

'I think I should go.'

'Why?'

'I—'

'Did I do something wrong?' Behind the intense dangerous beautiful stare was, I thought, some desperation. His fingers tapped the table. For the first time, I realised he was nervous too.

'Gideon, if I'm being honest, I don't know any of those teas. I've never tasted champagne, and when you invited me for tea, I thought it would be out of a mug. With biscuits like this.' I leaned over and pulled the Mcvities out of my rucksack.

Gideon's eyes widened. Then he smiled. 'Oh, I love those. I'll get a plate.'

'You're missing the point. This isn't me.' I waved my hand over the table. 'I'm sorry. I don't want to sound ungrateful after you've gone to so much trouble.'

'Honestly, it was no trouble. I only had to open the hamper.'

'You know what I mean.'

Gideon shook his head. 'I'm such a blithering idiot.' His lips were trembling. 'I just thought…no, damn, I didn't think. I just assumed when I said tea, it meant the same to you as it does to me.'

'Gideon, really, it's okay.'

'No, it isn't. I should have been more sensitive. Look, can I be honest?' He moved the cake stand aside and looked directly into my eyes. 'I…I'm so bloody lonely here.'

'Really?'

'I have no friends.'

'But the university is full of students all desperate to meet. You're handsome. You like U2, you…you…' I smiled to myself. I'd spent most of the first year too terrified to go out, but here I was offering advice as if I were some sort of party-going socialite.

'What's so funny?' Gideon said.

'Nothing.'

'When people hear my accent, I can see from their eyes, they're making all sorts of assumptions.'

'Such as?'

'That I'm a rich Tory boy—'

'Which you are.'

'I know. But they see some unfeeling buffoon whose daddy pays for everything. And yes, they're right, he does. I know I'm damn lucky. Many would kill to swap. But when people decide they know all about me by the way I pronounce "house" it hurts, really hurts.'

'I see.'

'They stop listening. Either that or their eyes light up when they know I'm rich.'

'But I made all sorts of assumptions about you.'

'You spoke to me like I was a human being like you didn't care that I was rich. Some things you said were bloody rude.'

'Such as.'

'The skull bashing, but it made me laugh. And you listened, and nobody else has.'

'Gideon, you'll find people...' I paused as I thought of the best words to use. 'From your class.'

'You mean like the five who voted for me? I'm sure they did so by mistake. Most of "my class," as you put it, are either at one of the top universities or they're slumming around Europe.'

'Why aren't you doing that?'

'I'm so thick, even Daddy's money couldn't get me into a top university.'

I couldn't help smiling at Gideon's misguided modesty. 'Surely nobody can be that thick.'

'There you go again. You just don't bloody care, and I like that.'

'So why aren't you slumming around Europe?'

'Daddy's exact words were, "I'm not paying for you to go rogering all over Europe. It's university or the army." I'm a coward so I chose university. Damn! I wanted to make this special for you, but I've messed it up.'

'Don't be such an idiot, of course you haven't. Look, this is all new to me. I'm nervous too. I mean, look at this place. This table probably cost more than all my parent's furniture. You don't need to impress me. I like you. I don't bloody know why, but I do.'

Gideon smiled. 'Really?'

'Yes, crazy I know. Maybe when we clashed heads, it did something to my brain.'

Gideon held his hand to his mouth and laughed as if he were releasing months of tension. When he'd recovered, he looked up. 'Okay, can I start again?'

I nodded.

'What tea do you want?'

'Anything tastes like Tetleys?'

Gideon snapped his fingers. 'I can go one better.' He left the room and came back with a packet of Tetley tea bags. 'Ta-da. Not mine, the maid's.'

'Obviously.' I grinned. I became more relaxed, especially when Gideon took one of the chocolate digestives.

'What are you studying?' I said.

'English Literature and Drama.'

'So I'm speaking to the next Olivier.'

'I see myself more as the devilishly handsome matinée idol. James Bond type.'

In many people that would be arrogance, but with his deep-set eyes, smooth skin, muscular build, and that magnetism, for Gideon stardom was highly likely if not inevitable.

'But Daddy wants me to get a proper job.'

'Oh, shame.'

'He said, "Study for three years but after that, you're bloody well coming to work for me".'

'Sorry to hear that.' I remembered Gideon's casual remark about Thatcher promising "Daddy" she wouldn't be closing the university. I was curious to find out more. 'What does he do?'

'He owns half the country.'

An exaggeration, obviously, but it was too early in our acquaintanceship to press him about it.

We chatted, laughed, ate and drank I'd never found it so easy to talk to anyone, and when one spoke the other listened and did not interrupt. We were both shocked when the grandfather clock chimed nine.

'Wow! Where did the time go?'

I shrugged.

'You know you're welcome to stay. I have a spare room.'

I was tempted. 'I need to get up early for a lecture. But thank you so much.'

'Lunch in the canteen tomorrow?' said Gideon.

'Oh yes. I'd love to.'

Almost out of nowhere, I'd made a friend. True, a friend who was a filthy rich Tory, but still a friend. I told myself the reason my heart raced when his eyes seared into me was because I was relieved to have made a friend. It wouldn't be until months later that I realised why my heart raced and why I almost skipped home.

3

After that, we met every day. There were no more misunderstandings like with the tea. At first, we'd arrange to meet, then after a few days, we just turned up at the places where we knew the other would be, at the times we knew they would be there. It was during our first visit to the student bar when Gideon said, 'Let's go to that.' He pointed at a poster for a student disco.

I'd only been to one. It had been during my short-lived getting out-and-about phase in Fresher's Week. I'd stood with my back pressed against the wall, sipping beer from a plastic cup. Too nervous to dance alone, too scared to approach a girl. I left before I'd finished half my drink.

'I don't know. It's not really— '

'Come on! It'll do us both good.'

If I went with him, at least I wouldn't be stuck on my own: the wall flower of all wall flowers. And perhaps being seen at a disco with such a handsome man would make girls curious about me. So I agreed to go with him.

As soon as we stepped into the disco, heads turned. Girls didn't look at Gideon, they ogled him, like he was a rock star. Something about the nighttime made him look even more stunning. At first, being noticed made me uncomfortable, as I imagined the girls were wondering, "Why the hell had that Adonis lumbered himself with such a dowdy companion?" but I reasoned being caught on the edge of Gideon's spotlight was better than being invisible, so I relaxed.

That night, two girls came and danced near us. They smiled and looked coyly at Gideon from behind their Princess Di fringes. Giggling and whispering to each other. When Gideon and I left the dance floor, they stood nearby. Gideon went over. At first, the girls were all smiles and giggles, but within a minute, they were frowning and edging away from him.

'What happened?'

'My sodding accent, as usual.'

We went to several discos, both on campus and in the city. There was only one occasion when the girl didn't look horrified or back away. She nodded and smiled at what Gideon was saying. I was pleased he'd scored as he'd been becoming increasingly frustrated. Before he left with her he came over. With a double thumbs up he exclaimed, 'Jackpot, she's deaf!'

But that night of triumph was his only success. All the other times he was rejected.

One night he said, 'Marky, unless we find another deaf girl I'm going to go crazy. I need sex.'

'So you want me to contact the RNID to see if they run discos?'

He laughed. 'No Marky, but you have to help me.'

'What? How?'

'Speak to the girls.'

'How can I? I'm bloody shy and don't have your looks.'

'Hey, don't do yourself down, you scrub up pretty well.'

'Thanks. But—'

'I don't know how to speak to these fillies.'

'Surely at school, you chatted to girls.'

'It was a Catholic boarding school, the only females were fat cooks or old nuns. At your comp you must've chatted to girls all the time.'

Although I'd attended a mixed Comprehensive School, I'd never chatted up a girl. I could talk to them. I was a good listener. But flirting, no. Gideon was the sexiest man I'd ever seen. And I could tell by the girls' eyes they were feeling the same gravitational pull towards him I'd experienced. And yet they were put off by him. I didn't understand it.

'I'd love to help, but I haven't spoken to girls much, not in that way.'

'Come on, anything.'

I shook my head trying to think. 'Oh yes.' I raised my finger when I thought of something. 'If you stopped referring to them as "fillies" that would be a start.'

'Really?'

'They're not at your father's stud farm waiting to be impregnated by the latest Derby winner.'

'How did you know Daddy owns a stud farm?'

'Shit, I was joking.'

'Anyway, don't call them fillies. Good, great stuff. Anything else?'

'Talk to them like they're human beings. And listen. Don't go on about yourself all the time.'

Gideon shook his head and his eyes widened as if I'd just told him the Earth was about to fall into the sun.

'But my life is so much more interesting than theirs. Do you know, most of these girls have never tasted foie gras, some don't even know what it is.'

'Well nor do I.'

'But you're different, you're Mark. You're interesting. And I'm not trying to get you into bed. Foie gras is something these fillies...sorry...girls, should be able to talk about. Especially if they want to hook a good husband.'

'Did you just say that?'

'Say what?'

'Nothing. Look, Gideon, I know Thatcher and her chums are trying to take us back to the nineteenth century, but these days, women have the vote.'

'That was a big mistake.'

For a moment, I thought Gideon was being serious, then I saw his grin.

'They want careers, and don't want to rely on some rich husband.'

'Not even a husband as bloody rich as me?'

'No!'

Gideon shook his head. 'No matter how hard I try, I always say something offensive. And Christ Marky. I bloody need sex. Please, help me, be my wingman.'

I wanted to ask what he'd done about sex before UEA, then thought it was better not to know. It would only make me feel even more forlorn about my lack of sexual experience. 'But what do I say?'

'Just tell them what a splendid chap I am.'

I certainly wouldn't be using the word "chap" or, indeed, "splendid".

'I know physically the girls are smitten by me. I can see lust burning in their eyes. But as soon as I open my mouth. It all goes to shit. Just make them see I'm not some rich idiot.'

'Tricky.'

'Thanks. Love you too. Marky, people *adore* you.'

'Do they?' I'd never noticed. I always thought they tolerated me because they were reassured by my blandness.

'They'll listen to you.'

Had he known how much time I'd spent hiding in my room before I'd met him, Gideon wouldn't have said that. 'I don't know.'

'Tell them you're my best friend.' Gideon turned his eyes to me. 'Which I assume you are.'

I nodded.

'And that I'm a good guy, just crap at chatting to girls. They'll understand that.'

'I suppose I can tell them you're a Tory and I'm a Commie, but I still like you.'

'Yes…yes very good. See, I knew you'd be good at this. So will you do it?'

I agreed. Not only because I wanted to help him, but I was worried if I didn't, he'd find someone who would.

The first time we tried this strategy was at Ritzy's a disco in Tombland, not far from Gideon's house. As usual, he attracted a lot of coy glances. This time, when he went over to speak to a couple of girls, he dragged me along with him. He made an impressive start by asking their names, Tracey and Carol. And what they did, both secretaries for Norfolk County Council Social Services. But then he started to boast about how his dad probably owned much of Norfolk and was a majority shareholder in the company that brewed the *Oranjebooms* the girls were drinking. The girls looked sceptical and began to look beyond him at other guys. He stared at me with a look that screamed, "Please help me!" I had no idea how to dig him out of the hole he'd already dug, so I just shrugged. Before I could say anything, he asked the girls.

'What's it like working with Norfolk nut-jobs?'

I could see from Gideon's eyes even he realised he'd made a mistake.

He said, 'More *Oranjebooms*?' As he headed to the bar, he whispered to me, 'Please clear this shit up.'

Tracey asked, 'Why are you friends with such a fucking twat?'

'It's just the surface. Believe me, underneath, he's really sweet.'

'That's very hard to believe,' said Carol.

'It's just his upbringing. He doesn't know how to speak to girls.'

'You don't say.'

'But you have to admit, he's the sexiest guy here.'

The girls nodded. 'But he's so bloody rude,' said Carol.

'Here's your chance to show him how to be nice. Reform him. Make him a better person.'

'I think he's beyond saving.'

'Look, I'm a Socialist Worker, he's a bloody Thatcherite Tory. I should loathe him, not give him the time of day. But he's my best friend. Doesn't that tell you something?'

The girls whispered to each other behind their hands.

'And look, he's bringing more drinks.'

'Two more *Oranjebooms*.' Gideon grinned as he gave

the girls their drinks.

Tracey and Carol stayed. As they drank, they became more relaxed. They giggled and towards the end of the night, when the DJ played "Endless Love", Gideon asked Carol for a slow dance. She accepted. During their dance, Gideon and Carol snogged. As they spun past me he gave me a double thumbs up.

'Thank you old man.' Gideon said at lunch the next day. 'Carol told me what you said, and it persuaded her to stay.'

'Was it a good night?'

'It was a fucking wonderful night. And did you, you know, with whatever her name was?'

'Tracey. No.'

'Why not?'

'Not my type.'

Over the months we continued with the same strategy. He did learn to be less obnoxious, and I had to do fewer firefighting operations. However, none of his encounters ever amounted to more than a one-night stand.

One day I asked him, 'Don't you want to find someone more permanent?'

'Look,' he said, 'I decided during that election I wasn't going to find a suitable wife here. They're all like you said. Independent, free-thinking lefties. Bloody Simone de Beauvoir and sodding Germaine Greer have a lot to answer for.'

'You've read them!'

'God no! But we all know feminism is just a load of Marxist claptrap sent to emasculate men.'

'Jesus. But what about your beloved Margaret? Should she be kept in the kitchen?'

Gideon frowned for a few seconds, then grinned. 'If you look through the history of this great country. Sometimes, in its moment of greatest need, it takes a woman to save it. Boudica, and now Maggie. But we only need one. The rest can stay home, baking and taking care of the kids.'

I thought about telling him to read some history. He'd see in the end things didn't go so well for Boudica. And Thatcher was destroying the country. 'Okaaay,'

'I want a woman who knows her place, can oversee a triumphant dinner party, give me an heir, a son, obviously. Doesn't go on CND marches to cavort with commie lesbians and jump onto Cruise missiles.'

'Jesus.'

'This is the only missile I'm going to let my girls get hold of.' Gideon thrust his hips forward. 'And it doesn't belong to Uncle Sam.'

'Bloody hell, Gideon, that's disgusting.' I wondered whether he was being serious or just saying stuff for effect. I'd noticed since he'd been getting lots of sex, far from quelling his appetite, it was feeding it. It was becoming an obsession. And what was worse, it was making him even less respectful towards women. 'Gideon, I don't feel right about this.'

'About what?'

'Helping you pick up girls to shag and then dump.'

'Are you jealous?'

'No, absolutely not. It's wrong.'

'These girls make their own choice. They don't have to sleep with me, but in the end, they can't resist. Maybe some of them hope for more, but too sodding bad.'

'I couldn't do what you do.'

'Oh come on, don't give me any of that, saving myself for the right girl bullshit. Look Marky, you just need to get started. Hey!' He slapped my shoulder. 'I know, tonight we'll get you a girl.'

'No, really, I'm fine—'

'How can you be fine? You're twenty, at your sexual peak, and still a bloody virgin. No wonder you're so fucking tetchy.'

'What?' I'd never said anything about my sex life or lack thereof. Was it so obvious I was a virgin?

'It's my fault. I should've noticed. All these months you've been my wingman, you've sacrificed yourself for me.'

It wasn't Gideon's fault. Sex intrigued and yet terrified

me. In Year 7, Mr Atkins drew diagrams on the blackboard. They made the male and female genitalia look more like UFOs than sex organs, and although Mr Atkins' explanation made it clear the male UFO had to be put inside the female UFO, his explanation gave no detail about the docking procedure. Many boys seemed to know. Every weekend, most of them boasted about "having it off" with some girl. I listened, hoping to pick up clues, but like with Mr Atkins, details were scant. All through the last years at school, I became more gloomy as I realised I was falling further and further behind in the sex scramble. All the boys were having sex every week, and all girls seemed so knowing and experienced. And at university, it was the same.

Gideon put his hands on my shoulders. 'Tonight, if you see a girl you like, don't think about helping me get laid. Give me a signal and I'll sing your praises.'

'Thanks, but I'm fine.'

'No.' Gideon squeezed my shoulders so hard it hurt. 'Tonight you're going to lose your cherry.'

I knew the only way to stop him from crushing my shoulders was to agree. 'Okay… okay, I'll let you know.'

But once Gideon had drunk a couple of pints and spotted a blond he liked, he forgot about his offer. He went over to her and without any help from me, he got her to dance.

'See you tomorrow,' Gideon said an hour later as they walked past, arm in arm. 'Go on, get one.'

I waited ten minutes to make sure Gideon had disappeared, then went back home. Relieved he hadn't gone through with his plan.

There was only one night that was different. Gideon left Ritzy's with a girl, Susan, but he came back a few moments later.

'Hey, Marky, come and look at this.'

Tombland was covered in snow.

'Isn't this wonderful?' Gideon threw a snowball at me. Susan threw one at him. The three of us had a drunken, giggly snowball fight.

After five minutes I said, 'I'd better go home.'

'No way Marky.' Gideon put his arm around Susan's shoulders. 'Getting to campus will be murder tonight. You better sleep at mine.'

'I'll be fine.' I brushed snowflakes out of my hair.

'You can sleep on the sofa.'

It was so cold, and I dreaded the trek back to campus through a snowstorm, so I accepted his offer. I wasn't sure why he'd offered me the sofa instead of the spare room he'd offered me the day I went around for tea. Had I been relegated in his affections?

We trudged under the Erpingham Gate and into The Close. The snow around the Cathedral was fresh, and unblemished. The yellow glow from the lamps made it look like a layer of frosted butter. I stopped for a moment admiring it, reluctant to spoil it.

'Come on Marky. You'll catch your death.'

Gideon and Susan leaned into each other, their arms around each other's waists.

The house was warm. I could feel my fingers and toes again as the blood suffused my body. I filled the kettle. After a minute, Gideon poked his head around the kitchen door.

'We're off upstairs. Will you be okay?'

'Yeah, I'm fine.'

'Have anything you want. See you in the morning.'

I made a cup of tea and sat on the sofa. After a couple of minutes, I understood why Gideon had wanted me to stay downstairs. Loud groans and grunts thundered from upstairs. I went to close the lounge door, I listened for a minute and was tempted to go up. I shook my head. Then went back to the sofa.

Even though the room was warm, I still needed the comfort of a blanket or a sheet. I searched the sideboard, but there was just china and cutlery. Except in one drawer, I noticed a photo album. Eventually, I found a tablecloth in the kitchen. I settled on the sofa and spread the tablecloth over my body. But still, I couldn't sleep. Curiosity got the better of me. I pulled open the sideboard drawer and lifted out the album.

It seemed as if all of Gideon's life was there. He'd been everywhere. Sydney, Rio, New York. Skiing in St Moritz. Christmases in the grand hall of some country pile. Birthdays in pricey restaurants. At the back of the album was a programme for a school play, "The Game". On the front cover was a photo of boys and girls dressed in tennis whites. When I looked closely, I saw one of the boys was Gideon. He must have been sixteen or seventeen. He played a character called Gervaise Sinclair. The "girls" were boys dressed in short skirts, blouses, and wigs. One of them had been ticked. I looked at the cast list. Vincent DuBoise played the "girl" who'd been ticked. None the wiser, I closed the album and put it back in the drawer.

I slept fitfully. At seven, when there were the first hints of daylight, I decided I didn't want to bump into Gideon and Susan in their post-coital bliss. So I went to Gideon's desk. Took out a sheet of paper and wrote.

"Thanks for letting me stay. You're a lifesaver."

I put the note on the kitchen table.

All the footprints of the night before had been covered by a heavy fall of fresh snow. Even though a beam of sunshine cut across my face it was too weak to warm me. Unlike the night before, when the walk had been filled with laughter, snowballs and friends, now I trudged through the icy wind, alone.

4

Towards the end of my second year, I neared the limit on my credit card. I hadn't been extravagant, but a fiver here and a tenner there on nights out with Gideon had built up. So I decided to work during the summer. When I told Gideon my plan, I expected him to say, "Good luck, see you in September". Instead, he said,

'What a wonderful idea. Can I come too?'

'What happened to Daddy's Monopoly money?'

'He's told me to apply myself. "Prepare yourself for the big bad world of work." I think he lined up some God-awful job in one of his beastly supermarkets.'

'Well, good for him.'

'No doubt with spies reporting my every move.'

'My heart bleeds.'

'I told him, "No thank you very much. I'll find something myself."'

'But any job I get is going to be God-awful too.'

'But at least we'll have a jolly good laugh together.'

I couldn't imagine any of the jobs available were going to be a "jolly good laugh". But it was good news. I'd never been abroad, so if Gideon came along, I'd be able to draw on his travelling experience. However, he'd spent most of his summers cruising around the Caribbean on "Daddy's boat". Long shifts in some menial job were going to be tough for me. For Gideon, it could be traumatic.

A week later we went to the Careers Centre. We browsed through *Student Summer Jobs '82*.

'This one looks good.' Gideon pointed at an advert. 'Waiter, Lake Como. You'd love Como. Italian girls are great. Dark and sultry. With all that Catholic angst.'

'Gideon, this isn't a holiday.' I looked at the advert, the pay wasn't great and I didn't fancy waitering. 'You've never been a waiter.'

'How difficult can it be, taking orders, carrying trays, and flirting with pretty customers?'

'I'm sure there's more to it than that. And how's your Italian?'

'Gucci, Armani, Ferrari,' Gideon said with an exaggerated cod-Italian accent and flamboyant hand gestures.

'Non-existent, in other words.'

'Okay, look at this one, South of France, wonderful, another waitering job. You got O-level French?'

'Scraped a C.'

'Good. I could chat up a pretty French starlet. Is Brigitte Bardot single en ce moment?'

I shook my head.

Gideon turned the page. 'Well look at this one. Summer Camp. No experience required. And it's in America, so they speak English. Well, sort of.'

The airfare to Orlando would take me over my credit limit. Something I didn't want to admit to Gideon. 'I don't want to work with kids.'

'You don't have to. There's cleaning—'

'Or spend my time wiping up their shit.'

Gideon tossed the book onto the desk. 'So you come up with a suggestion then?'

We'd been looking for almost an hour. It was going to be impossible to find a job we could agree on. Gideon wanted to go somewhere warm and exotic, where he could sleep with as many girls as possible. I didn't care if the job was in a Trappist monastery halfway up Mont Blanc, so long as the pay was decent.

There were hundreds of fruit-picking jobs, but they

didn't pay much and many of them started in August, which was too late. Whilst I was flicking through, a girl wearing a black and white Sex Pistols T-shirt sat at the table next to ours. Gideon picked up a piece of paper, rolled it into a tiny ball, then tossed it so it landed in front of her. When she looked at him, he grinned. She gave him the V sign.

'You know you want me,' he said.

'Shut up Gideon and concentrate.'

Gideon smiled at the girl and then leaned across the desk. 'Anything?'

I turned to the pages offering factory work. 'Look at this one, it's in Holland. They pay over a hundred quid a week.' I tried to hide the "**MALE ONLY**" stipulation at the bottom of the ad, but I was too late.

'Male only! You're kidding me.'

'I want to earn money, not spend the summer chasing girls.'

'Come on, there's a whole continent of girls just waiting for us.'

I wasn't sure whether Gideon had deliberately swapped the "o" in continent for a "u", or if it was just his accent coming through. Either way, the girl in the T-shirt snorted and left.

Gideon continued, 'Look. Our boys have just given the Argies a bashing in the Falklands. There must be thousands of European girls just waiting to sink their teeth into some victorious English flesh.'

'Christ Gideon! Boasting about giving the Argentinians a "bashing", as you put it, isn't going to go down well with anyone in Europe.'

'Why not?'

I shook my head. This was the first time he'd mentioned the Falklands War since we'd argued over the sinking of the Belgrano. I said Thatcher was a war criminal, as the ship had been sailing away from the Exclusion Zone. Gideon argued it didn't matter, it was war. "But more than three hundred sailors died." I had said. Gideon only shrugged.

We didn't speak for over a week. When we did speak again, we agreed no more mention of the war.

I was bristling to argue with him about the English flesh comment, but instead, I took a deep breath and continued looking through the book. The only suitable job was the one in Holland. Not only did it offer the best pay, it was close and didn't involve serving customers. And there was a part of me that wanted Gideon to get a taste of what tough working-class life was like. 'Look, if you want to come with me. It's going to be this one.'

'Why?'

'A hundred quid a week. Bed and food free. Bonus on completion. In two months I could clear more than a grand.'

'No girls! Marky, no fucking girls.' Gideon jabbed his forefinger six times on "**MALE ONLY**" like a Maths teacher pointing out the minus sign to a dim pupil. 'I can give you a grand, whatever you need.' He leafed through the pages and jabbed his finger at the Lake Como job. 'Then we can go here and have fun.'

'I don't want your money. You go to Lake Como if you want. I'm going to Holland.' I held my breath. Though originally I hadn't expected Gideon to come with me, over the last week I'd been assuming he would. Now the thought of going alone, after imagining I'd be going with him, made the prospect of working abroad alone, look a whole lot worse than it had when I first came up with the idea.

'Please Marky, if I go and work in Italy without you, I'll end up on some Mafia hit list.'

I smiled. Gideon's blue eyes were staring at me, pleading. It took all of my self-control to not say, "Oh all right, we'll go to Lake Como." But in the end, I decided I had to make sure I chose the job that paid the most. 'No, sorry Gideon.'

'You bastard.'

I was convinced Gideon would flounce out, but instead, after a few moments, he picked up the book and read the

Holland job ad again. 'It doesn't say much about it.'

'Factory work. It'll be tough.'

'I suppose, in a way that's good. When I tell Daddy I'm going to work in a factory, he'll say, "Man's work." It'll impress him.'

'So you'll come?'

Gideon jabbed his finger on **MALE ONLY**. 'It'll be like being back at school. And I've gotten used to spending my weekends shagging.'

That was true. I'd lost count of the number of girls Gideon had taken to bed. I was tempted to tell him perhaps a couple of months of celibacy would do him good.

Gideon grinned. 'But Holland's a small country. Amsterdam can't be too far away from the factory. We can visit, and I can show you the red-light district.'

'I want to earn money, not spend it.'

'We'll see.' Gideon took a pen out of his pocket. 'Let's apply.'

'Are you sure?'

'Yes, of course. Could be fun.'

5

When I stepped on the deck of the ferry, I said. 'That's it, the first Ludgrove to set foot outside our green and pleasant land.'

'Hooray!' said Gideon. 'I still can't believe you've never been abroad. Doesn't everyone jet off for a week in Marbella these days? Costa Del Crime and all that.'

I glowered at Gideon. 'Are you saying my family is a bunch of gangsters?' Over the months, I'd revelled in pretending to be outraged by some of his more ignorant comments. The look on his face, like a schoolboy caught masturbating in church, was an endearing contrast to his usual self-assurance.

'No, no of course not, sorry, I was just saying it's so easy to travel these days.'

I was too excited to explain not everyone, even those in work, could afford to fly abroad, let alone the millions Thatcher had put on the dole. I didn't want to get into a row with him and just wanted to enjoy the ferry crossing.

As the ferry pulled away from the dockside, I waved vigorously. 'So long Blighty, see you in a couple of months.'

'You're crazy.'

My excitement fizzled out, or more accurately, spewed out, when the ferry reached the open sea. It lurched, causing my stomach to churn. 'Christ,' I said, gripping a table.

'You'll be fine once you get your sea legs.'

'Where can I buy a pair of those?'

I spent much of the crossing in the toilet. Once,

when the ferry lurched so steeply, I shouted, 'We're capsizing.' Gideon gripped my shoulders. 'Relax Marky, this isn't *The Poseidon Adventure*.' He'd gotten his sea legs cruising around the Caribbean on his dad's boat, so was unaffected, and spent the night trying to chat up the waitresses in the canteen.

It was the longest night of my life. I have to admit there were moments when I wondered whether it might be better to jump overboard and drown, rather than have another dash to the toilet.

Eventually, as dawn broke, Gideon pointed to the horizon. 'Holland.'

'Thank fuck for that.'

Had I not been a committed atheist, when I stepped off the ferry I would've copied the Pope and kissed the ground. Instead, I stood stock still for twenty seconds until I was certain I was back on terra firma.

'Come on, let's sit down.' Gideon led me to a bench in the Customs Hall. Even though we sat for fifteen minutes, until my wooziness had passed, when we walked to the bus station, the ground was still undulating.

'Will I be like this forever?'

'Don't be silly, it'll pass.'

As our bus trundled through the Zeeland countryside, Gideon looked gloomily at the cold grey flat land and said, 'Congratulations Marky, I didn't think there could be anywhere flatter and more boring than bloody Norfolk, but you've found it.' He looked down the bus. All the passengers were male, then stared out the window again. 'This place is woefully bereft of both hill and tit.' He slumped onto his seat and within a few seconds, he was asleep.

I looked at him, his head leaning against the window. I still wasn't sure why he'd come. Yes, "Daddy" told him to spend the summer working. But he'd been so keen to go somewhere warm, with "Girls in tight bikinis". And Zeeland was never going to be that. Perhaps he was telling the truth when he said he needed me around to survive a working summer. I found that consoling, and even though there was a part of me relishing Gideon having to endure a taste of tough working-class life, I didn't want him to be miserable. He stirred, then swept a lazy forearm over the condensation. His sleepy eyes brooded for a moment, then he mumbled. 'Still bloody flat.'

'They reclaimed a lot of land from the sea.'

Gideon yawned as he spoke, which made what he said sound like the last groan of a dying bear. 'Why would anyone bloody bother?' His head fell against the glass and he went back to sleep.

I spent the journey studying the map and trying to work out where we were. It was tricky. There weren't many signposts, and I was still tired and shaky from the crossing. After thirty minutes, I pressed the button and gave Gideon a shake.

'Come on, we're here.'

Gideon looked out the window. 'There's nothing here.'

'Move. We wrestled our rucksacks down the aisle and then disembarked onto a narrow road. As the bus pulled away, I looked around. We were the only two people. The sky was a heavy threatening grey. The only buildings were a few ghostly outlines in the distance.

'Are you sure this is the place?' said Gideon.

I looked at the map again and realised we'd got off too early. I didn't want to discourage him, so I said, 'It shouldn't be far. This way.'

After we'd been walking for twenty minutes, Gideon took off his rucksack, dumped it on a grass verge, folded his arms and leaned against a lamppost. 'Are you sure we're even in the right country?'

'It should be around here.' I looked up from the map. 'What's that?'

Gideon looked to where I was pointing and squinted. 'It looks like black fog. That's all we bloody need.'

'I think it looks solid. Come on.'

Gideon groaned as he picked up his rucksack. 'If this

isn't the place, I'm sodding well going back to the ferry.'

I found it tricky because it was usually Gideon, who was the upbeat, optimistic one. I was sure if the black fog turned out to be just that, Gideon would leave and perhaps never speak to me again. But when we got close, I saw it was a mound of black barrels, as high as a two-storey house, and a hundred yards long.

'You know what that is?' Gideon pointed to the top row.

'No.'

'The highest point in bloody Holland.'

I was relieved to hear he hadn't lost his sense of humour. He squatted and gripped the rim of a barrel in the lowest row.

'Do you think if I pull this, Barrel Mountain will come tumbling down?'

'Don't be such an idiot.' I grabbed his arm and pulled him up.

'You're no fun.'

When we reached the end of the wall of barrels, we were on the edge of yet another field. But this one was strewn with the resting bodies of dozens of young men, most lying with their heads propped against rucksacks, others sitting, sipping from cans of beer or smoking.

'This must be it.' I stepped forward.

'Wait.' Gideon leaned toward my ear and whispered, 'Do they look like students to you?'

I squinted. 'Well, they're all young and scruffy, some are smoking weed, so yeah.'

'They look like a bunch of yobs.' Gideon nodded towards two prefab buildings. 'And I've seen nicer prisons than that.'

I doubted whether he'd ever seen a real prison: the prefabs looked similar to some classrooms I'd had at school. But he was right about the guys on the grass. I would never be as dismissive as Gideon and call them yobs, but had to admit they weren't how I'd imagined.

'Come on Marky, we could still go somewhere hot,

teeming with girls.'

As I stood beneath the grey sky, with the bank of bleak black barrels behind me and an icy breeze biting my earlobes, the thought of blue skies and girls in skimpy bikinis was tempting. But I was shattered and couldn't take another minute of travel, even if I'd had enough money to get to Italy. 'Gideon, I can't.'

'Come on, let's go before anyone sees us.' He touched my forearm.

'I have to stay here.'

Gideon turned and looked along the length of the bank of barrels towards the road as if contemplating heading to the ferry. Now I had seen who I'd be working with, I wasn't sure how I'd manage on my own. I needed a friendly face, at least at the start, so I desperately wanted him to stay. But I didn't want to plead with him, so hoping to tempt him with an offer of immediate rest. 'Look, we're both knackered. The nearest food and bed will be in there.' I pointed at the buildings.

Gideon's bloodshot eyes looked around. 'You're right about that, I'm bloody knackered.'

'So come on, let's go.' I pulled my blue anorak out of the rucksack and spread it over the grass. When I lay down, weariness swept over me, my eyelids became heavy. But a survival instinct told me not to sleep, so I forced myself to sit. The guys were in groups of three or four, except for one black guy who was sitting on his own. The only accents I could hear were Mancunian or Glaswegian, which was puzzling. I'd expected more variety, just like at university. I'd imagined evenings after a day's hard work, sitting in small groups, sharing university experiences, speculating about the future. If there'd been some more philosophy students, maybe even the occasional discussion about Plato. These guys looked more like the sort I'd seen going into dole offices back when I used to sell copies of *Socialist Worker*.

After ten minutes, the door of one of the prefabs burst open. A blond man whose frame almost fitted the doorway appeared. He was wearing faded denim jeans and a Holland football shirt. He glared at us as he tapped a baseball bat on the concrete. After twenty seconds, he roared, 'What are you lazy English fuckers waiting for?'

Those who were awake lifted themselves off the ground, then prodded the ribs or kicked the backsides of those still asleep.

'Come on.' I picked up my rucksack.

Inside the prefab was a canteen. Plastic tables, wooden benches, chipped linoleum. There was a strong smell of bleach with just a hint of another familiar smell, but I couldn't work out what it was. Without being asked, guys were forming a queue leading to a serving hatch. I looked at Gideon. We shrugged, then joined the queue. It turned out to be a queue for breakfast.

Everything was sliced; bread, cheese, ham, tomatoes.

'Is this it?' Gideon shook his head. 'Nothing hot?'

The Dutch guy pointed his baseball bat at a metal teapot. It was the size of a tin bath, and covered in scratches and dents, as if someone had used it to fend off a battalion, and lost.

'Great. I bet the tea comes in slices too,' said Gideon.

We filled our plates and found a table. Gideon sat looking gloomily at his food. He picked up a slice of ham, but it fell apart before he could put it in his mouth. 'Jesus Christ.'

'I'm sure it'll get better.'

'I wouldn't count on it.'

By spreading some cheese over a slice of ham, like concrete, Gideon constructed a sandwich, which didn't disintegrate before it reached his lips. As he bit into it, his eyes widened.

'What?' I had my back to the canteen so turned to see what he was looking at. Behind the hatch, a girl had managed to lift the teapot and was pouring the most insipid looking tea I'd ever seen into rows of plastic cups. However, what I assumed Gideon had noticed wasn't the watery tea, but the girl's blond hair and firm breasts, which were wrapped in a tight-fitting Pink Floyd T-shirt, like grapefruit.

'Things are perking up. Tea?'

I nodded and watched as Gideon strode towards the hatch. When he tried to chat with the girl, she ignored him and carried on pouring. The black guy was looking from table to table.

I waved to him. 'Hey! There's a spare seat here.' I pushed a chair away from the table and he came over.

'It's pretty scary isn't it?' I said.

He put his plate down and took off his rucksack. 'You can say that again.' He held out his hand. 'Thanks for that. I'm Lance.'

'Mark.'

Gideon came back carrying two cups of tea. 'She's WTGT.'

WTGT was an acronym he'd come up with ever since he'd started being successful in bedding girls. It stood for Waste of Two Great Tits, and he used it whenever a girl rejected his advances. It meant he thought she had to be a lesbian.

I shook my head. 'Gideon, this is Lance.'

'Hi.' Gideon looked at the cups for a moment, then back at the hatch. 'Here, take these.' He handed one cup to me and the other to Lance and went back.

'Sorry about him. When he sees a pretty girl, everything else ceases to exist.'

Lance sipped his tea. 'This is foul.'

'Jesus…you're right. Still, this bread is so dry anything wet is—'

'Hello ladies.'

A guy in a denim jacket plonked himself in Gideon's chair. He was older than the other workers, late rather than early twenties. He had bloodshot, swollen eyes, but nothing unusual there: we were all shattered. But both his hands were clenched as if he'd just come from a fight, or more worryingly, was spoiling for another one. Given his appearance and the fact the word "HATE" was tattooed on the backs of the fingers of *both* hands. I, surprisingly, managed to say, 'Hey! That's taken,'

'Oh, really?'

'My friend's sitting there.'

The guy raised his right hand and pointed a finger down the end of the table. 'Your fucking boyfriend can sit there.'

'He isn't my boyfriend.'

He grinned and leaned back in the chair with the assurance of someone who'd made it clear who was boss.

When Gideon came back, I said, 'I put your food next to Lance.'

I was worried about how Gideon would react. I feared he might argue, but he just stared at the guy for a moment, then sat. I assumed the guy chose our table in the same way a predator in the wild finds a victim, by selecting the weakest member of the herd. I tried to hide my nervousness by biting into a ham sandwich. It fell apart.

The guy laughed then said. 'I'm Kenny, from Manchester.'

At first, I hoped by ignoring him he'd go away. But fearing what he might do with his "HATE" bearing fists if he was ignored, and as neither Gideon nor Lance showed any inclinations to engage with him, I said, 'I'm Mark from Norwich. What are you studying?'

'Fucking hell, why do you students always assume everyone else in the world is a fucking student?'

'But didn't you find this in *Student Summer Jobs '82?*'

Kenny leaned back and laughed. 'I saw it in the fucking *Daily Star.*'

I began to understand why I'd only heard Mancunian and Glaswegian accents. *The Daily Star* was a tabloid especially popular in the unemployment hotspots in the North. Gideon shook his head.

'I guess you expected this to be like university, full of stuck-up ponces going on about the fucking meaning of life?' said Kenny.

'No, of course not.'

'Last year, I reckon there were only five students, at least to start with.'

'Jesus,' said Gideon. 'So what goes on here?'

Kenny stared at Gideon for a few seconds. 'And where are you from, the University of Toffee Nosed Gits?'

'Typical Socialist, making all sorts of incorrect assumptions.'

'Okay, point taken.' Kenny mimicked a posh accent, 'My humblest apologies, you better get used to it, you'll get much worse.' He looked at the three of us. 'After a week you'll be so sick of fucking onions you'll want to jump into the machine.'

'Onions. Ahh…that's the smell,' I said.

'I thought this was factory work,' said Lance.

'You're gonna see millions of onions, and tons of fucking soil, shit and anything else the fucking diggers scrape out of the ground.' Kenny picked up his empty cup and pretended to pour from it. 'Filthy shitty onions go in one end of the factory. We poor fucking buggers clean, sort, polish them. And they come out the other end as white as your mother's tits. Not yours, of course.' He smiled at Lance.

'How do you polish an onion?' said Gideon.

Kenny shook his head. 'I guess you better call your butler.'

'What?'

'He's winding you up.' I caught Gideon's eye and mouthed, "Relax".

Kenny looked at Lance. 'You a student too?'

'No. I'm from Brixton.'

Lance looked so nervous I thought for one moment he was going to choke on his sandwich.

Kenny reached across the table and squeezed Lance's forearm. 'Don't worry pal, we'll take care of you.'

Kenny puzzled me. When I'd first seen him I thought he was an arrogant, ignorant working-class racist, like the skinheads I'd seen wearing Union Jack T-shirts on National Front marches. But he was clearly intelligent and not only was he reassuring Lance, he touched his arm.

'Most guys here are on the dole. They do six weeks on

onions, then up to Amsterdam for a few days of well... a bit of How's Your Father.' He looked at Gideon. 'That means sex.'

'I do know what How's Your Father means.'

Kenny grinned. 'Anyways after getting their dicks sucked, they fuck off down to France for the grapes, then Spain for the olives. A week of sun and Sangria on the Costa del Crime, then back to fiddle the dole in Maggie's Britain.'

'I see.' Gideon looked at me and nodded his head towards the door.

I knew what he was going to say, so I didn't want to go with him.

'Lover's tiff?' Kenny smirked at Lance.

Gideon stood and glared with such a burning intensity, it compelled me to follow him. As soon as we got outside he said, 'Onions Marky! Bloody onions!'

'I know.'

Gideon looked at his watch. 'If we're quick, we might just catch the ferry back to England.'

As much as I would have liked to pick up my rucksack and run away from the barracks as fast as possible, I couldn't. I needed to earn. And even if I didn't need the money, I was sure my body couldn't take another twelve hours on the ferry, not so soon. As I looked back at the canteen, a plastic cup hit someone's head, and the guy who was hit grabbed the thrower by the throat. Kenny got up and pulled the two apart. I knew it was going to be tough, but I had no choice.

'I need to stay here.'

'Come on, I know what you expected. You thought you'd be sitting around log fires discussing Plato. But this lot.' Gideon pointed at the canteen. 'Probably think Plato is Italian for plate.'

I couldn't help laughing. Gideon could always cheer me up, even in the worst circumstances. But even though it would be much harder to survive the ordeal without him, I had to give him a chance to go.

'Gideon, I can't leave, but you don't need to work here.

So if you want to go. Go. I'll be fine.'

Gideon's deep-set eyes stared at me so intently I had to look away. 'If I leave you, you'll get eaten alive.'

'I'm sure once I get used to it—'

'I can't believe I gave up Lake Como for this.' Gideon looked into the canteen. The girl in the Pink Floyd T-shirt was clearing plates away. 'But she's pretty nice.'

'I thought you said she was WTGT.'

'Which makes her a challenge. And you know what? If I can stick this out, Daddy will be impressed.'

'But this is going to be hell for you.'

'I can stick around, at least for a few days.'

'Are you sure?'

Gideon nodded. 'Bloody crazy, I know.'

It surprised me how relieved I was knowing Gideon was staying. I didn't want to show it so I bit my lip and said, 'Just one thing, don't refer to your parents as Mummy and Daddy.'

Gideon sniggered and then saluted.

When we got back inside, Kenny was saying, 'You don't want to be on the belt.'

'What's that?' said Lance.

'You sit on your fucking arse, chucking out bad onions.'

'What's a bad onion?' Gideon said as he sat next to Lance.

'Oh, you're back.' Kenny stared at him. 'I thought you'd be halfway to Harrods by now.'

'Harrods is for deluded plebs who think it's classy. And besides, the company here is so charming.'

Kenny nodded as if impressed by the banter. 'Anyways back to fucking onions. They only want white ones.'

'I know all about that,' said Lance.

'Good one,' said Kenny. 'You need to work on a machine where you move about. But don't fucking do barrels. Last year one guy went arse over tit, knocked half his teeth out.'

'Jesus!' I said.

There was a crash. Everyone looked towards the hatch.

The Dutch guy was whacking his baseball bat against a metal bin. After he bashed it three times, he shouted, 'Now I have your attention.' He looked like a seal hunter choosing which head to bludgeon first. 'I should say welcome back, but after what happened last year.' He gave us the finger. 'Fuck off back to England.'

'Hey John, some of us are naw fucking English,' said a redhead.

'Can someone translate?' said John.

There was a lot of giggling and pointing at the guy who'd spoken. John slammed the bat against the bin again and there was silence. 'That's why this year I'm prepared. With this.' He swung the bat as if hitting a home run. 'And with my little boy. Frans! Come out!'

A blond, even taller than his father, humped from behind the counter, a golden-skinned monolith carrying a baseball bat like a toothpick.

'Frans is a black belt in everything. So any trouble from you drunken Brits.' They lifted their bats.

'One, two, three.' On three, they started bashing the bin.

After John and Frans stopped bashing, it toppled forward. Frans kicked it like a Mafia hitman, making sure their target was dead.

'Tomorrow I will choose one corridor for day shift, and the other will do the night. You swap every week. Understand?'

'Which corridor, which shift?'

John swung the bat as if hitting another home run. 'That's my little secret. I know you guys fucking kill to be on the night shift first.'

There were cries of, 'No! No, we won't.'

John raised his bat and pointed at the flattened bin. 'You, if you don't fucking shut up. You will find out tomorrow. Now find your beds.'

'Guys.' Kenny leaned forward and in a low, urgent voice said. 'I don't want to be in a room with a load of drunks. So we all go down the right corridor, to the very end room. Okay?'

'Why should we do that? You're hardly the most endearing person on the planet,' said Gideon.

'Because I know which fucking corridor is doing the night shift.'

'Really?' I said.

'Shhh… come on.'

Despite my first impressions of Kenny, I thought it wise to stick with him. He'd been here before, so he could guide us, and the way he'd treated Lance showed despite his aggressive appearance, he was a sensitive guy. I looked imploringly at Gideon, who shrugged. We all followed Kenny down the right corridor. It was dusty and the smell of onions was even worse than it had been in the canteen; I sneezed three times before we reached the end of the corridor. Kenny kicked the door open and let us file inside. The smell of onions was stifling. I sneezed again.

Kenny pointed at the windows. 'Lance, can you open those?'

After he'd opened the windows, Lance joined us in the middle of the concrete floor. We stood staring at the bunks like we were gazing at our own graves.

'Now I assume you two lovebirds will share a bed.' Kenny grinned at me and Gideon. 'I wonder who's top and who's bottom?'

I stepped towards one bed and tossed my rucksack onto the lower bunk.

'Thought so.' Kenny winked at Lance, who just looked bemused.

I whispered to Gideon, 'What's all that top and bottom crap about?'

'I'll tell you later.' Gideon climbed onto the top bunk.

When I sat on my bed, I noticed, written on the wall, in black felt tip, right by where my head would be lying, "ONYUNS ARE THE ERTHS SHIT."

The door burst open and the redhead who'd shouted at

John strode in.

'Fuck off Jimmy, this room's full,' said Kenny.

Jimmy glared at Lance. 'We kin kick the fucking nig-nog oot the windae.' He stamped his Doc Martens as he strode towards Lance. Then leaned into his face. Lance looked like he was going to faint.

I was too scared to intervene. Gideon was gazing out the window. Kenny jumped off his bunk and pulled Jimmy away from Lance.

'Lance stays. You go.'

Jimmy resisted. 'What the fuck? Ye wanna share wi' that piece a—'

Kenny grabbed Jimmy's shirt and pushed him against the wall. 'Fuck off. Or I'll fucking kill you.'

Jimmy's face went red and his eyes bulged. 'Okie, okie.'

'This corridor is on day shift. So if you want a lie-in, you better fuck off.' Kenny let go.

Jimmy spluttered. 'Ye lying.'

Kenny grabbed Jimmy's shirt again. Jimmy raised his arms in surrender. 'Okie.'

When Kenny loosened his grip, Jimmy stepped towards the door.

'Where the fuck are you going?'

'Oot.'

'Not before you apologise.'

'I nae gonnae apologise tae tha.' Jimmy pointed at Lance.

Kenny moved towards him, his hands reaching for his throat.

Jimmy stepped back. He stared at the floor and mumbled, 'Sorry.' Then left.

'Wow! That was...I've never seen anything like... Well done,' I said.

Lance stared at Kenny, his eyes wide, tearful. 'No white man has ever...'

'Hey, you shouldn't have to thank me. I'm just sorry

there are wankers like him around.'

'So you lied to us.'

'Gideon!'

'He said we'd be doing the night shift, but he just told that guy this is the day shift.'

'It doesn't matter.'

'It bloody well does.'

'Look, I just told him that to make him fucking leave, we're on nights.'

'Well, we'll soon see, won't we?'

'Gideon!'

'What I can't understand is why you chose to share with us, out of all the guys out there,' said Gideon.

'Do you really wanna know?'

'You don't have to tell us.' I glared at Gideon.

'I'm all ears.'

'Because you all look so fucking boring.'

'Wow! How to win friends and influence people.'

Kenny lifted himself onto his bunk and then rolled back onto the mattress. 'I'm not here to fucking make friends. I don't want to spend six weeks sleeping with a load of drunks and druggies.'

'You look like a druggie to me.'

'Gideon!'

'Look, we can't all be poncy students. Some of us were born with shitty spoons in our mouths. It's not my choice to be on the fucking dole, pal.' He wagged a finger at Gideon. 'It's courtesy of your pal Maggie.'

For a moment, I panicked. Gideon looked like he was about to boast Thatcher was a family friend.

'Kenny, we're all grateful for your help.' I said.

'I'll be grateful for the rest of my life,' said Lance.

'Gideon, aren't you thankful we don't have to share with that racist?'

Through thin lips and gritted teeth, Gideon said, 'Yes.'

Kenny lay back on his bunk. 'Okay, stop all this

thanking nonsense. I'm fucking knackered. So you lot better shut the fuck up.'

I was angry with myself for having made so many ignorant and stereotypical assumptions about Kenny. And not intervening to help Lance. I dreaded to think about what would have happened if Kenny hadn't been there to confront Jimmy. What was going to happen if the place was full of Jimmys? Maybe Gideon was right, perhaps we should leave. I looked up at the curve of the mattress formed by his body. For a moment, I thought about waking him and then both of us sneaking out. But I turned to face the wall. "ONYUNS ARE THE ERTHS SHIT". Stuck in my head like a malign mantra until I fell asleep.

6

That evening, as the four of us were sitting in the canteen, Jimmy stormed towards Kenny.

'You're a fucking liar!'

Kenny coated a slice of chicken in gravy, examined it like a food critic checking its appearance then lazily looked at Jimmy. 'What did I lie about?'

'You know. The fucking night shift.'

Kenny raised his fork to his nose then sniffed the chicken. 'No fucking aroma.' He shook his head. 'Oh, that. Sorry.'

'You fucking lied.'

Even though Jimmy was now only a foot away from Kenny and leaning over him, Kenny didn't flinch. 'Why would I lie?'

'Coz you wanna fuck your nig-nog loverboy.'

Kenny's demeanour changed. He slammed his knife and fork onto the table so hard all the plates bounced. He grabbed Jimmy's shirt then pulled him so close, he looked like he was going to eat Jimmy's nose instead of the flavourless chicken. 'Are you fucking calling me a poofter?'

'I…I.'

Kenny twisted Jimmy's collar so tight his face turned redder than his hair. 'Are you calling me a fucking poofter?'

'I jus wanna—' Jimmy spluttered.

'Maybe I should swap,' said Lance.

'Shut up Lance,' said Kenny.

'See the nig-nog dunnae mind.'

Kenny tightened his grip again. 'He told you his name.'

'But...but...'

'What's his name?'

'Lance,' Jimmy spluttered.

'So call him Lance and leave him the fuck alone.' Kenny shook Jimmy so hard his head wobbled like a broken doll.

'Sorry...Lance.'

Kenny released him. 'Now go and eat.'

Lance whispered, 'He's never going to give up.'

'Lance, he's a fucking racist. We'll look after you, won't we guys?' Kenny looked at me and Gideon.

'Yes, yes of course.'

Gideon said nothing.

Jimmy went from table to table, pleading for someone to swap.

'Why is he so bothered? It's all the same work,' I said.

'Fuck knows. He won't remember any of it when he's sober.' Kenny slurped his last drop of water. 'Look, guys. For the next two months we're gonna be living up each other's arses. There'll be times we wanna fucking kill each other. But we stick together. Right?'

Lance and I nodded. Gideon didn't respond.

'Fucking wankers!' Jimmy threw a plate on the floor, scattering a chicken leg and chips over the concrete. Then stormed out of the canteen.

'I guess still no takers,' I said.

After dinner, Gideon and I sat on the grass. Gideon turned his face to soak up the sun as it sunk behind Barrel Mountain. Nobody was in earshot, so I asked the question that had been bothering me since Kenny commented about the bunks.

'What did Kenny mean by top and bottom?'

'Christ Marky. Have you been thinking about that all day?'

I nodded.

'He was making a cheap joke about poofs.' He looked at me as if expecting that to be enough.

'I still don't get it.'

'Jesus Marky! Where've you been living? Some poofs like to have another guy ram his cock up their arse.'

'Bloody hell!' I was shocked, yet again, to find out how naive I was about sex. At school, I'd heard boys talk about "bumming". But been too scared to ask what it meant. 'And they enjoy that?'

'I guess.'

'Jesus! So when I took the bottom bunk and Kenny laughed—'

'He was saying you like to take it up the arse.'

'Shit. And that you—'

'Yep.'

'Bloody hell.' I looked into the canteen. Kenny and Lance were still there. 'We have to tell him it's not true.' I moved towards the door.

Gideon grabbed my arm. 'Marky, no!'

'But it's disgusting.'

'Charming. I love you too.'

'The idea of it... with anyone...Yuck. I mean Jesus.' I tried to break free of Gideon's grip. 'Why aren't you pissed off about it?'

'I don't damn well care what some Mancunian scrounger thinks. After two months, we'll never see any of these wankers again.'

'But the thought that people think we... that you...and me—'

'Who cares? At school, there was always gossip about who was shagging who. A lot of it turned out to be true.'

'Really? Jesus. So did you? I mean...have you ever?' I stared into Gideon's deep-set eyes, but as usual they gave nothing away. 'No, sorry, of course not. It's ridiculous. You like girls.'

The girl in the Pink Floyd shirt came out of the canteen.

'Yep, I'm addicted to pussy.' Gideon grinned at her. 'Hi

there.'

She emptied a bowl of dirty water, most of it on the grass but some on the concrete so it splashed towards Gideon's shoes. The grin on her face suggested she'd done it deliberately.

'She loves pussy too, unfortunately.' He slapped me on the thigh. 'Anyway Marky, now you know. Coming back inside?'

'In a minute.'

I needed time on my own. At university, the one thing that made my enforced celibacy almost tolerable, was the thought the greasy, spotty cadavers I'd seen sitting at the Gay Soc stall during Fresher's Weeks, weren't getting any sex either. All too ugly, too skinny to have girlfriends: I assumed they were only pretending to be gay until some girl was desperate enough to sleep with them. But If what Gideon had said was true, even those ugly guys were having sex with each other. Not as some consolation prize, but because they enjoyed it. I felt even more like an alien who'd crash-landed on Planet Sex. Where everybody else knew all about it, was having it all the time, and not telling me anything about it.

I gasped as I remembered a wet dream I'd had whilst I was at school. It happened during the hot summer of '76. And involved a boy called Nick.

Nick and I were the same height and weight, so one day, during circuit training, we were paired. We had to brace against each other and push. As we pushed, my thigh brushed against Nick's, sending a tingling sensation straight to my brain. I shivered and was so shocked I stopped pushing, allowing Nick to force me back. In the next tussle, I pushed hard, forcing Nick to push harder, and then I deliberately stopped resisting. Nick pushed me so hard that when my back hit the gym wall his momentum pressed his firm body against mine. As we "embraced", I shivered as a wave of tingling sensations flowed through my body.

'Don't fucking stop pushing,' he said.

During the summer holidays, I went to Marine Lake, the tidal pool by the estuary, pretty much every day. One day,

Nick was sitting outside the changing huts.

'They're all occupied,' he said.

I was so excited to sit close to him, my breaths became short and the more I tried to control them the more I was sure he'd noticed. The silence was awkward but I couldn't think of anything to say. So I just stared at a line of ants that was crossing in front of my feet. I wondered if Nick was remembering the moment in the gym and if so, was he remembering it with fondness or with disgust? All things considered; the fact he played football for the school, always had a girlfriend on the go and was one of the boys who most often boasted about "having it off". I concluded, he probably remembered it with disgust. Just as I reached my conclusion one of the doors opened. Nick jumped up and went inside. A few seconds later, he poked his head out. 'We can share.'

'That's okay, I can wait.'

'Don't be fucking silly. Come on.'

I gulped as I looked at Nick's bobbed blond hair shining in the sun, his smooth skin glowing and his kind smile. I shuffled towards the hut. Nick closed the door and tossed his blue *Adidas* duffel bag onto the bench. I did the same. The hut was cramped and hot. Boiling, as if all the heat from the scorching sun had combined with the rampant heat of our adolescent bodies to form a duvet that was tightening around us, pushing us together. I stood motionless as if I'd forgotten how to undress. Using all my concentration to quell the desire to touch his skin.

'Are you going to swim in your fucking clothes?'

'No.'

'Well, get changed then.'

Nick pulled up his shirt. I'd never been so close to him when he was topless. I noticed for the first time he had the early signs of chest muscles, so different from my skinny white chest. I yearned to touch his honeylike skin. And stroke the curve of his pubescent muscles. Nick shook his hair back into place and tossed his shirt into his bag.

'Hurry up.'

I nodded and undid the buttons of my shirt. The heat coming off Nick's skin was more intense than the heat searing from the corrugated iron roof. My breathing became short and rapid.

'Are you sick?'

'No, just hot.' I folded my shirt and slid it into my bag. When I turned around, Nick was pulling down his shorts, revealing sinewy thighs covered in downy hair. I longed to rub my leg against him again. I fought to stop it but I was getting hard, I looked away and stared at my bag, and even though I noticed, for the first time *Adidas* backwards was "sad Ida". I became fully erect.

'Do you fucking want to swim or not?' Nick kicked his underwear so it curved in an arc towards his shoulder then caught it in his left hand. As he was rifling through his bag I couldn't help staring at his cock, which was as unerect as any cock had ever been.

'Come on,' he said, pulling on his trunks.

I was still hard so before taking off my shorts I pulled my towel out of my bag and wrapped it around my waist.

'Wow! Why so fucking shy?' Nick grabbed the towel. 'You've got nothing I haven't got.'

'No! No! No!' I shouted so loud I was sure people outside looked up at the sky expecting to see Concorde.

Nick was so stunned by my shout he let go. 'Okay, okay, it was just a fucking joke.'

I was still fully erect. For a crazy moment, I contemplated dropping my towel to show him how excited I was. After all, he'd invited me inside the hut. Perhaps... he was even attracted to me? Maybe he'd enjoyed our "embrace" in the gym and was longing for us to touch again. Was that why he grabbed my towel? But then I remembered how soft his cock was and how he always had a girlfriend.

'You're right, I'm fucking shy.' I turned away and with some difficulty, managed to change into my trunks.

With my towel still around my waist, I turned. Nick's bare back was in front of me. I yearned to stroke it, to wrap my arms around his waist. Pull him towards me so we could kiss and snog, then swim together. Slowly I leaned forward, when I sensed the tingle as my nipple neared his skin, I told myself to move back, but I didn't stop, I took a deep breath so my chest lifted slowly and my nipple brushed against his back. I held my breath, for the milliest milli of a millisecond. Sensations rippled from my chest all over my body. My cock throbbed. I trembled so much I thought I was going to fall. I closed my eyes and braced for the punches.

'Cramped in here, isn't it?' he said.

I leaned away. 'Yes, and hot.'

Nick turned around. 'Fuck you're slow. I can't waste any more time.' He picked up his bag and grabbed the door handle. 'Karen must think I've fucking died.'

'Sorry. Thank you for letting me in.'

I slumped onto the bench, my heart thumping. Elation. Shame. Fear. What if Nick told? I'd get beaten up. How could I have been so stupid? But the joy of touching his skin, even for a moment, made me realise, for the first time, how much pleasure my body could experience. But it was wrong. It should have been with a girl.

When my erection had subsided, I stepped outside. Nick was walking with his arm around Karen's waist, his fingers tucked inside the strap of her bikini bottom. I positioned myself high on a rock as far from them as possible. But when I saw them frolicking in the water, I decided to head home.

That was the night I had the wet dream. I couldn't remember much about it. I was in the hut with Nick, when I woke, I was hot and I could feel something, his presence in bed with me. And it was weird. It felt like there was something in my arsehole. I didn't understand it. But as I sat outside the canteen and remembered what Gideon had told me about poof sex, I realised I must have dreamt of Nick fucking me. Way back then. When I knew nothing about it. I also realised the only other time

I'd felt anything like what I'd felt when I was close to Nick was when I was close to Gideon.

'Fuck!'

I got up and wandered inside. Gideon was already asleep on the top bunk. I lay on the bottom bunk, then wriggled into my sleeping bag. At first, I lay on my back, but even in the grey gloom, I could see the curve in the mattress created by the weight of Gideon's body. I reached up and touched it. And even though I wasn't touching his skin, I got an erection. I turned onto my front so I couldn't see the curve and put my pillow over my head . But even though I ran the words "ONYUNS ARE THE ERTHS SHIT" through my brain over and over, I couldn't stop thinking about him and hoping I'd have another wet dream, this time starring Gideon.

7

The next day, just before 6 pm, Kenny led us out of the barracks for our first shift. As we reached the far end of Barrel Mountain, the day shift came around the corner.

Lance said, 'Oh shit!'

'Don't worry.' Kenny slowed, so Lance could catch up with him.

Jimmy was in the middle of the day-shift workers, staring at the ground, too shattered to notice us as we crossed. Kenny gripped Lance's shoulder. 'See, he's forgotten all about that fucking shift nonsense.'

Beyond Barrel Mountain was a concrete compound. Down one side was a car park, down the other a high wall with a gate opening onto the road. Opposite us was the factory, long, squat and grim: the red glow of the setting sun soaked up by the pores in the breezeblock walls and the thick grime on its windows. In the middle of the compound was a blue mound. Kenny shuffled towards it, squatted, then plunged his arm into it.

'One, two, three.' He pulled out a pair of blue overalls and shook it in the air. 'Knew it, fucking ripped.' He sniffed the armpits. 'At least they cleaned them this year.'

I took a pair from the top of the pile. 'Ripped too.'

'Those day shift wankers grabbed the best ones.' Kenny tossed another pair back.

Gideon held up two pairs, both with gashes. 'This is bloody appalling.'

'No, it's bloody capitalism,' said Kenny.

I found a pair with only one small split in the right sleeve. As I was loosening my belt to take off my jeans, Kenny said, 'What the fuck are you doing?'

'These are my best jeans.'

'It's going to get fucking cold in there.' Kenny pointed towards the factory. 'Without those, by midnight your cute little bollocks will be ice cubes. And we wouldn't want that, would we?' Kenny winked at Gideon. 'Shit! You too?'

Gideon had removed his jeans. 'Where are the lockers?' he said.

Kenny pressed an index finger to his lower lip. 'Oh yes sir, let me think, oh of course.' Then, like a camp Club Med tour guide, he waved a limp hand in the air. 'You'll find them just over there between the cocktail bar and the Swedish sauna.'

'Very funny. So what am I going to do with these?'

'Give them to me. And yours.' Kenny grabbed Gideon's and my jeans. 'Lance, you going to treat us to an impromptu striptease too?'

Lance shook his head and put his overalls on over his clothes. Kenny ran across the compound and handed the jeans to a group of women who were walking past the parking area. When he came back, he said, 'You can collect them from the canteen at the end of the shift. Now, where are the boots?' He looked around the compound. 'Ahh...over there.' He strode towards the open door of a shed next to the factory.

Inside were rows of Wellington Boots. Dirty, smelly and not in any order. It took ages to find two that fitted. When I was ready I sat on the concrete with my back leaning against the wall.

'Look out, here comes God!'

I turned to see where Kenny was pointing. When I was a kid, I often wondered what God looked like. I never pictured a short man in dirty white overalls, with wisps of grey hair poking out from under a black beret.

'That's French Pierre,' said Kenny. 'If he doesn't like

you, he'll kick you out. Anyways see you suckers later.'

'Where are you going?' said Lance.

'To my car.' Kenny bowed and headed towards the parking area.

When French Pierre saw him, he reached out his hand. 'Ahh! Kenny! Welcome back.' They shook hands so vigorously and smiled so warmly, I half expected them to kiss like two East European dictators. After they'd finished their greeting, French Pierre showed Kenny to a forklift truck.

'How did the wanker wangle that?' Gideon said as he shook half a withered onion out of his right boot.

French Pierre came back and shouted at us. 'Anyone over one eighty stand on right, anyone less stand on left.'

'What's one-eighty?' said Lance.

Although I'd been brought up on metric, I'd never known my height in metres. 'God knows.'

From the seat of his forklift, Kenny shouted, 'Fucking six foot, you idiots!'

Guys started moving around, not forming one line, just groups of three or four of varying heights standing near each other.

French Pierre held up his hands. 'Stop! Stop!'

He scanned the line-up like a failing basketball coach, desperate to find the tallest players. Lance was the shortest, so French Pierre grabbed his arm and dragged him to the left. Then he ordered people around. I wanted to work with Gideon, but as he was over six foot and I was only 5' 10", I feared we'd get parted. So when French Pierre got close, I took a deep breath and pushed my shoulders back as far as I could. He stopped in front of me, narrowed his eyes, and looked me up and down. When he curled his lip, I was sure he was going to drag me out and send me left, but he grunted and moved on.

Once French Pierre was satisfied with the lineup, he said, 'Follow me.'

The dull gloom of the factory made the silent machines, spread around all four walls, look like the ruins of a medieval castle. French Pierre stood in the middle of the factory floor, his arms on his hips, tut-tutting like a sergeant major with a bunch of useless recruits. Starting with the tallest, he gesticulated and despatched guys to different machines. He sent Gideon and me to the machine nearest the entrance.

I climbed a ladder to a platform on the left, and Gideon did the same on the right. In front of me was a metal mesh, five metres long, punctured with identically sized holes. Parts of the mesh were clogged with dirt and grass. In the centre, looking like a pimple, was a single white onion. I sent a quizzical look to Gideon, who shrugged. In the gloom, we looked like tired sentries on the ramparts of a remote castle.

French Pierre led Lance with a group of the other shorter workers to the back of the factory. Ten minutes later, he returned. He climbed onto Gideon's platform and picked up a scraper which he used to slice the grass. When he cut through the single onion, one half dropped through the hole onto a belt, leading up towards the ceiling. He pushed the other half along to the end of the mesh, where it fell onto a conveyor belt leading to the next machine.

'Understand?'

We nodded. French Pierre jumped from the platform and ran into the compound. I crouched and peered through the window behind me. Two lorries thundered through the gate, turned into the compound then reversed towards the factory. A minute later I almost jumped out of my skin as the machine roared to life. The platform shuddered, and the mesh shook.

I covered my ears.

A clump of dirt, stones, and grass dropped off the higher belt onto the mesh in front of me. A small white onion popped out and rolled until it fell through one of the holes. Gideon picked up his scraper, pushed it over the mesh, slicing the grass. Then pushed the cut grass and grit until it dropped onto the conveyor belt below. I took my hands off my ears, picked up a scraper, and did the same.

Five minutes later, the smarting started.

At first, it wasn't too bad, like I'd chopped a particularly pungent onion. A few itches, a few tears. But it got worse. The smarting became stinging. I blinked, but it didn't help. And when I rubbed my sleeve over my eyes, I almost screamed from the pain. I blinked faster, trying to clear with tears. It was as if someone was holding my eyelids open and spraying hot onion juice onto my eyeballs. I sneezed, then cupped my hands over my eyes. But tears kept flowing. It was so bad I thought the only way to make the pain go away was to pop my eyeballs out of their sockets.

Gideon was sneezing and tearing, not scraping. Our mesh became clogged. I made a feeble sweep but didn't clear much before the pain in my eyes forced me to turn away. There was a fine spray coming from a metal pipe running the length of the machine. I moistened my fingers under it, then dabbed my eyes.

'Fuck!' It made the stinging even worse. To distract from the pain, I stamped my right foot on the platform. As I raised my leg, I banged my knee against the side of the machine. 'Fuck!'

'Snell! Snell!'

I turned around. Through the blur, French Pierre was standing below my platform. He was bent forward, making scraping motions in the air.

'Snell! Snell!' he shouted.

I wanted to say, "I'll fucking snell your fucking beret off your fucking head." Instead, I pointed at my eyes.

French Pierre made a kicking motion. He wasn't showing off his footballing prowess, and remembering Kenny had said he was God. To avoid the indignity of being the first to get the boot, I turned around to face the mesh. Somehow, I managed a few half-hearted sweeps. As soon as French Pierre moved away, I stopped, put my hands over my eyes and lifted my face as close to the open window as possible. It gave some relief.

There was no way I could survive twelve hours of this. I wanted to toss the scraper on the mesh, jump off the platform and run out of the factory as fast as possible. No amount of money was worth this agony. My boots had filled with water, so every time I took a step, my feet squelched. I took off my right boot. As I was pouring the water out, I noticed Gideon's side of the mesh was clear, so different to my side, which was like a jungle floor.

'Come on Marky! Before Froggy Pierre gets back.'

'I can't. My eyes.'

Gideon stretched further and cleared a bit of my side of the mesh.

'Hang on.' He jumped off his platform, then came bounding onto mine. He grinned, bent forward and scraped. He sliced through the grass like a highly efficient lawn mower, then he swept the cuttings to the end of the mesh.

I stared at him. Gideon was helping me, saving me. He could so easily have let me get fired and said, "Told you so. Let's go to Lake Como." Instead, he was scraping like crazy. The effort was making his biceps flex, pressing against the cotton of his overalls. I'd never noticed how muscular his arms were. I became aroused so looked away.

Once Gideon had cleared my side, he grinned and squeezed my shoulder. I trembled.

'We make a great team.' He jumped from my platform, then climbed back onto his own. I could still feel the pressure of his strong fingers pressing into my shoulder.

When French Pierre reappeared, he stared at my side of the mesh. He looked surprised and perhaps a little disappointed he couldn't fire me. After ten minutes, the stinging eased. There were fewer tears. After another five minutes, all the stinging had gone.

Two hours later, our machine stopped. The factory fell silent. The last onion dropped onto the mesh, rolled a couple of feet, then dropped through a hole.

'Hey, wankers!' Kenny was below our machine, pointing towards a trolley in the middle of the compound. 'Drinkypoos!'

Gideon and I climbed off our platforms. 'Thanks for that.'

'No problem,' said Gideon.

'Weren't your eyes really bad too?'

'Of course. I guess not as bad as yours.'

'Ahh… the stinging.' Kenny grinned. 'Tomorrow, bring some water.'

'Why didn't you warn us?' Gideon frowned at Kenny.

'No fun that way.'

Gideon pointed at the forklift. 'And how come you get to be on that?'

'I fucked the right people.'

'What?' said Gideon.

Kenny shook his head and smiled at me. 'These rich bastards, so fucking gullible. Of course I didn't fuck my way onto the forklift truck. Last year I was on your machine. Never. Again. So I got a license.'

I rubbed my eyes. 'Will it always be this bad?'

'Only for the first week. But it'll be a lot better with water. I promise you that.'

Gideon and I each took a cup of tea from the trolley and went to sit on a pallet.

'Gideon, I'm so bloody sorry. I had no idea it was going to be so terrible.'

Gideon smiled. 'I know. Don't feel too bad. Look at my hands. Blisters.'

'What?'

'Evidence for Daddy. Sorry, for my dad. Will you take some pictures?'

'Of course.'

'I know this is going to sound crazy, but I enjoyed that. The stinging was hell, but after that it was fine. My muscles feel like they've done some proper work.' He flexed his biceps.

Remembering what happened on the machine, I looked away. 'How can you enjoy scraping grass and shit?'

'Maybe tomorrow I'll hate it. But at the moment, I'm

invigorated. My sinuses...' He spread his arms wide and sang, 'Have never been so clear.'

I was relieved at how Gideon was reacting, but wasn't sure if he was pretending. 'If you keep doing bloody Julie Andrews impressions, people definitely will think we're poofs. And stop trying to make me feel better.'

'I'm not.'

Lance joined us. 'I never want to see another fucking onion.'

'What did they get you doing?' I said.

'I was on the belt. Throwing out bad onions.'

We were all so tired, we just sat drinking until French Pierre told us to go back to work.

At the end of the shift, I was exhausted. At breakfast, we all ate and stared at our food like knackered zombies. After a shower, I slumped onto my bunk and enjoyed the best sleep in years.

I woke at 1 pm. and lay on my bed, staring at the bulge of Gideon's mattress.

'Hey Marky,'

The springs of Gideon's bunk creaked. A second later, his upside-down head appeared as he leaned out of his bunk. 'Let's go to Amsterdam at the weekend.'

'Gideon, I can't.'

'Don't worry, I'll pay.'

It wasn't just the money. After what had happened on the machine, I feared if I spent time alone and close to him, I might want to touch him, as I had done with Nick in the changing hut. That could destroy our friendship.

'Look out!' Gideon leapt off his bunk then squatted next to my bed. 'Come on Marky, we need to have something to look forward to.' He leaned towards me. 'And I bloody need a shag.'

'You go, I'll stay here.'

'I'll get into trouble without you. You know that.'

No, I didn't, yes he could make offensive remarks, but

I'd never seen him get into any trouble or danger. And even if he had, Daddy's Millions would soon get him out of it. But he was right about one thing. After the dreadful first shift, I needed to have something to look forward to. Being able to get away from the barracks for a couple of days would make surviving the shifts easier. A trip to Amsterdam could be that.

'Come on, you know you want to say yes.'

Perhaps I could make sure we didn't get too close. Then I had a brainwave. 'Can we bring Lance?'

'Why?'

'Because he's one of us and he needs to have something to look forward to as well.'

'But we barely know him.'

I gave Gideon a stare, which he interpreted correctly as, "Either Lance comes with us or I don't."

'Okay, if he even wants to.'

'But not this weekend.'

'Why the bloody hell not?'

'Look, we finish our shift at six on Saturday morning, even if we left immediately, it would be afternoon before we got to Amsterdam. Then, to be ready for our first shift Monday morning, we'd have to leave Amsterdam on Sunday evening.'

'Why are you always so bloody sensible? '

'If we go next weekend when we swap back to night shifts, we'd have a whole weekend in Amsterdam.'

'I wasn't planning on a million canal tours, just a few quick shags, then back.'

'More time, more shags.'

'Good point. And shags for you too?'

I thought he was joking, so said. 'Yes, of course.'

'But how am I going to last another week? Lisa the Pink Floyd Lesbian clearly isn't interested.'

'You could go on your own this weekend.'

Gideon sat on the concrete floor. 'You're right. This weekend would be a rush. I'll just have to throw myself into onion processing.'

'But we'll have to stay in a cheap hostel or something.'
'Don't worry, leave everything to me.'

When he said "leave everything to me", I should have suspected Gideon was likely to plan something I didn't want. I should have gotten involved because what happened on our trip to Amsterdam ruined our friendship and changed my life forever.

8

Following Kenny's advice, for the next shift I took a bottle of water. Whenever the stinging became unbearable, I splashed my eyes. It helped. By the end of the week, even though I was exhausted and had blisters within blisters, I had a sense of accomplishment. I'd survived and earned a hundred pounds.

We were all so tired we spent the weekend resting. On Sunday evening, Gideon and I sat on the grass outside the prefab. He rolled a spliff with weed he'd bought from one of the women who worked in the factory canteen. 'Marky, you were right. I was too knackered to go to Amsterdam this weekend.' He held up his spliff. 'Thank God I got this stuff. Sure I can't tempt you?'

'No thanks.'

'You don't know what you're missing.' He took a puff, closed his eyes, and leaned back.

The whole week, I'd been so tired, I'd fallen asleep pretty much as soon as I lay down. And struggled to get up. I feared if I smoked weed, I'd be so drowsy it would be even harder to wake up.

'Still on for next weekend?' he said.

'Yep, by then I'll be screaming to get away from this place. And so will Lance.'

'Yes.'

I could tell by the tone of Gideon's one-word reply he still didn't want Lance to come with us. I could understand. Although we both liked Lance, we weren't as close to him as we were to each other. He wouldn't understand our in-jokes and comments. But I needed a buffer between me and Gideon's sexual allure. The sheer joy on Lance's face when we invited him to join us had been one of the few uplifting moments of the week.

Kenny, of course, had commented. 'I take it I'm not fucking good enough?'

'Sorry Kenny, we thought it better just us three newbies — '

'I was kidding. I've been to the 'Dam too fucking often.'

And I could tell from the smile on Kenny's face he was overjoyed that we'd included Lance.

After the first day shift I fell asleep quickly, but woke at 2 am. It took a long time to get back to sleep. The same thing happened on Tuesday. So on Wednesday, I decided, rather than spend the time tossing and turning in my sleeping bag, to take a book into the canteen and study.

It was strange being alone in the silent canteen. Usually it was filled with shouted expletives and the scraping of cutlery, but now it was calm. With windows all around, darkness surrounded me, except for the mustard-coloured light of the factory glowing on the other side of Barrel Mountain. The stillness was excellent for studying. After I'd been reading for twenty minutes, I thought I heard something outside; I looked up but could see nothing. A couple of seconds later, the door burst open and Lance staggered in.

'Lance!' I jumped off the bench and ran towards him. Blood was dripping from cuts on his face and his right eye was swollen.

'What happened?' I helped him to a bench.

Lance winced as he sat down. 'Nothing.'

'It doesn't bloody look like nothing.' I crouched to get a clearer view of his face. 'You look terrible.'

'Thanks.'

'Some of these cuts are really bad.' I looked around for some tissues.

'It's fine. I'm fine.'

'What happened?'

'I just told you, nothing.'

'Bloody hell Lance, do you think I'm stupid? It's bloody obvious something has happened.'

He stared at me. It was clear from his eyes he wanted to tell me what happened.

'Come on, Lance.'

He glanced over both his shoulders. 'Promise not to say anything.'

The state of his face would make a promise to remain silent pointless, but he wanted to hear it. 'I promise.'

'I couldn't sleep, so I went outside for some air. When I was walking by Barrel Mountain someone jumped me.'

'Shit! Who?'

'It was too dark.'

I found that difficult to believe. There was a floodlight near Barrel Mountain. 'Really? We should tell the police.'

Lance gripped my arm. 'No! Don't say anything to anyone, please.'

'But the bastard needs to be stopped.'

'Mark, I don't know who did it.'

When I looked at his eyes, he avoided my gaze, perhaps a sign he wasn't telling the truth. But if my face had been treated like a punching bag, I'd probably do the same. 'It was the Nazi bastard, wasn't it?'

'I don't think it was him.'

'How can you be so sure, if it was dark? Is he threatening you?'

'No, no.'

'What's going on here?' Dutch John appeared in the doorway.

'Shit!' Lance bent forward and tried to hide his face.

Dutch John strode towards us. 'Fuck, what happened to you?'

Lance shook his head. 'Nothing.'

Dutch John touched the side of Lance's face and looked

at the cuts. 'You need stitches. I'll get something.'

When Lance shifted on the bench, his shirt fell open. His chest was covered in cuts and bruises.

'Bloody hell Lance!'

'How did this happen?' said Dutch John.

Having seen Lance's chest, I regretted promising not to tell anyone. Clearly the attack was much worse than I'd first thought. Dutch John had to know. 'He was—'

Lance scowled at me. 'I got into a fight in the village.'

Dutch John lifted the hem of Lance's shirt. 'You could have a cracked rib or even bleeding inside.'

'I'll be fine.' Lance winced as he shifted his weight.

'No. If you die, there's lots of fucking paperwork.' Dutch John stood up. 'So, come on, hospital.'

'But I can't afford that.'

'You crazy guy. The factory pays. Insurance.'

Dutch John's genuine concern surprised me. He always behaved like he'd be happy to see us all die. 'Come on Lance, at least you'll get a decent bed for the night,' I said.

Lance winced again. 'Okay.'

Dutch John helped him over the field and eased him into the passenger seat of his car.

'Do you want me to come with you?'

'You get to bed. You don't wanna miss your shift,' said Lance.

The car pulled away. I couldn't understand how anyone would attack Lance, such a sweet harmless guy. Despite what he'd said, I sensed he knew who'd done it. But why was he protecting him? It had to be Jimmy. He'd hated Lance from the moment he saw him. I shuffled back into the canteen, picked up my book, but wasn't in the mood to study. So I went back to the dorm.

I thought about telling Gideon what had happened. Perhaps he was right, maybe we should leave. The factory work was bad enough, but knowing a racist attacker was prowling around made everything a million times worse. But I wanted to persuade Lance to do something about it, not pretend it never happened. So I had to stay. I tossed and turned on my bunk until the first grey light of dawn appeared.

Kenny sat up and stretched his arms. 'Ahh, another wonderful day of onions.'

'Good morning,' I said.

'Awake already? Not like you.' Kenny got down off his bunk. 'And Lance too. He's usually dead to the fucking world. Where is he?'

'Dutch John took him to hospital.'

'Fucking hell!' Kenny flopped onto the end of my bunk and leaned towards me. It was the first time I'd seen him look in any way unsettled. 'Why?'

Despite my promise to Lance not to say anything, I decided the attack had been far worse than when I'd made the promise. Even though I knew Kenny would get angry, perhaps *because* I knew he'd get angry, I said, 'Someone beat him up.'

'Fuck.' Kenny punched the mattress so hard the metal bed frame shook. 'I'm gonna kill that fucking Nazi.' He leapt off the mattress.

'No, Kenny, you can't.'

'Just fucking watch me.' He grabbed the trousers hanging on the end of his bed.

'Lance doesn't know who did it.'

'Well, guess what? I fucking do.'

I jumped out of bed and grabbed Kenny's arm. 'It was dark. He couldn't see.'

'How the fuck do you know all this?'

'I was in the canteen after the attack.'

Kenny paused. 'How bad is he?'

'A swollen eye, bruises, cuts. I don't think it's too bad.'

'But he's in the fucking hospital.'

'Dutch John wanted to get him checked.'

Kenny grabbed his bunk and shook it so hard it banged against the wall. 'I promised to fucking look after him.'

'Kenny, it wasn't your fault.'

Gideon sat up in his bunk and stretched. 'What's going on?'

'Lance has been attacked,' I said.

'Shit!'

'He's in the fucking hospital.'

'Precautionary.' I made to reach for Kenny's arm, but he pulled it away. 'Kenny, please, we don't know anything,'

Kenny stormed out of the dorm.

'As if this place wasn't crappy enough already. I guess the shift goes on.' Gideon jumped off his bunk. 'Thank God we're going to Amsterdam.'

Amsterdam! I'd forgotten about that. 'We can't go, not after this.'

'Now we should go more than ever.'

'It wouldn't seem right after what's happened.'

'Christ Marky, you make it sound like Lance has died.' Gideon gripped my shoulder. 'He'll be fine, and we'll be fine if we get away from this shithole for a couple of days. Come on Marky.'

I pulled my shoulder out of Gideon's grip. 'Hopefully, Lance will be well enough by the weekend.' I pulled open the wardrobe and took out my overalls.

'But even if he's not we should still go.'

'I wouldn't be able to enjoy it.'

'Believe me, you'll feel a whole lot better after a trip. We both will.'

Gideon was right. I wanted to get away for a few days more than ever now. As we walked down the corridor I looked at the other guys, to think one of them had attacked Lance made me want to leave. I was relieved when we reached the canteen to see Kenny there, eating his breakfast. At least he hadn't done anything stupid. When the other shift arrived, I stared at Jimmy. I tried to get a glimpse of his knuckles, but I couldn't see them clearly.

Kenny just glared at him. 'If that fucking Nazi attacked Lance, he's fucking dead.' He slurped the last drop of tea out of his cup. 'After today's shift, I'm gonna visit the hospital and find out who fucking did it.'

'I'll come along too.' I said.

'You don't need to,' said Kenny.

'Why go?' said Gideon.

'I'm concerned about Lance.' Which was true, but I also wanted to make sure Lance was still up for going to Amsterdam.

'Do you even know where to find him?' said Gideon.

'They always use the same fucking hospital.'

'This has happened before?' I looked at Kenny.

'Last year, there was a riot. A few people got hurt.'

After the shift, Kenny and I showered and grabbed a quick bite. As we were walking to the bus stop, I asked, 'Do you think we should buy Lance something?'

'Like what?'

'Flowers?'

'Do you think a bunch of fucking roses is going to make him feel better?'

'Isn't it what people do…on hospital visits?'

'I don't give a fuck what other people do. I just want to find out who did this to him.'

'Then what will you do?'

'It's better you don't know.'

The bus pulled up, and we climbed aboard.

'But shouldn't we go to the police?'

He glared at me with such contempt I think if we'd been near the door he would have kicked me off the bus. 'What are the fucking Dutch police gonna do about some black British boy, getting attacked in some poxy onion factory—'

'But still.'

'They'll do fuck all.'

I realised it was going to be hard, maybe impossible to dissuade Kenny from taking revenge on Lance's behalf. There was a part of me that agreed, the police would probably do nothing, and I didn't want whoever attacked Lance to get away with it. But I feared the violence might escalate.

The hospital was a five-minute walk from the bus

station. It was surrounded by a neat lawn dotted with linden trees and pink rose bushes. As we approached the entrance, I caught an aroma of apricot; I paused for a moment, soothed by the fragrance: such a contrast from the pungent onion juice laced with sweat I'd been smelling for almost two weeks.

'Are you fucking coming or what?' said Kenny.

'Yes, sorry.' I followed him into the hospital.

Lance was in a bed at the far end of the men's ward, sipping something through a straw and staring out the window.

Kenny shouted, 'Hey Lancey! Are y'all right?'

Lance turned, spilling some of his drink. 'Kenny.'

'Hi. How are you?' I said.

'Why are you guys here?'

'Well that's fucking charming.' Kenny plopped himself on the edge of Lance's bed.

'Sorry, I didn't expect anyone.' Lance winced as he stretched to put the glass on the cabinet next to his bed. The swelling around his eye had gone down a little and the cuts on his cheek, cleaned and stitched, looked a lot less severe.

'We just came to make sure you were okay.'

'Sorry, no flowers. This do-gooding bastard wouldn't let me nick any,' said Kenny.

Lance winced as he laughed.

'Hey, you don't look too good,' I said.

'I'm okay.'

'So when you coming back?' Kenny raised his hand as if he was about to pinch Lance's cheek like he was a seven-year-old. He reconsidered and instead gripped his shoulder.

Lance shook his head and coughed. 'Guys, I'm not coming back.'

'Fuck! No.' Kenny glanced at me and used his face to hint I should say something encouraging.

'Lance, in a couple of days, you'll be buzzing again. And then there's Amsterdam.'

'I was really looking forward to that, but sorry guys. I can't sit on my arse for twelve sodding hours a day? No way.'

'I can ask French Pierre to give you a different job,' said Kenny.

'Kenny, I can't.'

The tattoo of the word "HATE" on the knuckles of Kenny's right hand seemed to get bigger as he twisted the edge of the blanket in his fingers. His quick breaths sounded like the snorts of a bull getting ready to charge. 'Who the fuck did this to you?'

'It all happened so fast.'

Kenny twisted the blanket tighter. 'It was that fucking Nazi bastard, wasn't it?'

'It was dark.'

Kenny punched the mattress. 'Come on Lance, tell me that fucking Nazi did this and I'll make sure he doesn't walk again.'

'Kenny, calm down,' I said.

'I won't fucking calm down. Look what he did.' Kenny slid off the bed. 'Did you hear his voice?'

Lance shook his head. 'He didn't say anything.'

'I bet he stank of fucking beer, that Nazi—'

Lance shook his head.

'Has he threatened you?'

'Nobody has threatened me.' Lance looked imploringly at the two of us. 'Please guys, I just want to forget about it.'

Kenny gave me a "You have a fucking try" look.

'Lance, I understand you just want to forget about this and get away from here, but this guy needs to be stopped—'

'He needs to be taught a fucking lesson.'

'So just tell us. We won't do anything hasty, will we Kenny?'

Kenny snorted and paced up and down by Lance's bed.

'Honestly guys, I don't know who did it.'

'Just give me a fucking hint.'

'I can't.'

Kenny went over to the window. He looked around as if searching for something to throw through it. After a few seconds, he put his hands on the sill, bent forward and took long breaths. 'If it was that fucking Nazi, just nod. I'll do the rest.'

'Kenny, the guy did me a favour.'

'How the fuck can you say that?'

'I hated every second here. You could see that. The bed, the barracks, the work, the racists. I hated everything. I tried, I really did.' Lance winced as he leaned towards Kenny. 'And thank you so much for standing up for me.' Lance's voice began to shake. 'I'll never forget it.'

Kenny gave a brief smile.

'Come on Kenny, Lance doesn't need us causing him any more strife.'

Kenny took a long, calming breath. He nodded at Lance. 'Okay, because I fucking like you so much. I'm going to do what you want and leave it. But it's fucking wrong.'

'Thank you.'

'But if you remember anything, you tell me. Even years from now, you fucking tell me, right?'

Lance nodded.

Kenny looked around. 'Pen?'

'Maybe outside,' I said.

Kenny headed to the corridor.

'Lance, are you just trying to stop Kenny from killing someone?'

'No, honestly, I don't know.'

'You can tell me. I won't go crazy like him. I'll just tell Dutch John.'

'I saw nothing.' Lance looked away.

I was sure he was lying. But could also tell he wasn't going to change his mind. I couldn't understand why he was protecting whoever it was.

Kenny came back in. 'Okay, here's my number.' Kenny handed Lance a piece of paper. 'You remember anything you call, right? Tomorrow, next week, fucking ten years from now, you call me, okay?'

Lance nodded. 'Now guys, I need to rest.' He held out

his hand.

I shook it. 'Good luck. What about your stuff?'

'Oh yeah, I called Dutch John. He's going to bring everything over.'

Kenny grabbed Lance's hand. 'Sorry I couldn't protect you.' For a moment, it looked like he was going to resume the interrogation.

'Come on, Kenny.' I touched his arm and led him to the door.

'Good luck, guys.'

As we walked out of the hospital, Kenny said, 'He's fucking lying.'

'Maybe.'

'There's no maybe about it. I'm not going to drop it.'

'Kenny, we should just do as he says and forget about it. He's not coming back, so why bother?'

'It's not fucking right, that's why.'

'But if you beat up the wrong guy.'

Kenny was silent for the whole of the bus journey. I wasn't sure whether it was because he'd decided Jimmy had attacked Lance and was planning what to do with him, or if he was so angry with himself for allowing Lance to be attacked.

When we got back to the barracks, Gideon was in the canteen.

'How is the little soldier?'

'He isn't coming back.' I dragged a chair from under the table and sat down.

'That's a real shame. I liked the little guy.'

'You hardly said a fucking word to him,' said Kenny.

'That's not true.'

'If it wasn't for stuck-up fucking bigots like you, he'd still be here.'

'It sounds like you think I did it.'

'Did you?'

'Kenny!' I looked up at him. 'You can't go around accusing people.'

'Someone in this fucking factory did it, and he's going to get away with it.' Kenny kicked a chair over, then stormed out of the canteen.

'Well, someone's a teeny bit touchy.'

'Shut up, Gideon. He's angry and rightly so.'

'Come on Marky, these people don't matter, don't get so involved. Look, in a couple of days we'll be in Amsterdam. Forget all this macho nonsense and think of that.'

I looked beyond him at the grey sky behind the blackness of Barrel Mountain, as the millionth lorry carrying the billionth onion trundled past. Gideon was right, we needed to get away more now than ever. I wished Lance was coming with us, and I was anxious about what might happen between me and Gideon. But I remembered the apricot aroma from the roses outside the hospital. I needed more moments like that, when the sheer beauty of the world cut through the grey onion-stinking reality of life in the factory.

'Amsterdam's gonna be great,' said Gideon.

'I hope so.' I smiled, then coughed as the wind picked up and carried an overwhelming onion stench from the factory.

9

'Stop here!' When the taxi stopped, Gideon pushed open the door, flung his rucksack onto the pavement, then gesticulated for me to follow. 'Come on!'

I manoeuvred myself out of the taxi, then picked up the rucksack Gideon had dumped. 'I'm too knackered for jokes. Let's get to the hostel.'

'But sire, your room awaits.' Gideon bowed.

'Very funny, haha, now come on.'

'Seriously Marky, I booked two nights of five-star luxury.'

Gideon took his rucksack from me and skipped down the steps towards the entrance of the Ambassade Hotel. 'Come on, we've earned it.'

I should've guessed there was no way Gideon was going to slum it in a hostel, even a one-star hotel would have been way beneath his standards. Somehow, he'd survived two weeks in the barracks. Hard work, terrible food, the constant ribbing from Kenny, not to mention the total lack of sex. My admiration for his endurance was only exceeded by my bewilderment that he hadn't given up. But I'd told him I wanted to stay somewhere cheap, and the Ambassade was definitely not that. The door to the hotel swung open, a woman wearing a flowing yellow silk dress and more diamonds than The Crown Jewels glided up the steps like a yellow rose caught on the breeze.

'If I'd known you were going to do this, I'd never have come.'

'That's why I didn't tell you. Don't worry, I'm paying.

Come on Marky, it isn't even loose change.' He turned his head in the little boy lost way he did whenever he knew he was pushing his luck.

I had no idea how much a room in the Ambassade cost, probably more than I'd earn in the whole time I would be working at the factory, so there was no way I would have been able to pay, even if I'd wanted to. But I was angry Gideon had overlooked my wishes. I looked at the darkened glass door of the hotel entrance. My reflection, me in faded jeans and lumberjack shirt, looked like a man-sized smudge on the pristine glass. 'Will they even let us in?'

'Of course they bloody will. I've booked the Grande Suite.'

The closest my family ever came to staying anywhere posh was Aunt Maisie's guest house in Weston-Super-Mare. It had no suites, Grande or otherwise. Just tiny rooms with shared bathrooms and an ever-present smell of boiled potatoes. "Grande" sounded expensive. 'Gideon, it's too much. Come on, there must be a cheap hotel nearby.'

Gideon shook his head. 'Too late, it's all been paid for.'

'Why the hell did you do that?' I thought about abandoning him and going to find a cheap hostel for myself, even heading to the station and going back to the factory. But I was shattered. My lower back ached from all the bending I'd been doing on the onion sorter, and the thought of a long soak in a warm bath was a whole lot more enticing than lugging my rucksack around Amsterdam.

'Come on Marky! Surely you can swallow your Marxist conscience for a couple of nights.'

I bit my lip, then said, 'Okay. But I'm only going along with this because I'm so bloody tired.'

'Great.' Gideon held open the hotel door. 'After vous.'

As soon as we entered, a porter wearing a dark blue uniform and a peaked military-style cap approached us.

'Good afternoon, this is the Ambassade Hotel.' There was a long pause, he looked us up and down as if both coping with the idea that such a pair of smelly tramps would even contemplate setting foot in his domain, and deciding how to address us. Eventually, he hissed, 'Gentlemen.'

'I'm fully aware of where I am. Thank you very much, my good man. Can you direct me to reception?'

I couldn't help but admire Gideon's haughty aplomb. The porter's eyes widened as if he'd been expecting us to turn around and walk out, and not treat him with the same disdain he'd shown us.

'Did you hear me?' said Gideon.

'Yes sir. Over there, sir.' He bowed his head slightly and pointed a gloved hand at a chalk-white reception desk in the corner of the lobby.

'Thank you.' Gideon strode towards it.

'Good afternoon, sir.' The receptionist sneezed.

'Bless you.' Gideon opened his rucksack.

She sneezed twice more. 'Excuse me, sir.'

'Bless you again. Gideon Grieve, I've booked the Grande Suite for two nights.'

When the receptionist sneezed again, I wondered if it was because of the smell of onions. I turned so my nose was over my shoulder, then lowered my head as surreptitiously as I could and sniffed. There was an onion whiff, but it didn't seem very strong. I feared perhaps I'd been immersed in the smell for so long it had become part of me and it no longer stood out.

The receptionist filled in the register, beckoned the porter and handed him the keys. Gideon and I followed him along a corridor to a tiny lift. In the cramped space, the onion smell became so strong the porter had a fit of sneezes. I had to avoid making eye contact with Gideon because I knew if I did, we'd both have hysterics. The door opened, the porter gave one last loud sneeze and stepped into the corridor. He held open the only door.

'Thank you.' Gideon slid some cash into his gloved hand. Then bowed to me. 'Sire, your room.'

'Stop it.' I shook my head, then stepped inside.

The room was so ornate I felt like I'd stepped into a giant jewellery box. There was a thick blood-red carpet, patterned with gold fleur-de-lis. The walls were cream, and they repeated the fleur-de-lis pattern. The furniture was the sort I'd only ever seen in stately homes, cordoned off behind thick velvet ropes and covered in cards embossed with "DO NOT SIT" in big black letters. I took a deep breath of the soft breeze blowing through the French windows and stepped back into the corridor.

'What are you doing?' said Gideon.

'I'm filthy.'

'Don't be so bloody ridiculous.' He swaggered into the room, then tossed his rucksack onto the floor.

'Gideon!'

He flopped onto one sofa, tossed the two duck egg blue cushions onto the floor, then tapped the seat. 'Join me.'

I looked around. Every surface was expensive, old, scuffable.

Gideon jumped up. 'Oh come on, stop being so bloody mothery.' He pulled the rucksack out of my hands and dumped it next to his own. He strode over to a spiral staircase. 'Come and have a look, it's a duplex.'

I didn't even know what duplex meant and wondered if it was yet another sexual practice I'd missed out on. With some trepidation, I followed him up the staircase.

'We don't have twin beds.' Gideon flung open one door. Then crossed to the opposite side. 'We have, ta-da... twin rooms.' He did the same with the other door.

'Christ! Gideon, this must've cost a bomb.'

'Stop being so Thatcherite about money. If I'd come alone, I would've booked the same suite.'

'Not like you to mock the Beloved Margaret.'

Although shocked by the extravagance, and angry Gideon had done all this without asking me, I was relieved we had two rooms. I wouldn't have to be alone in a room with him and wouldn't see him undressing. So no danger of any Nick-type incidents.

'Look Marky, I just want us to enjoy the weekend. Sod the expense.'

I knew what Gideon meant when he said "Enjoy the weekend". Sex. Lots of sex. I sighed. I didn't want to spend two nights being his wingman. Going from bar to bar, helping him find girls to bring back to this palace. 'Does twin rooms mean you'll be bringing girls back?'

'Good God no.'

'But—'

'I don't intend wasting my time chatting up, paying for drinks, dinner, whatever, all for some disappointing shag. We only have what?' He looked at his watch. 'Forty hours until we're back with the onions.'

'So how are you going to, "enjoy the weekend"?'

Gideon leaned back and let out a long laugh. 'Brothels Marky, brothels. Look, I haven't had sex for weeks. I'm going fucking crazy, literally. So I'm gonna pay and I don't care.'

I was relieved. Whilst he was off getting his end away, I could go to a couple of museums. Maybe the trip wasn't going to be so bad after all.

'So I'm going to a brothel.' He stepped toward me and gripped my shoulders. 'And you're coming with me.'

'What? No way. No, Gideon.'

'Yes Gideon. My mission this weekend, apart obviously from getting in a few quick shags, is for you to lose your cherry.'

My calmness evaporated. The idea that Gideon was going to drag me to some dingy flea-bitten brothel, so I could lose my virginity to some toothless whore, filled me with dread and embarrassment. Despite the time when he'd made a token offer to help me find a girl at Ritzy's, he'd shown no interest in my sex life whatsoever. So I'd always imagined he regarded my virginity as largely irrelevant and possibly endearingly eccentric. But the realisation he'd thought about it enough to want to help me lose it in a brothel was humiliating. 'Really, Gideon, I don't need to.'

'Oh you do Marky, you bloody well do. I've seen you

ogling girls at Ritzy's. Too nervous to do anything. We all have to start somewhere.' He gripped my shoulders again. 'And where better to lose your virginity than Amsterdam?'

'I'm happy to wait.'

'That waiting for the right girl crap ends here. Just think, after this, when you're back at UEA, you'll be so confident you'll get all the girls you want. And don't worry, I'll pay for everything.'

'No Gideon.'

'Don't even bother to argue about that. You've helped me get sex often enough.'

He could be right. If I had sex with a prostitute, a total stranger, someone I'd never see again, I wouldn't be so anxious. Then after I'd done it, I'd know I wasn't a poof, and all those memories and regrets about Nick, and those moments when I found myself attracted to Gideon, would be a thing of the past.

Gideon sniffed his armpit. 'You know you're right. We bloody reek of onions. Hang on.' He went downstairs and came back with the rucksacks. 'Let's unpack. Have long baths and then go shagging.'

I went into my room and stood by the window, staring at the boats on the canal. Even though I was terrified, I was also curious. Gideon was giving me the chance to banish all doubts about my sexuality. I would never have thought of going to a brothel to do it. I just wished he'd told me sooner so I could have had time to prepare. I went into the bathroom and ran the bath. On the shelf was a row of small plastic bottles, one blue, one red, one orange. I chose the red one because I like strawberries, but mainly to show solidarity with the Trotskyite gods so they wouldn't let Helga and Bryony know I was about to exploit a woman for sex. After I'd scrubbed every inch of my body, the bath water was a filthy onion colour. I pulled the plug, showered, then ran another bath. I lowered myself into the water and let out a long, slow breath as it soothed and calmed me.

A knock on the door woke me. Gideon, wearing a white cotton dressing gown, was leaning against the doorjamb. He was holding two glasses of red wine. He grinned like a Parisian roué about to seduce a young virgin and offered me one of the glasses.

Whilst I'd been sleeping, I'd gotten hard. I sat up, making sure my cock was fully immersed. 'Gideon!'

'Hey, why so jumpy? Change of plan. All my clothes stink. Forget tonight, we better go to the brothel early tomorrow.' He picked my jeans and shirt off the floor. 'Get your rucksack.'

'Why?'

'Christ Marky, I'm not rummaging through your filthy undies.'

'I'll sort it out later.'

'No, now. I'm going to call reception to get everything cleaned for tomorrow. So chop-chop.'

I sighed and lifted myself out of the bath.

'Wow!' Gideon grinned. 'I envy the first girl who's going to have that inside her.'

'Shut up!' I grabbed a towel and wrapped it around my waist. Hoping he hadn't noticed the slight cock-throb when I heard his admiring comment.

'Spoilsport.'

When I stepped out of the bath, Gideon pointed at the mirror. 'Who are those two devastating Adonises? Oh, it's us. I reckon the girls should pay us.'

I went into the bedroom, pulled my clothes out of the rucksack, and dropped them in the laundry bag.

Gideon swung the bag over his shoulder. 'See you bright and randy tomorrow.'

I stood for a moment, relieved we had postponed the brothel visit: it gave me time to prepare. I went back to my bath. Lay in the water until it was cold. Then went to bed.

10

'Look at this, proper food!' Gideon slid his overloaded plate onto the table. 'Come on Marky. I've seen you eat more of Dutch John's crap.'

I stared at the half-eaten slice of toast and the smudge of strawberry jam on the side of my plate. 'I'm not hungry.'

'You need to build your strength. Big day ahead.' Gideon stretched his fingers in front of his chest, then made a squeezing motion. 'In a couple of hours, you'll be clinging onto an enormous pair of knockers, like a life jacket.'

'Gideon!' I looked around at the other guests.

'Don't worry, everyone here's doing the same.'

I looked at the two grey-haired women at the next table. With matching beige cardigans and frowns, they were picking at their food as if eating were a mortal sin, I doubted whether brothels were high on their itinerary.

'Please eat some more.' Gideon nodded towards the buffet.

I was too nervous to eat, but to appease him, I shuffled over to the food. I'd had a rough night. Every time I woke up, I decided I didn't want to go to the brothel. I tried to come up with excuses. I was sick. Tired. Desperate to see Van Gogh's *Sunflowers*. But I knew Gideon would see right through me. And maybe he was right. A shag with a prostitute could be just what I needed. I half-filled a bowl with Corn Flakes and headed back to our table. As I brushed past the beige women one of them scrunched her nose.

'Do we still stink?'

Gideon buried his nose in his armpit and took a noisy sniff. 'Not a trace.'

'Do you need to be so obvious?'

'We can't still stink.' He tugged his t-shirt. 'Freshly laundered, and how many showers have you had since we arrived?'

'Lost count. But people are looking at us, or me, at any rate.'

'Who can blame them, a virile young buck like you?' When Gideon noticed one of the women looking at him, he flexed his biceps. She shook her head, tutted, then lifted her cup to her thin lips.

'Jesus, Gideon.' I munched my Corn Flakes like they were iron filings as Gideon devoured yet another rasher of bacon. I kept quiet for the rest of the meal, not wanting him to make any more embarrassing comments or gestures.

I was surprised. I'd expected the brothel to be in a seedy part of the city. Instead, Gideon led me to another canal house just behind the hotel. I assumed it had been built at the same time as the Ambassade because it was the same height and style. But there, the similarities ended. Its paint was flaking and all the windows were grubby and opaque. However, I could still see my reflection in one of them, only this time, I saw a terrified boy.

'Come on Marky, you'll be fine.'

Gideon slid his arm around my waist. He guided me down the steps to a green door. No stuck-up porter this time. The door was opened by a young woman in a black dress and white apron. I wasn't sure whether she was dressed as a waitress because she was genuinely one or because she was part of someone's fantasy. She led us along a corridor lit only by dusty swan-neck crystal chandeliers. When she opened the door at the end of the corridor, I half expected Joel Grey to burst through the doorway singing "Willkommen".

Although the bar was gloomy, there was still enough light for me to see it had a thick blood-red carpet, I smiled when I noticed, unlike the carpet in the hotel, instead of fleur-de-lis it was decorated with cigarette burns. And the only fresco on the ceiling was a swirl of nicotine stains.

The girl said, 'Can I get you some drinks?'

'No thanks,' said Gideon.

He pointed to a stool. Its cushioned, ivory-coloured plastic seat was dotted with cigarette burns as if it had been tortured. 'You sit here Marky.' He turned to the waitress. 'May I have a word with the Madame?'

The waitress looked surprised. 'I will call her.'

'No. Take me to her.' Gideon pulled a ten-guilder note out of his wallet and slid it into the pocket of her apron. She smiled and led him towards the door.

'Where are you going?'

Gideon put his finger to his lips.

I sat on the stool. I was relieved and surprised there were no other customers. It was 10 am., which I assumed was early for a brothel, even in Amsterdam. Gideon had been aggravated about missing out on sex yesterday because of our smelly clothes. So he'd woken me up at seven.

'Come on Marky. Breakfast. I want to have as many rounds as possible.'

In my bleary state, I'd assumed he meant rounds of the buffet, he actually meant rounds at the brothel. I wondered whether he'd even paid to have it opened especially for us; I decided I'd rather not know, so didn't ask.

It amazed me how at home he was. He strode around the place like he owned it, which, given his family's wealth, I suppose wasn't entirely out of the question. But there was more to his swagger. It was as if he knew how brothels worked. Perhaps a clue as to what he'd done for sex before he came to UEA.

He reappeared. 'Right, I told the madame you're a virgin.'

'Bloody hell Gideon, why did you do that?' As if I wasn't already cripplingly self-conscious enough.

'Because it's the truth.'

'I know but—'

'Look Marky. She's got a lovely girl lined up for you, who specialises, in, well,' Gideon paused, obviously trying to find a word or phrase that would accurately describe my inexperience without making me feel smaller than I already did. 'She specialises in rookies. She'll guide you gently into the wonderful world of sex.'

My nerves kicked in. I trembled and thought I was going to vomit, so swallowed hard. 'Maybe I should just sit here and wait for you.'

'No way. No chickening out now. It's all arranged.' He pulled a stool over and sat close to me. He pointed to the corridor. 'Just think about it Marky, in less than an hour you'll be walking, walking? No, you'll be bloody dancing down that corridor. Ready to go out and shag the world.' He slapped my back, which had I eaten a bigger breakfast could well have triggered a bout of severe projectile vomiting.

'Maybe another time?'

'First-time nerves, old man. First-time nerves. Once you're in the room, you'll be fine.'

'What about you?'

'Don't worry about me.'

Two girls crept into the bar and slunk over the carpet like hungry leopards crossing the savannah. I swallowed hard. And tried to calm my thumping heart. One girl was black. She was wearing a pink bikini; she looked to be in her early twenties. The other was white, slightly older, wearing a crimson one-piece.

'See you later.' Gideon winked at me and slapped the white girl's bum as she led him out.

'Hi, I'm Feather. What's your name?'

'Nice to meet you, Feather. I'm Ma...Ma....Martin...' I had no idea why I gave a false name. I just wished I'd thought ahead and come up with something sexier than Martin.

'Hello Martin, let's go somewhere quiet.' She leaned into me and whispered. 'So we can get to know each other.' She took my hand and led me up to the first floor and into another dimly lit corridor. She pushed open one door with the tips of her flamingo-pink fingernails and stepped inside. I hesitated in the doorway.

'Don't be scared Martin.' She pulled me inside and then shut the door. She leaned so close, my lips were warmed with the heat from hers. There was a hint of wine on her breath. When she brushed her lips against mine, I shuddered. When her breasts pressed into my chest, I stepped back.

'Oops sorry.'

'That's okay Martin.' She slid her hands behind my neck and kissed me again.

I recoiled. 'Sorry, I've never done this.'

'That's why you're so special to me. Come.' She drew me towards the bed. 'Just open your lips a little bit.' This time when we kissed, she slid the tip of her tongue along the inside of my lips.

I shuddered.

'Let's take this off.' She undid a button on my shirt and caressed my chest. 'Wow...so strong.' She undid two more buttons, then tweaked my left nipple.

I moved back.

'Don't you like me?'

'I like you, at least what little I know about you. Given we've only just met.'

She giggled. 'You're funny. So let's get to know each other, very, very.' Her fingers tugged the top of my jeans. 'Well.' She slid her tongue over my lips again.

I gulped. 'Yes...yes we... that would be nice.' I noticed a small fridge. 'Actually, I'm a bit thirsty. Do you have anything... water, maybe?'

'Of course.' She sidled over to the fridge, took a swig out of a bottle as her eyes seemed to eat me up, then leaned towards me.

I stepped back. 'Actually Feather, no offence. I'm sure you're very clean. But would you mind if I drank from the bottle?'

She giggled and handed it to me. Then knelt and slid her fingers over the zip of my jeans. Making me swallow the wrong way which gave me a coughing fit.

'Martin, are you okay?'

I cleared my throat. 'Fine! I'm... fine.'

The tips of her fingers pressed against my dick. 'Still sleeping. I'll wake him up.' She slid her fingers inside.

I gasped. 'Shit.' I leaned towards a ledge, trying to put the bottle on it, but it was out of reach.

When she pulled down my jeans and underwear and then cupped my balls, I coughed again.

'Hey Martin, I'm not a doctor. You don't need to cough.'

I laughed nervously.

'Just relax.'

I didn't dare look down, too embarrassed to see her fingers desperately stroking and tickling. I clenched my buttocks, trying to force blood into my flaccid dick. I couldn't understand. It got hard at some very awkward moments, but now when I wanted it to, nothing was happening. The soft touch of Feather's fingertips on my balls made me shiver.

'Now you know why I'm called Feather.'

'Yes, yes, very... feathery. Is there somewhere I can put this?' I shook the bottle.

'Just drop it on the floor.'

There was some irritation in her tone. I couldn't blame her. When she licked the tip of my dick, I looked down. It looked smaller than usual as if cowering from her lips. She took the bottle out of my hand and put it on the floor. Then slipped my left hand under her bikini. I decided to at least show willing so I put my right hand on her other breast.

'That's good, Martin.'

Still nothing. I imagined her later, laughing with her friends as she told them about the young English guy who couldn't get it up. It shouldn't have bothered me, but it did. Maybe if we sat and talked, got to know each other at least a little, that might help. Maybe if we talked so much, she might even forget about doing anything at all. But I had no idea what an Amsterdam prostitute would want to talk about. Canals? Tulips? Windmills? I just wanted her to stop. When she slid my dick in her mouth, like it was a floppy chipolata, the only thing I could think of to say was…

'Does my dick smell of onions?'

She took it out of her mouth and looked up at me. The skin of her beautifully smooth forehead was creased for a moment with a frown. After a few seconds, she said. 'Yes, it does.'

'Oh no, I'm really sorry.'

'It stinks and your balls are like two rotten red onions, you dirty, dirty boy.'

I wondered why people had recently taken to making unflattering comments about my balls. Kenny had compared them to ice cubes and now Feather to rotten red onions. What next? Lumps of coal? Brussels sprouts? Dead mice?

'But I showered and bathed three times.'

'Not enough. Next time you dirty, dirty boy. Shower and bathe six times before you come to see Feather or… I will crush you like this.' She squeezed my balls.

'Ow…ow…ow.'

'And if you come here dirty after that I will get my whip, and whip you till you bleed.'

'Whip! Blood! That's a bit harsh.'

'So you must stop being such a dirty, smelly boy.'

'But I did clean. I used half a bottle of shampoo down there. I can't help it if I'm working in an onion factory.'

She stopped, leaned back, and looked at me. She tilted her head and frowned. 'Onion factory?'

'Yes, with my friend.'

'You're being serious?'

'Of course, I'm being bloody serious. That's what I'm doing in Holland. What did you think?'

Feather let go of my dick, put her hand over her mouth

and laughed, her whole body shaking.

'What's so funny?'

'I thought...my God...I thought.' She leaned back against the side of the bed, both hands over her face as she laughed. 'I thought onion talk turned you on.'

'How the hell could anyone be turned on by bloody onions?'

She sat on the bed and wiped the tears out of her eyes. 'Some men have very weird tastes.'

'So I don't smell of onions.'

'No Martin, you smell sweet and taste even better.' She leaned forward and kissed my dick.

I hoped that moment of levity would have relaxed me and enabled me to get hard. But when she slid my dick in her mouth and I clenched again, all I had was the image of a worm wriggling on a hook.

Feather sucked, licked, purred, groaned.

No reaction.

'Don't be nervous. Just relax and let Feather do all the work.'

As I was trying to think of how to get away without embarrassing myself even more or offending Feather, I heard sex noises coming from next door.

'Fuck yeah, fuck yeah. You like it?'

Judging by the volume, very passionate sex. Which only made the flaccid non-event happening below even more awkward. As I heard loud groans, I realised it was Gideon.

'Shit.'

'What's the matter?'

I shook my head. 'Nothing.'

Gideon's groans and the squeaking of the metal springs were so loud it was almost as if he was in the room.

'You like that, you sexy bitch?'

'Yes, yes, harder, harder.'

This was now officially the most embarrassing moment of my life. Next door someone was showing how it was done, and that person was bloody Gideon, and it was underlining just how hopeless I was. As I tried to think of how to get away, Feather said,

'Yes Martin. Here he comes.'

I noticed the first stirrings of an erection.

'Yes, yes, yes,' said Gideon.

I got harder.

'Wow Martin! I knew you were a big boy.' Feather looked up at me and smiled.

When the bed next door started banging against the wall, I visualised the girl lying on her back. Gideon on top, his sweaty muscular biceps flexing as he thrust into her.

'Martin, soon you can fuck me,' Feather said.

Gideon's voice got louder. 'Wow…yeah fuck…fuck.'

'No, stay like this.' I closed my eyes.

Gideon let out an ear-piercing groan, then, 'Oh yeah…yeah…yeah…'

When I imagined Gideon's sweaty, spent body pressing down on the girl as her hands gripped his buttocks, I shot into Feather's mouth. She recoiled and fell back against the side of the bed. I bent forward, my heart thumping. My dick still spurting. Images of Gideon's sweaty body now lying on top of me.

'Fuck.' Feather jumped up and pulled open a drawer. She took out a flannel and cleared her mouth with it.

'I..I'm really sorry. It just…I lost control.'

Feather picked the bottle up off the floor, swigged the remains of the water, swirled it around her mouth, then spat into a basin. 'You should've warned me.'

'Sorry.'

She handed me some tissues. I wrapped them around my still hard dick and leaned towards next door, trying to hear what was going on, but there was silence. When I was soft. I unwrapped the tissues and tossed them into a bin. I dressed and stood in the middle of the room like a blade of grass stuck in the onion sorter mesh, helpless as a scraper was about to slice it in two.

'Martin, show's over, you can go.'

I didn't move.

'Martin! Martin!'

Eventually, I remembered I'd given a false name. 'Yes, sorry.'

Feather held open the door, and I gave her a weak smile as I walked past. 'I'm really sorry,' I said.

I paused outside Gideon's room. I wanted to see inside. I wanted to be inside.

With him.

I reached for the handle but pulled my hand away. Then crept back to the "Cabaret" room.

'Would you like a drink, sir?' said the waitress.

'No, I'm just waiting.'

I had no idea what I was going to say to Gideon. He'd expect a blow-by-blow account, literally, of what had happened. And expect me to be brimming. But I never wanted to be naked with anyone ever again. I would read books, study, and if I ever thought about sex, I'd have a cold shower, or a hot shower, whatever worked. I never wanted to be intimate with anyone ever again. The time with Feather would have been bad enough. But then Jesus, I shook my head. What was a million times worse was hearing Gideon's grunts and groans. And what was a billion times worse was getting hard when I heard him. Now I knew for definite I was a poof, which would have been bad enough, but I was a poof who was desperate to be fucked by his straight best friend.

'Thank you, Bambi, I bloody needed that.' Gideon's booming voice came from upstairs.

A few seconds later, he appeared in the doorway.

'There he is. There he is.' His pointed index fingers flicked up and down as if divining my loss of virginity. 'The boy who just lost his cherry.'

One moment, I wanted to grab him and show him I could kiss a million times better than Bambi. The next moment, I wanted to turn and run and never see him again. I gripped my stool, looked at him, and somehow managed to smile.

11

Gideon slapped my back. 'Well done Marky boy! Next term it'll be you getting all the girls.'

He lowered himself onto a stool, then like a boxer resting between rounds he lolled, his arms falling to his sides, legs spread wide so his ankles dug into the carpet. 'God, I needed that.'

I looked towards the door. If Feather appeared, he was certain to say something to her. That was the last thing I needed. I was hungry, tired and deeply ashamed. I needed to get out of the gloom and breathe air that didn't reek of stale tobacco, cheap cologne, and disgrace.

'I'm really hungry, can we go and eat?'

'I told you to eat more brekky.'

'Please.'

Gideon frowned, then nodded. 'Okay. But I'll definitely come back.' He pressed his hands to lift himself off the stool, arched his back, launched then landed just in front of me. 'Come on, let's go.'

As soon as I stepped outside, I took a deep breath, trying to clear the clammy smell from my nostrils. I couldn't help tilting my head so my face soaked up the sun, as though I hoped the heat would burn every last cell that had come in contact with the air of the brothel.

'Look at you, the cat that got the cream,' he said.

We crossed the road, and Gideon leaned against the railing that ran alongside the canal. I gripped hold of it and leaned forward, staring at the water.

'That was incredible.' He was squinting at the brothel's facade as if trying to work out behind which of the grubby windows he'd just had sex.

I managed to stop myself from saying, "I could tell."

'Really?'

'Don't get me wrong, I love the girls back in Norwich. But I've never...Jesus... that Bambi, she bloody knew what she was doing. I'm almost tempted to go back and do her again, right now.'

A glass-topped canal boat glided past. I stared at the tourists chatting and taking pictures. A young girl in a pink dress waved at me. I didn't wave back.

'Marky! Did you hear me?'

I looked at him.

'I'm tempted to bang on that door and get some more.'

I was about to tell him to go ahead. But then realised he might bump into Feather. Was there some sort of Seal of the Bordello, like there was of the confessional? Were prostitutes bound to secrecy like priests and lawyers? Even if there was such a code, it would probably only take a small bribe or even one of Gideon's irresistible grins to get her to break it. 'Don't you think if you go back so soon, you'll be having too much of a good thing?'

'No!' Gideon looked at me with a mixture of shock and contempt. 'You can never have too much sex. Now you've tasted it, you must know that.'

'Yeah, yeah of course.' I looked back at the canal boat.

'So you come back too. And get more wonderful sex memories to take your mind off those bloody onions.'

I would rather be loaded into a barrel, put under one of the factory chutes, then have raw onions poured over me. 'Once was enough. For now, at least.'

'Are you sure?'

'Yes, I need to...to... assimilate.'

'Assimilate! Marky, it isn't one of your weird

sociological theories. It's just sex. Just bloody enjoy it.'

'I need to savour it.'

Gideon closed his eyes. Then nodded. 'Yes, that's what I should do.' He lifted his face to the sun then with his eyes still closed, he took a long slow breath through his nose. As he breathed out he purred, 'Savour it, Gideon, savour it.' He opened his eyes and grinned at me. 'Well and truly savoured. Happy now Maharishi?' He tilted his head. 'Actually, now that I think about it, after my first time I was in a spin for days, took a while to go again.'

'Really?' I was tempted to ask for details but didn't in case they excited me.

Gideon smiled. 'Couldn't do it now. I need it every day. Shit! Every sodding hour. How the hell do I survive in the factory?' He looked at the brothel door. 'But maybe you're right, a little rest would be good. I'll definitely come back later though, and tomorrow before we catch the train. Come on, let's get you some nosh.'

We headed to the nearest McDonald's where I ordered a Double Cheeseburger, large fries and a Chocolate Shake. Gideon ordered a shake. He'd only drunk a mouthful when he said, 'Okay Marky spill the beans.'

'What?'

'How was it?'

I knew it was pointless saying I didn't want to talk about it, but I was also sure he'd know I was lying if I tried to brazen it out. 'Well, to be honest, it was pretty nerve-wracking.'

'Understandable, it is your first time. But your girl, what was her name?'

'Feather.'

He laughed. 'The names these girls come up with. Still, she must have helped you.'

'She was very patient and…tender, yes tender, that's the word.'

'Tender? Well, that's a new one.' Gideon looked straight into my eyes. 'Details Marky, details.'

If I tried to make something up, he was bound to know I was lying. Yet again I was suffering because of Mr Atkins' sketchy UFO sex-education drawings. 'It's all a bit of a blur.'

'Come on Marky, you must be able to tell me something. Was she a good kisser?'

I nodded.

'Was she a good header?'

'Header?'

Gideon looked down at his crotch.

'Oh, yes, amazing.'

Gideon reached across and squeezed my forearm. 'It's okay. I can see you're embarrassed talking about it. I won't probe any more, at least for now. So long as you enjoyed it.'

'I did...very much.'

'Good. Lost your little cherry, that's the main thing.'

I looked back at him and with as much assurance as I could muster said, 'Oh yes, cherry well and truly crushed.'

'Excellent.' He looked towards the counter. 'You know what? I think I will eat something. Build up my strength.'

He came back with two apple pies and handed one to me.

'Thanks. When you go back, will you choose Bambi again?'

'Maybe, she was great. But I like variety. What was Feather like? Never done it with a black girl.'

He'd never shown an interest in any of the African students, which was odd, considering they were female and breathing. Was he racist? That would be handy. He did engage with Lance, but not with any great enthusiasm, but he treated everyone at the factory like that. So I couldn't rely on him being racist to stop him from choosing Feather. So I did something shameful. 'She was nice, but she...she...'

'She what?'

'A bit.' I squeezed my nostrils. 'You know...whiffy.'

'Oh shit, no really? I'd heard that about black girls.'

I looked away from him. It had only been a couple of

days since I'd visited Lance and wanted him to do something about the racist attack. Now I was re-enforcing a racist stereotype to save myself. The combination of Gideon and this bloody city was bringing out the worst in me.

'Maybe one to avoid. I guess I'll see how the mood takes. What will you do whilst I'm having fun?'

'Museum or something.'

'Jesus, Marky, sometimes I think you're a different species. Art over sex. Crazy! You'll regret it when we're back, scraping onions.'

'Maybe.'

'I'm gonna come here every weekend. You should too.'

No! The last thing I wanted was to go through this every week. It made me say things I didn't believe and made me lie. 'I can't accept more of your charity—'

'It isn't charity. I love having you here.' He leaned forward so his elbows were on the table and stared directly at me. 'Sometimes you're like the Pope at an orgy, but it's wonderful being here with you.'

'Really?'

'Of course you clown.'

'I need to spend the weekends studying.'

'Oh Marky, you're the last person who needs to bloody study.' Gideon leaned back in the seat.

'I'm sorry.'

'Don't apologise, that's you, the perfect student.' Gideon gave a wry grin and shook his head. 'But I guess that's why I love you.'

I didn't dare look at him. If I did with the words "I love you" repeating in my head, I might not stop myself from leaning across the table and kissing him.

'You've gone all misty and quiet.'

I needed to put some distance between us. 'I'm fine. You want another drink or ice cream?'

'What a bloody good idea. Ice cream. Strawberry.'

I went to the counter. Part of me wanted to turn

around and shout, "Please don't go back to the brothel, come to the hotel with me!"

We'd shower together, and I'd wipe every drop of Bambi's foul sweat from his skin. We'd sleep together. And whilst making love, Gideon would groan even louder than he had with Bambi. His sweaty body pressing against me as my arms enfolded him and I cried, "I love you!". The thought made my legs so weak I had to grip hold of the counter to stop falling.

'Are you okay?' said the server.

I closed my eyes and took a deep breath.

'Sir?'

I looked up. 'Two strawberry ice creams…please.'

Gideon was sitting with his arm stretched across the top of the bench as if waiting for the whole world to sit next to him. When he noticed me looking at him, he grinned and gave a thumbs-up.

As I sat down, he said. 'You know Marky, I don't think I've ever been happier than I am right now.'

'I don't believe that.'

'I really don't think so.'

'But you've lived in luxury all your life.'

'I know, but after the factory, the onions and all the other bloody crap. After having great sex with Bambi. And now sitting here with you, eating this.' He took a spoonful of ice cream and slid it into his mouth. 'It's joy, just pure, pure joy. Don't you think?'

That was the moment I knew I couldn't go back to the factory.

I had to look away. I wanted to kiss him. I managed to fight the desire, but every time it was getting harder to resist. Back in the factory, living so close together, round the clock, there'd come a time when I'd succumb. That would be the moment our friendship ended.

'Don't you think?

'Do I think what?'

'Bloody hell Marky, where are you today? Don't you

think this is a wonderful, perfect time, just us here together?'

I nodded. 'Yeah, it is, never happier.'

Maybe a few weeks away from Gideon's intense presence would kill the desire. In the autumn, back in Norwich with my studies and other distractions, there'd be no yearning to kiss him. And this dangerous, futile aching would be dead and forgotten.

When we got back to the hotel, Gideon went to his room and I to mine. After showering, I lay in bed. I decided to leave as soon as he went to the brothel. I wouldn't go to a museum, I'd catch a train to Flushing and get the first ferry home. I'd be losing two months of well-paid work. I'd just have to find a job back in England. I'd also be abandoning my books. But I had no choice about any of it. I fell asleep to the sound of water lapping against the sides of the canal.

When I woke, I sat up and noticed a piece of paper had been slipped under my door.

Sorry, Marky! Woke up desperate for more!!! Couldn't wait!
Quelle Surprise! Gone for young pussy.
Enjoy your Old Masters?!
See you later.
G

I went back to my bed and pressed the note against my chest. So much of me wanted to stay and have more time with Gideon. I sighed, rolled off the bed, and crammed my clothes into my rucksack. On the back of Gideon's note, I wrote,

Gideon
I'm really sorry, but I feel guilty about taking all of this, silly I know, but you know me.
Thanks for a wonderful time.
I've decided to head back.
I hope Bambi was even better this time.
See you soon

When I was in Gideon's room, I couldn't resist lying on his bed. I hugged and kissed one of his pillows, sniffing it for any hint of his aroma. I kissed the note and laid it on the bed. When I left the hotel, I wandered to the road behind, paused for a few moments, staring at the brothel, imagining Gideon inside having fun and no doubt making the same noises he'd made earlier on. I shook my head, blinked back tears, turned on my heels and walked to the station.

12

The cold-hearted, ruthless side of London hit me as soon as I stepped off the coach. A man in a grey pinstripe suit, clutching a black leather briefcase, knocked me to the ground.

'Sorry mate, didn't see you.'

With my nose at exhaust pipe level, the fumes from a dozen departing National Express Coaches blasted my face. I staggered away and plopped onto a bench. I coughed so much I thought I was going to vomit. The next firing squad of coaches was forming, so I retreated into the ticket hall.

The destination board listed routes to pretty much anywhere in the country. I was tempted to go where people weren't in a hurry, where if they knocked you down, they'd help you up. Perhaps a quiet market town or some fishing village tucked away in a far-off cove. But I only had forty pounds. I couldn't afford to fritter cash on a fare to somewhere unknown and find there was no work. There was another possibility, I could go home. Spend two months with the family, get looked after, even pampered. But I'd have to explain why I was back from Holland so early. And I couldn't tell my mum the truth. Besides, I was twenty. I couldn't keep running back home the moment things got tough. Another possibility was an early return to Norwich. But Gideon. I guessed once he found out I hadn't returned to the factory, he'd go off gallivanting, so it would be unlikely if I did go to Norwich I'd run into him. But I didn't want there to be even the remotest chance of seeing him until the new term.

People with bags, cases and rucksacks bustled past me,

their eyes fixed straight ahead as if they knew exactly where they were heading. I envied them. When I'd left Amsterdam, everything seemed so obvious; get away from Gideon as fast as possible, get back to England, get a job. But now, standing in the middle of Victoria Coach Station, jobless, homeless and alone, with forty quid in my pocket, in a city where people pushed you to the ground, nothing was obvious. I couldn't decide where to go or what to do. After a lot of hesitating, I figured it would be easier to find casual work in London than anywhere else, so I decided to look around.

Buckingham Palace Road was mostly offices; nowhere looked likely to have work. When I got close to Victoria Railway station, I noticed a Wimpy. I remembered I hadn't eaten anything since the time in McDonald's. I went inside and ordered a Wimpy Special Grill. I sat by a window, munching, as I stared at the black cabs, cars, red buses, and the hordes of people bustling past. London was daunting, but at the same time, exciting. I could just disappear. Be anonymous. Become whoever I wanted. An attractive idea, especially after the constant scrutiny in the barracks.

The only obstacle, I had no bloody idea who I was, or wanted to be.

Did I want to be a poof, or rather, a gay boy, and find someone who I truly loved, perhaps even tell Gideon, and hope he'd been living a lie too? Or did I want to be straight, find a girl, settle down and have 2.4 normal, i.e. straight children, then die prematurely of a heart attack on some third-rate golf course? I had no idea.

A man with a long straggly beard and two plastic carrier bags in each hand slid against the glass. He lowered himself to the ground, then pulled a bottle from a pocket and took a swig. Seeing him made me even more anxious. Things could go wrong in London, a couple of bad moves and I could end up like that.

I ate as slowly as I could. I wondered if the Wimpy needed staff. Perhaps someone to pick up trays or clean. So when

I'd finished, I asked the manager. He eyed my rucksack and said. "No".

I had to ditch the rucksack. It made me look desperate. I stored it in a locker in Victoria Station, then went down to the Underground.

Oxford Street, Covent Garden, Waterloo, Baker Street. The map was covered in familiar names. Being so close to them excited me. I could go to any or even all of them. The entire city was waiting. But I shook my head. I had no time to explore; I had to find work. I decided to get onto the Circle Line and head towards Liverpool Street. The City. The big banks. The place where money was made, and spent.

When the train pulled into Sloane Square, I realised I was going in the wrong direction. I was about to get off but decided the train would get me to Liverpool Street eventually, so I settled against the glass partition. The warmth made me drowsy, and I fell asleep. When I woke and looked up, I had to look twice because I was back in Victoria. It was 3 pm. I'd wasted hours sleeping as the train completed several circuits.

'Shit!'

The woman sitting next to me snorted.

'Sorry.'

I'd wasted so much time. I had to get to the surface, so I got off. I was in South Kensington. All I knew about the area was the Science Museum was there. I'd visited it once on a school trip. It was a posh area, probably not the place to find a casual job.

When I got to the ticket hall, I headed towards the subway. Halfway along the tunnel, a busker in a dirty trench coat was sitting cross-legged on the concrete, his back pressed against the wall. He had a guitar and was singing. Screeching would be more accurate. It took me a while to recognise, "Streets of London". Its theme of the downtrodden of the city didn't lighten my mood. After twenty minutes, I found myself at the Science Museum. As I stood outside I thought, "Why not? No harm in asking."

I went inside to the information desk.

'Yes?' said a young woman in a crumpled uniform.
'Do you have any vacancies?'
'Vacancies?'
'Jobs, do you have any jobs?'
'Haven't you heard, the government runs these places called Job Centres?'
'Yes, of course.'
'Well, bloody well go to one of them then.'
'Thanks for nothing.'
'Anytime.'

I shook my head. How rude, how cruel. I could have been desperate. Shit! I am desperate. And not thinking straight. I was angry with myself for wasting so much time. Around the corner from the museum, I found a small cafe. When the owner, a middle-aged Italian, brought a mug of tea to my table, I asked. 'Do you have any work? I'll do anything.'

He smiled as if remembering when he'd once been a young man, down on his luck. 'I'm so sorry I have all staff I need, and money not so much.'

'Anything. I'll do the washing up.'

He gave me a sympathetic smile. 'Sorry.' He went to the counter and came back with a cheese and ham sandwich.

'I don't want charity.'

'You look like boy who needs a little kindness.'

The only way I stopped myself from crying was by pressing my lips firmly together. It wasn't so much the gift of a sandwich that made me emotional; it was because I realised I was at rock bottom. When I went to pay for my tea, the owner refused to take any money.

I had to find somewhere to sleep. I'd assumed I'd find a job easily and then have been able to find somewhere. With less than forty pounds, I couldn't afford to fritter any more money. A bed, even in a hostel, would be reckless. I shook my head. Only two nights earlier, I'd been sleeping in luxury. Even a tenth of what Gideon had spent on the Ambassade would have been invaluable now.

I noticed the dome of the Royal Albert Hall, something I'd seen many times on TV. I climbed the steps to the entrance. People in evening wear were going inside. According to the posters they were attending *The Trojans* by Berlioz, I guessed it must be an opera or something equally tedious. I walked around until I saw the Albert Memorial and, beyond it, the trees of Kensington Gardens. That might be somewhere I could spend the night. It was late July, and the air was sultry. I'd survive.

I crossed Kensington Gore and carried on to the park entrance. Inside, the sound of traffic diminished, and the air was less heavy. I walked along a path until I came to the Serpentine Bridge. My legs were aching, so I sat on a bench. Opposite me was a statue of a boy on a bronze tree stump blowing what looked like a flute. As I looked more closely, I realised the boy was Peter Pan, "The boy who never grew up." Even Kensington Gardens was mocking me.

For the first time, I wondered if I'd done the right thing. What had happened in the brothel had been a shock, but maybe I'd been too hasty. Perhaps I could have coped and made sure I resisted the urge to kiss Gideon. Behaved like an adult rather than a boy. I hadn't thought it through. If I'd known I'd be spending a night in a park, virtually penniless. Would I have left? Probably not. And if things weren't bad enough…

I bloody missed Gideon!

If he'd been with me, no way would I have drifted around all day. I yearned to be with him. To find out what he was doing. Whether he was still in Amsterdam or somewhere exotic. I got up and walked until I found an oak tree out of sight of the paths; I sat beneath it and dozed off.

When I woke I was feeling hungry again. I tried to ignore it, but the pangs became so strong I knew I wouldn't be able to get back to sleep until I'd eaten something. So I left the park and bought a sandwich from a mini-market. I ate it on a bench outside the Royal Albert Hall. When I finished the sandwich and dropped the bag into a bin, people were coming out of the concert, they were chatting, smoking, some were sipping wine.

'What did you think of the first half?..... Hey! I'm talking to you. What did you think of the first half?'

I turned around. Behind me was a man. I guessed he must be in his late forties. He was wearing a loose cream-coloured linen jacket, matching chinos, and a purple cravat. He was holding the flame from a gold lighter to the end of a pink cigarette.

'What?'

'The prom, Berlioz's *Les Troyens, The Tro...jans.*' He flicked open a gold case and offered me a cigarette.

'No thanks. Sorry, I wasn't at the concert.'

'Oh I see, I thought because you were sitting here—'

'No, I was just eating a sandwich.'

'Ahh... just eating a sandwich, of course.'

'Is it good...the concert—'

'Opera dear, a tad long. Jessye Norman is divine as always. Do you like opera?'

'Never been.'

'Oh, really.'

'U2 is more my scene.'

He leaned towards me, his eyes studying me like a surgeon. 'Are you sure you weren't inside? I could have sworn I saw your cute little bum swaying with the Promenaders.'

I took a step away from him. 'Not me.'

He grinned. 'So it's pure coincidence that you're sitting here eating sandwiches right next to the Albert Hall, during the interval.'

'Yes, it is.'

'I find that very hard to believe.'

'Why?'

'Come on, stop being so obtuse. You're a Dilly boy?' He pointed the cigarette at me.

'A what?'

'Don't play all innocent with me, you're rent?'

'What?'

'An escort, a prozzie, a whore....shall I go on?'

He was staring at me with lascivious eyes, with the same voracious glint I'd seen in Feather's as she'd approached me in the brothel, but this was different, he wasn't faking. He looked me up and down, then stared at my crotch.

'Fuck off! I'm not a poofter.'

'Really dear? Are you quite sure about that? Why else would a handsome and clearly uncultivated boy like you be sitting here during a Proms concert, in your tight, grubby but oh so irresistible jeans?'

'I was just here eating and minding my own bloody business, so fuck off.'

He took the last draw from his cigarette, then flicked it over the ledge.

'Actually, I'm studying philosophy in Norwich.'

'I see. Well, good for you dear.' He narrowed his eyes. 'Then you must have a very interesting story to relate.'

'It's the most boring story in the world.'

He sat on the bench and tapped it. 'Well, sit down. I love to hear beautiful boys telling me boring stories.'

I shook my head.

'Come on. I won't bite. Sorry about before, I was stood up and I was taking it out on you. Please.' He tapped the bench again.

I knew the sensible thing would be to leave, but it had been a terrible day when I'd felt completely alone, tired, hungry and couldn't see any future. And here was someone who wanted to listen. Yes, I knew he had dirty motives. But I just needed to talk.

As I sat next to him, he sniffed the air. 'I'm inclined to believe you. No way a Dilly boy would come out stinking like that. When was the last time you washed?'

'Sorry. It's the onions.'

'Onions! Do tell.' He lit another cigarette.

I shifted along the bench, trying to get as far out of sniffing and groping range as possible. I had the urge to tell him everything, about the factory, Amsterdam and, of course, Gideon. I needed to tell someone. And have someone tell me I'd done the right thing. But I wasn't sure I could trust him. 'I arrived in London today—'

'From where dear?'

'From Bristol, I came here looking for work.'

'I see.' His eyes narrowed as if he didn't believe me.

'I'll return to UEA at the end of September.'

'And have you...found work?'

I thought about trying to brazen it out by saying I had options but decided not to lie. I shook my head.

'So what are you going to do now?'

A bell inside the Albert Hall rang.

'Doesn't that mean the show's about to start?'

'Opera dear. Yes, it does. But I think I'm going to give it a miss.'

'Why?'

'As I said, I was stood up. And being on one's own isn't the same. I'm sure you know what I mean?'

I certainly did.

'So, if I may, I'm going to stay here and smoke my little cheroot. And listen to your boring story.' He let out a series of small smoke rings. 'But you've avoided my question. What are you going to do now?'

'I was going to spend the night in there.' I nodded towards Kensington Gardens.

'Tremendous.'

I smiled weakly. 'But tomorrow will be different once I get a job.'

He sniggered.

'What's so funny?'

'You really think someone's going to hire you, smelling like that?'

'Obviously I'll find somewhere to clean.'

'Really?'

'A public lavatory.'

'You mean a cottage?'

'What do you mean, cottage? This is London, not a village?'

He laughed. 'Oh, my dear sweet boy, you're so innocent.'

'If you're going to mock me, you can just sodding well go back to your concert.'

'Opera dear.' He squeezed my arm. 'Sorry. I'm Barnaby.' He held out his hand.

I didn't shake it.

'Come on. I'm sorry if I offended you. I'm just a bitter old queen who got stood up.'

I shook his hand. 'Mark.'

Barnaby nodded. 'It's getting a bit chilly out here.' He pressed his arms across his chest.

He was right, the temperature had dropped and there was a breeze blowing off the park.

'Would you like to go for a drink?'

'Isn't everywhere closed?'

'This is London dear. You can always find somewhere. If you know where to look. So?'

I guessed wherever the somewhere was would be expensive, classy. I looked down at my dirty jeans and trainers. I couldn't imagine walking into somewhere posh looking like I did. 'No, thank you. Besides, where would let me in smelling like this?'

'You're probably right.' He took a long draw on his cigarette and held the smoke in his mouth as he watched a Number 52 bus go by. He exhaled slowly. 'Mark, do you need money?'

'I'll be fine.'

'Are you sure?'

'I told you I'm not a chilly boy.'

'Dilly boy dear, dilly boy.'

'I'm not one of them.'

I looked into his eyes. The smart clothes, the perfect

haircut, the pricey cigarettes, the same assuredness as Gideon. 'I'm not a poof.'

'Really dear? Are you sure about that? Look, I can see you're in trouble. And need help. And I can help you.'

'I'm not in that much trouble.'

'I don't know what's up with you, or what you're running away from, but you clearly are running away from something.' He pulled out his wallet.

'I don't need your money.'

'Oh, you do, you most certainly do. It's a question of whether you're prepared to take it.' He pulled out three twenty-pound notes.

'My arse isn't for sale.'

'I can tell you, Mark,' he leaned over and whispered in my ear. 'I could go to Piccadilly Circus and find much cuter, cleaner arses than yours for much less than sixty quid.' He leaned away again. 'I'm going to give you a choice.' He held up the money. 'You can take this and find yourself a warm bed for the night. No strings attached. We'll never see each other again.'

'Why would you do that?'

'I don't know. Perhaps I'm feeling generous. And you haven't heard the rest of my offer. Which is. We can get into a taxi and go back to my home.'

'I told you I'm not selling my arse.'

'Hold your horses, I'm not finished. You can come back with me, have a bath, a shower, whichever you prefer, you can put on some clean clothes, and get something to eat. Then you can sleep. Alone. In a wonderful four-poster bed.'

'I don't believe you.'

'Up to you, you can take this money and disappear or you can come with me and, well, you'll just have to see, won't you?'

My hands were itching to take the money. With it, I'd have nearly a hundred pounds, enough to pay for a few of nights in a decent hotel and give me plenty of time to find a job. But part of me was curious to go to Barnaby's house. I knew it would probably be the craziest, most dangerous thing I'd ever done. But I wanted to find out. 'I could be a serial killer?'

'You could well be. But what is life without risk?' Barnaby held up the money. 'The decision, as they say, is yours.'

'Do you live around here?'

'Highgate.'

'Oh...where Karl Marx is buried.'

Barnaby smiled. 'I don't actually live in the cemetery but yes, nearby.'

'Is it far?'

'We'd go by taxi. I can see you look sceptical, so here's another offer. You can take the sixty quid now and disappear, goodbye, so long, have a nice life, or you can come back to my place and if you don't like it, you can leave without even coming inside. You can still have half, so that's... thirty quid, plus a taxi fare to take you to wherever you want. How about that?'

I wondered why was he so keen, even desperate to get me to come with him. What would Gideon do? He'd have probably kneed him in the ghoulies as soon as he opened his mouth. But I wasn't Gideon. I was desperate and hungry, but most of all, curious.

'It's getting bloody cold now. You better decide before we both freeze to death.'

13

'Okay, I'll come.'

'Excellent.' Barnaby handed me the money. 'Take it.'

'But I've just agreed to come.'

'Treat it as a mark of good faith.'

Was he toying with me? Giving me some malign test? Was I just his plaything?

'No, I agreed to come without taking the money. And that's what I'm going to do.'

Barnaby smiled. 'I'm impressed. I'm not sure I wouldn't have just taken the money and run.' He slid the notes back into his wallet.

'But we agreed, no hanky panky.'

'Absolutely, no hanky panky.'

'And I'll leave first thing in the morning.'

'Whenever you want.'

Barnaby strode down the steps towards Kensington Gore. A black cab slowed into the kerb, apparently without Barnaby signalling for it to stop, or at least if he'd signalled it was too subtle for me to notice.

Barnaby pulled open the taxi door. 'After you,' he said with a bow.

I slid into the seat. 'Can we go to Victoria Station first? I need to get my rucksack.'

'Of course.'

I was relieved to be in the cab. I'd been outside for much of the day, worrying about getting work and finding somewhere to sleep. My body sank deep into the seat and I realised for the first time how exhausted I was. I looked across at Barnaby. He was real, not some apparition. Before we got to Victoria, we passed the Wimpy. The tramp was still propped against the window. I shook my head. But for the grace of God and Barnaby.

'Something wrong?' he said.

'No, just … it's nothing.'

When the taxi stopped outside the station I ran inside. I lifted my rucksack out of the locker, paused for a few moments. Should I go back to the taxi? I could find a bench in the station and spend the night there. At least I'd know I'd be safe. I couldn't help wondering what Barnaby wanted. Everyone wanted something. If I went back to the taxi, I was going into the unknown. Into possible danger. But the way he'd still offered the money after I'd accepted his invitation meant I was inclined to trust him. Perhaps it was the craziest, most reckless decision I'd ever made. I'd made a few of those recently, but still I went back to the cab.

'Is that it?'

I nodded. 'I abandoned my books.'

The traffic was heavy, so the taxi took a while to travel along Victoria Street. Barnaby didn't say anything. I wasn't sure whether he expected me to charm and flatter him. I was too exhausted to think of anything to say. The longer the silence continued, the harder it became to break and the worse the atmosphere got. It was like I was in a paddy wagon, with Barnaby the taciturn policeman escorting a convicted mass murderer to his execution. Just before crossing into Trafalgar Square, we stopped at a set of traffic lights.

'Amazing to go from Jesus to porn.' Barnaby pointed at the Whitehall Theatre, which was putting on a play called *Private Dick*.

Relieved the atmosphere had been broken, I leaned across and looked out the window to where he was pointing. 'What?'

'Didn't Robert Powell play Jesus on the telly a few years back?' said Barnaby.

'That's right, he did. I watched it with my mum.' Keen to keep the conversation going, I continued. 'But I think *Private Dick* means private eye, not you know—'

'Oh, really.' Barnaby shook his head.

'Sorry, I didn't realise you were kidding. I'm just tired. Have you seen it?'

'Good God no.'

After Trafalgar Square, the journey up Charing Cross Road towards Tottenham Court Road was a blur of neon lights. Once we got clear of the West End, it got darker. The deathly silence inside the cab was becoming increasingly awkward, so I pretended to be asleep.

Fifteen minutes later, Barnaby said, 'Mark, wake up.'

I opened my eyes and shook my head so I looked lost as if I'd just woken from a deep sleep.

'Wakey, wakey.' Barnaby leaned towards me. 'We're here.'

I picked up my rucksack. When I stepped out of the cab, the first thing I noticed was how quiet it was, and dark. Such a contrast to the shimmering lights and cacophonous streets of London.

Barnaby smiled and pushed open a high metal gate. I followed him onto a gravel driveway leading towards a silver glow, curving like a halo over the top of a bank of trees. The only sound apart from the leaves fluttering in the breeze was the dull crunch of our shoes on the gravel. When we turned a corner, I had to stop. Stunned by the sight of the house, not a house, a mansion. It stood in a blaze of shimmering silver light, which gave it an unreal, almost illusive quality. As if the lighting were saying, "Here I am, look at me. I exist only in your fantasies."

'Jesus!'

Barnaby, who was several steps ahead of me, turned. 'Chop-chop.'

'Is this your house?'

'It was when I left it earlier this evening.'

'But it's...it's huge.' It was the sort of place I'd imagined Gideon's family lived in. Was I destined to spend my life meeting rich men? Would that be so bad?

It had five bay windows on the upper floor and four on the ground. A Palladian entrance. Georgian? Regency? I had no idea. Expensive, bloody expensive, I knew that much. The sort of place not even the BBC could afford to use for filming. And the sort of place, if and when the Socialist Worker paradise arrived, Bryony and Helga would seize and turn into a commune for lesbian mothers.

'Are you okay?' said Barnaby.

'Yes, it's just, do you own all of it?'

'No, just the coal cellar. Of course I own bloody all of it, been in the family for over two hundred years.'

Even though the silver light gave the mansion an icy feel, there were glints of amber behind the downstairs curtains. Hinting at comfort, warmth, security.

'What do you think?'

'It looks...nice...cosy.'

'Is that all you can say?'

I shrugged.

Barnaby shook his head. 'Right, if I ever want to sell. I'll tell the estate agent to forget about saying the house was built in 1749, has ten bedrooms, three reception rooms, God knows how many bathrooms, two acres of landscaped garden, a lake, a gazebo and a pool, heated, and has housed one of the richest families in London for more than two hundred years. I'll tell him to scrap all that, just use three words, "nice and fucking cosy"!

I couldn't help laughing. 'That's four words.'

'I'll probably drop the fucking.'

'Sorry. I'm just overwhelmed.'

'So are you willing to stay in my nice, cosy house?'

I was exhausted, my body ached. In the taxi, I'd imagined Barnaby living in a flat. Admittedly, I'd pictured a big one, luxurious. Never a mansion. Once again, my Socialist

Worker's conscience made me feel guilty. But I decided if Trotsky was as tired, dirty and hungry as I was, even he would accept Barnaby's offer. 'Yes. But I'll leave first thing.'

Barnaby nodded. 'Of course.'

He led me to the entrance. I expected us to be greeted by a retinue of bowing and curtseying butlers, maids and whatever other sundry members of the proletariat Barnaby was exploiting. But he opened the door himself and there was nobody in the hallway. It was vast, with pure white walls, and a creamy marble floor which reminded me of the virgin snow around the Cathedral the night I'd played snowballs with Gideon. At the end of the hallway was a stone bifurcated staircase with a duck-egg blue carpet. Weirdly, the only pieces of furniture in the hallway were a small wooden table on which there was a classic black Bakelite phone. And a pair of brown art déco leather armchairs.

'Off with those.' Barnaby pointed to my trainers.

I stepped across to one of the chairs, which was surprisingly comfortable, and pulled off my trainers. The overwhelming stink embarrassed me.

'I think those are beyond saving.' Barnaby disappeared through a doorway. He came back thirty seconds later with a plastic bag. 'Dump them in here.' He leaned away from me like a scientist about to receive a glowing nuclear rod.

'But it's my only pair.'

'Even Jesus on a good day couldn't save those. I've got millions upstairs. I'm sure we can find a pair to fit.'

I wondered whether he wanted to take away my shoes to make it harder for me to leave, so held on to them for a few seconds.

'Come on, the longer those are in the open air, the more butterflies in China die.' Barnaby shook the bag.

I dropped them inside.

'Follow me.'

He led me into the lounge. I had a feeling similar to when I stepped into the Grande Suite at The Ambassade. The furniture was even older. The oak floor was covered in thick woven rugs. Facing each other in the middle of the room were two matching three-person Red Chesterfield sofas. Between them was a glass-topped coffee table: at least it was something that looked like it had come from the 20th century. On top of the table was a copy of *The Guardian.* That was a surprise. I'd expected him to read, or rather take, as no doubt was Barnaby's preferred verb when referring to his newspaper of choice, *The Times* or some other right-wing rag. It was open at the cryptic crossword. Which had been completed. Next to the paper was a half-finished glass of red wine and, next to that, a bottle of *1978 Barton and Guestier Chateauneuf-du-Pape.*

'Sorry about the mess.' Barnaby picked up the paper and glass. 'I left in a bit of a rush.' He examined the bottle and realising there was still some left, said, 'Can I tempt you?'

I shook my head. 'I'm really tired. Can I just get clean and get to bed?'

For a moment, Barnaby looked a bit hurt. 'Yes, yes, of course. Okay, the first thing is to get you cleaned up. Just let me dump this wine.' He scurried through a doorway, then returned a moment later. 'Come on.' He led me upstairs. 'Now, which one shall I choose?'

We were in the middle of a long corridor. Barnaby touched his lip with his index finger, like a boy in a sweetshop. 'Any preference?'

I shook my head. Barnaby opened the nearest door.

'You'll find everything here. Here's the ensuite bathroom. The water takes an age to heat up, just be patient. Can I get you anything? Oh, towel.' He skipped through one of the other doors, then came back. 'Sorry, not used to putting people up. Here you go. Anything else?'

I wanted to ask him why he was doing this. Oddly, he seemed more nervous now he was in his own home than he had been when we'd first met outside The Albert Hall. I could have understood if the house had been a dump, but this was almost a palace. But his nervousness and obvious desire to please were endearing.

'And if you're still scared I'm going to jump into your bed.' He leaned around the door and pulled out a key. 'You can lock yourself in.'

I clutched the towel to my chest, barely able to believe this was happening, and almost on the verge of tears at his kindness. 'I really can't thank you enough.'

He waved his hand in front of his face as if swatting away an irritating fly. 'It's nothing. Have a good bath. I'll see you in the morning.'

'My rucksack—'

'Don't worry about that. I'll run your filthy clothes through the machine.'

'You don't need to do that.' Was that something else to make me stay longer? But he'd been so kind and done nothing to suggest he had any motive other than to help, so I didn't mention the clothes had all been laundered at the *Ambassade*.

He disappeared for a moment, then returned carrying a red dressing gown. 'One of my old ones, I'm afraid, but good enough to keep you warm and decent.' He handed it to me. 'Good night.'

'Good night,' I said.

I was about to lock the door but then decided I wanted to show Barnaby I trusted him, so I left it unlocked.

It did take an age for the water to warm up. There were so many bangs, gurgles and spurts, I thought I was in the engine room of the ferry. I wondered who was the last person to use the bath. Barnaby when he was a kid? His grandfather? Jesus? The water only ever reached tepid. Still, it was better than having to scrub in some public toilet, or cottage, as Barnaby had called them. As I lay in the water, I thought it would be so easy to stay longer, spend the summer living in luxury. I was sure Barnaby wouldn't mind. He seemed lonely and glad of the company. But I decided to stick to Plan A. I would leave in the morning and make sure I didn't muck around like I had today. I would definitely find a job.

14

I woke at eleven, lifted myself off the mattress, and shuffled over to the window. Below me was a landscaped garden with a lawn like Wimbledon Centre Court before a ball had been hit. Trimmed, manicured, perfect. Crisscrossed with hedges, cut so precisely, their edges so rectilinear, they looked like they were made of brick. At the end of the garden, just in front of a high stone wall, was a white gazebo. Beyond the wall, there was a church spire and beyond that, the London skyline, ghostly in the grey haze. For the first time in weeks, I was calm as from the safety of a house surrounded by a tranquil garden; I glimpsed the world beyond, a city with its noise, its dirt, a world filled with uncertainty and confusion, but a world that no matter how cruel could never breach those high stone walls. Did I want to stick to Plan A and cross back into that world? Barnaby stepped into the garden. Wearing a red dressing gown and gliding lightly over the grass, he looked like a red-robed angel. He had a copy of *The Guardian* in one hand and a glass of red wine in the other. He stepped onto the gazebo. Then lowered himself onto a wicker chair. Just like his garden, he seemed of another world, where his only hassles came on days when *The Guardian* came up with an especially baffling cryptic crossword.

I was grateful to him, but as much as I was grateful, I was suspicious of him too. After all, he was a poof. I'd always assumed they were predatory and dangerous. That's what all the tabloid papers said. Had he been generous just to get me into bed? But if that was true, why didn't he do anything? What did he want? Perhaps he was just a kind, generous, possibly lonely man, nothing more than that. It didn't matter; I was going to leave soon, anyway.

When I thought about it, the Fleet Street tabloids were always making up lies about The Socialist Workers Party. Maybe they made up lies about homosexual men too. Was I now thinking that because I was, what? Eighty, maybe ninety per cent certain I was one. But I hadn't actually "done it" with a man. I held onto that hope like a lifebuoy. Nothing was official until, well, it was official. Maybe this would pass.

I went downstairs, through the lounge and the open French windows into the garden.

'Ahh,' Barnaby looked up from his paper. 'Sleeping Beauty awakens at last. Sit, sit.' He motioned to a chair, then folded the paper and put it on a table. 'Sleep well?'

'Yes, an incredible sleep actually.'

'Excellent. You must be starving, I can rustle up some eggs…bacon—'

'Just tea and toast and I'll be on my way.'

'Come on Mark, that isn't nearly enough for a growing boy like you.' Barnaby picked up his glass and walked back to the house.

I followed. 'This is a beautiful garden.'

'Thank you…none of it my work. I just sit and admire it.' Barnaby stopped and held his face up to catch a sunbeam. 'It's going to be a beautiful day.' He led me into the kitchen. 'Sit yourself down.' He switched on the kettle and then cut two slices of bread. 'Are you sure this is going to be enough?'

'Yes.' I looked at my watch. 'I can't afford to waste time like I did yesterday.'

'Job hunting?'

'Yep.'

'What sort of work?'

'Anything. Just to tide me over until I go back to Norwich.'

When the kettle had boiled, Barnaby filled the teapot.

He dropped the two slices of toast into a rack and laid it on the table. 'I only have butter I'm afraid, none of this margarine nonsense.'

'That's fine.'

'Are you sure you won't stay a little longer, at least until Mrs Carter can iron your clothes?'

'They'll only get creased when I cram them in my rucksack.'

Once the tea was ready, Barnaby sat across from me. It was the first time I'd seen him close to, in daylight. His face was more wrinkled than I'd expected and there were a few grey hairs on his temples. When we'd met outside the Albert Hall I'd guessed he was in his mid to late forties. Now I thought he must be in his fifties. I munched some toast. 'I really don't know what I would've done if you hadn't turned up last night.'

Barnaby shook his head. 'Oh you would've survived.'

'Nevertheless, thank you so much.'

Barnaby waved his hand dismissively. 'It was nothing. It's just good to have some young life around the place.'

'If you don't mind me asking, why did you do it? It was a very risky thing to do.'

Barnaby raised one of his bushy eyebrows. 'Mark, I have absolutely no talents, no skills, no expertise, in anything, either learnt or inherited. I'm of no practical value to the world at all.'

'Oh, come on.'

'But the one gift I do possess is an almost infallible instinct when it comes to judging people.'

'Infallible? Is that even possible?'

'Maybe not one hundred percent but at least ninety-nine percent accurate. Once I saw your eyes, I could tell you were just lost, not a hustler, not a danger. The eyes, you can tell everything from the eyes.'

Barnaby's eyes were very tricky to see. Had he deliberately let his eyebrows grow bushy to make him difficult to read? 'I was sure you wanted sex.'

He laughed, then took a sip of tea. 'You're full of yourself aren't you? I suppose beneath that unkempt exterior, you're relatively presentable.'

'Thanks.'

'But you're no Richard Gere, are you?'

'No, but—'

'Look, when I saw you at The Albert Hall, munching cheap sandwiches, you looked washed out. Something told me that boy needs help. I could almost hear my friends shouting, "Barnaby, leave well alone". But I suppose being stood up, and not enjoying *The Trojans* as much as I'd expected, I had to speak to you.'

'So sexual desire had nothing to do with it?'

'That would be overstating it, I suppose in the back of my mind I did hope. But once I started to speak to you—'

'You realised you didn't stand a chance.'

'No, well yes, but I still knew you needed help and that became my priority.'

I wasn't sure I believed him. 'I must go.'

'Don't rush away.'

'I need to get moving.'

'Wait, wait. Please sit…please.'

After pausing a few seconds and seeing the look in Barnaby's eyes, I sat back in the chair.

'I admire your determination to go out there and do the Thatcherite thing, and get a job. But you're perfectly welcome to stay here.'

I wondered whether he'd deliberately made the Thatcher comment, knowing it would irritate me, and dissuade me from going. Perhaps he did have an uncanny ability to assess people. 'No, I need to go.'

'To where?'

No idea. The prospect of traipsing around London again, begging for work and trying to find somewhere to sleep filled me with dread.

'My place is vast. And I live here on my own.'

Why would anyone live alone in such an immense house? There had to be family, friends, even a lover. If there was nobody, what did that say about him? 'It wouldn't feel right.'

'Why not? You need a bed. I have the room. If you feel guilty, you can earn your keep by sweeping leaves off the lawn.'

'You must have people for that.'

'There's always stuff that needs doing. Why not stay here until you find a job?'

That was tempting, to have somewhere secure, a base from which I could search without all the panic and desperation of yesterday. I feared if I stayed, I'd become lazy, and spend the whole of the rest of the summer festering.

'Look, Hampstead Heath is just down the road. It's going to be a gorgeous day. I was planning a dip in the Men's Pond. Why don't you, just for today, forget all this job-seeking nonsense and come with me?'

'I really must get on.'

'I have friends, businessmen, who swim there. I can ask them about work. Come on.'

'Really?' Barnaby's friends had to be rich. Any job they offered would surely be better than any I'd find on my own. 'I don't have any trunks.'

'Oh, that's easily solved. I have dozens. I'm sure we can find something to fit.'

'I don't know.'

'It's a ten-minute walk, tops. And there are so many lovely boys.'

'I'm not interested in boys.'

Barnaby looked sceptical, but I was pleased he chose not to comment.

'We can swim, sunbathe, chat. Though I must warn you, there is a naked area.'

'Naked! I don't want that.'

'It isn't compulsory. Come on, it'll be fun.'

I had to admit, it sounded a lot more appealing than getting hot and sticky from traipsing around London. 'Okay. But just for today. Tomorrow you wake me up early.'

'Deal!'

Barnaby found me some trunks, a shirt, and shorts.

'Perfect, let's go,' he said.

The Pond was a ten-minute walk from his house along a narrow lane lined with hedges. We arrived at a grass bank the size of two tennis courts. At the foot of the bank was a path and a line of trees. Between the leaves was the wavering glint of sunlight on water.

'This way.'

He led me down the bank to a fenced-off area. On the wooden gate in red letters was the word "CAUTION". Before opening the gate, he paused. 'Be warned. Prepare to see some wizened old ball sacks.'

When he opened the gate, all I could see were mounds of sunburnt naked flesh, supine on concrete, like butchered pigs on a slaughterhouse floor.

'Jesus Christ!' I couldn't move.

If any of the carcasses were Gideon's businessmen friends, they were so old they must have sold wood to Noah. I doubted any of them could help me.

'We only have to stay in here whilst we change.' Barnaby walked to a section of the fence where there was space and dumped his bag. He beckoned me. I couldn't move. One of the carcasses shifted and a pair of weary eyes squinted at me. Barnaby came back to the entrance. He leaned towards me. 'They're harmless.' He tugged my forearm. 'Come on, it'll be fine.'

I tiptoed between the mounds of pink flesh and put my bag next to his. I stared at the wooden fence.

'They won't bite. Most of them can barely move.'

'How can they lie like that? It's...it's—'

'I know, hardly love's young dream, but they're happy.'

One wizened, grey-haired man, he must have been in his eighties, was leaning on his side. Next to him was another body, face down. The grey-haired man picked up a bottle of suntan oil and held it above the other man's nutbrown buttocks.

He squirted oil over the folds of flesh with the same relish a hungry teenager drenches syrup over a plate of waffles. I looked away before I caught even a glimpse of him rubbing the oil into the skin.

'Come on Mark, don't be shy.'

A couple of the carcasses came back to life, their heads lifted and turned in my direction as if their nasal passages had detected the aroma of young live flesh. One of them put on his glasses stared at me, then pouted to his friend.

'I don't like it here,' I said.

'The quicker you get changed, the sooner we can get out.'

I made sure the hem of my shirt was as low as possible. I pulled the trunks Barnaby had lent me out of my bag. I removed my shorts and pants as fast as I could, grabbed the trunks, and pulled them up so hard I crushed my balls.

Barnaby smiled. 'That was the swiftest change since the closing night of *Dreamgirls*.'

'What?'

'Nothing. Ready?'

I nodded.

Barnaby led me through a door onto a jetty. As soon as he stepped onto it, he trotted along it until he reached a diving board. He bounced onto the end of it, did a swan dive, then disappeared into the water with barely a ripple. Seconds later, his head appeared by the side of the jetty. 'Come on in! It's wonderful.'

I stood aside to let someone else run and dive. I'd never been keen on diving. At Marine Lake, I'd only ever gone into the water feet or bum first.

'If you don't want to dive, you can use those.' Barnaby nodded his head toward a set of wooden steps.

I stood on the first step, then lowered myself. When my foot touched the water, I gasped. A shiver shot from my toes to my head.

Barnaby swam up behind me. 'It always feels cold at

first.'

I carried on descending. When the water reached my crotch, I took a deep breath. Let go then fell back into the water, gulping for air as I was wrapped in an icy blanket. My legs kicked, my arms flailed. My blood froze.

'Well done.' Barnaby turned and did a neat crawl towards the middle of the pond.

I trod water for a few seconds, then doggy paddled away from the jetty. My body was shivering. But as I swam, I started to feel my extremities again. Barnaby's head was bobbing in the distance. There was no way I was going to catch up with him. So when I saw an area of water in sunlight. I did a sort of breaststroke towards it. Once I reached the sunny water, I stopped.

Barnaby swam back to me. 'Are you okay?'

'It's fucking cold.'

Barnaby laughed. 'Follow me.'

He swam towards a pontoon. Once I reached it, I put my hands on the side and lifted myself, then flopped onto the plastic. I held my arms across my chest. My teeth were chattering. Barnaby was reclining like he was on the French Riviera.

'Jesus! Why aren't you cold?'

'I come here most days. Sun, rain, even snow.'

'You're crazy.'

'On the really cold days, it's just a quick dip in and out. But on days like this, there's nowhere better in the world.'

I had to admit sitting under a warm but not scorching sun, surrounded by the trees of Hampstead Heath, as the pontoon undulated on the water, would have been idyllic if only my balls didn't feel like they were about to drop off.

'Once you get warmed up, you'll be fine.'

I leaned back with my hands on the deck and held my face to the sun.

'I bet you're happy you changed your mind about staying.'

I nodded. 'But—'

Barnaby raised his hand. 'Stop, don't go on about feeling guilty and needing to get on with your life. That can start tomorrow, today just relax and enjoy yourself. Anyway, I need to put in some lengths. Coming?'

'Can I stay here?'

'Of course. Do whatever you want.'

Barnaby dived into the water and swam away from the pontoon. He turned and swam beside a line of rings. There were two other people on the pontoon. Two old white men sitting on the edge with their feet in the water.

'Vada him dear, I'd love to get my lills into his basket.'

'And all over his luscious lallies.'

I had no idea what they were talking about. I looked to where they were staring. A tall guy was striding along the jetty. He had blond, shoulder-length hair and golden skin that seemed to glow in the sun. He flittered along the diving board and then launched himself high into the air, then like a golden arrow, he cut into the water. The two queens giggled, and one of them banged his chest with his fist as if trying to beat his heart back into life. The swimmer headed towards us.

'Ooh, he's coming this way. Primp your riah dear, primp your riah.'

They ran their fingers through their grey hair.

'You look like a ghost dear. Dolly your old eek.'

They pinched their cheeks and leaned back as if they were models on bonnets at a car show.

The golden boy's body cut through the water, heading towards where Barnaby was still swimming.

'That's a shame, isn't it dear?'

'After we'd gone to all that trouble.'

The golden boy turned his head to take a breath as he swam past us. He carried on for a few strokes, then changed course and headed towards the pontoon.

One queen nudged the other. 'Ooh, he must have vada'd us dear.' They giggled.

When he reached the pontoon, he placed his hands on the plastic, his biceps flexed as he lifted himself out of the water. His skin appeared to catch all the sun and reflect it. Even the two old queens were silenced as he sat, his thigh muscles spread over the pontoon surface like honey. He ran his hand through his hair, then flicked the water into the pond. He winked at me, smiled, then nodded. He dived into the water and swam towards the jetty.

'Follow him dear,' said one of the old queens.

'What?'

'That was the biggest come-on I've ever seen.'

'Yes, it was huuuuge.'

'I don't understand. Follow him to do what?'

'Oh, don't play all innocent. What do you think?'

'Just follow him dear, and find out.'

'Then toddle back and tell us—'

'Every inch of detail.'

The queens giggled.

The swimmer stopped halfway to the jetty. He looked towards the pontoon and smiled.

'See, he's gagging for it.'

'Follow him where?'

'To the cottage.' One queen pointed at a brick building to the side of the wooden compound.

They looked incredulous. 'You're really gonna say no to that dish dear?'

They giggled. 'Just let him do whatever he wants. I know I would.'

'I'd be like that bloody Mark Spitz trying to catch him.'

'I'm not like you poofs. I'm normal. You're disgusting.'

The two queens turned away from me and whispered to each other. The golden boy climbed the steps. When he was halfway along the jetty, he turned, took one last look at the pontoon, then shrugged.

'Apologise,' said Barnaby, lifting himself onto the pontoon.

'What?'

'I heard what you said, apologise to them.'

'Why? They were implying I was a poof and I'm not. Absolutely not—'

'Apologise. Now.'

I looked at the two queens, staring at me, their arms folded.

'They were trying to help.'

I took a long breath. 'Okay, I'm sorry, I shouldn't have said what I said, it's just I'm not a …not like that.'

The two nodded, turned away from me, then whispered to each other again.

I shook my head. 'It's just I'm not like that.' I looked pleadingly at Barnaby.

'Okay, okay, so you've said many times. You need to relax.' Barnaby sat next to me.

'What did he want?'

'You. Obviously. Usually, he swims a few lengths. I guess he saw you and made a detour.'

'Really?' I was horrified and flattered. The boy looked so like Gideon, and of course, like Nick would probably look now. 'But I'm nothing to write home about.'

'You're young, fresh, available and he's randy. That's all it needs.'

I pointed to the toilet block. 'Why would anyone want to do it in there?'

'And with that, I must agree. I've never been keen on cottaging.'

'Does a lot of sex go on here?'

'Loads.'

'People actually do it with complete strangers?'

Barnaby laughed. 'Last night I thought your coyness was an act, a pretence, even a come on, but now I see you really are that naive. What's your story?'

'There isn't much to tell. And I'm sure your story is far more interesting.'

'Sadly for me, the book is nearing its end.'
'No, you're barely halfway.'
'In the gay world, that is pretty much the end.'
'That's sad.'

A breeze blew across the pond.

'Time to go for a sunbathe.' Barnaby launched himself into the water.

I took a deep breath and followed. I swam to the jetty, climbed out, and followed Barnaby into the compound. As we entered, the golden boy came through the opposite door, followed by a young guy in pink trunks. He passed me, stared into my eyes, with a mocking look. As if saying "You had your chance."

'I usually sunbathe in here.' Barnaby dried himself. 'But I reckon you wouldn't like that.'

I noticed some of the old men lifting themselves off their towels and ogling me again. 'This is so tawdry.'

'Come on, let's go onto the grass.'

We picked up our stuff and went out to the grass bank. We spread our towels and stretched over them.

'You haven't been anywhere like this before, have you?' said Barnaby.

'That's what I keep telling you.'

'Sorry, I guess I'm so used to young hustlers pretending to be all innocent and coy.'

I looked towards the hedge surrounding the pond. Through the branches, I could see the golden boy walking along the path towards the toilet, and a few seconds later, he was followed by the guy in pink trunks. I was hurt. The boy's desires had shifted so swiftly to someone else. It also made me feel better about refusing. It would have been one of the most significant moments in my life, but for him, just another quick shag or whatever.

'We can go into Hampstead for lunch later,' said Barnaby.

'I can't afford—'

'Don't be so sodding ridiculous, I'll pay.'

'Please, you've done so much already, and if you're expecting me to…you know.'

'Expecting what?'

'To do whatever you gays get up to.'

Barnaby leaned back and laughed. 'Well, at least you're calling us gays now. That's progress. What do you think I am?'

'I don't know. I just can't understand why anyone would be so kind. Unless they were looking for a shag.'

'Look, I admit when I saw you last night. I did think you were someone to keep my bed warm. But when I spoke to you, that desire diminished.'

'Oh, thanks…that's—'

'Not because you're not attractive, you are. You're too refined, too well educated. I like my shags to be more rough and ready. And I don't like virgins.'

'So why still invite me back?'

'Maybe I'm just a kind-hearted soul who wants to help.'

I smiled. Then pursed my lips in an effort not to cry.

'Please don't switch on the waterworks.'

'I'm sorry, but it's been such a tough few days.'

'Okay, okay…make me a living saint of the Roman Catholic Church. Just as long as I've made it clear, I'm not about to pounce on you. You can stay as long as you need. Look, I like you, God knows why. There's an earnest vulnerability about you. I can see you're in trouble, or you need help in some way. And I can help you, look at the ridiculous size of my sodding house.'

'Don't you like it?'

'I love it, bloody love it, but sometimes it feels so dead, lifeless.'

'You could find someone to share it with.'

Barnaby looked up at the leaves, blinking as if trying to stop tears. 'Bloody pollen. When I meet someone, I always wonder do they want me or the house. And usually, in the end, I discover it's the house. And do you know how painful it is to live with someone who's waiting for you to die?'

I almost made a joke about hiring food tasters to make sure any lover wasn't trying to poison him, but there was a deep unfathomable sadness in his eyes. And a joke might hurt him greatly. 'Why don't you live somewhere smaller?'

'A pied-à-terre you mean, for when I'm out looking for love?'

'Rent your place out, and live somewhere smaller.'

'But if I did that dear boy, I wouldn't be able to rescue rapscallions like you, would I?'

'Just a thought.'

'You're right, but it's my home. I promised Mama nobody else would live there, not so long as I live.'

'So you're stuck.'

'I suppose, but what a place to be trapped.'

The gate opened and the golden boy came out dressed in cycling shorts and a T-shirt.

'Now's your chance,' Barnaby said.

The boy looked in my direction, then unlocked his bike. He straddled it and cycled along the path, his buttocks firm in florescent orange lycra.

'He'll probably be back tomorrow,' said Gideon.

We lay on the grass until two, then climbed over the hill to Hampstead. After the meal and the second glass of red wine, I felt warm, calm, serene, I reached out and squeezed Barnaby's hand.

'Hey. Everyone will think I'm your sugar daddy.'

'You're the sweetest, kindest man I've ever met. I'll never forget what you've done for me.'

'It's nothing, really.'

'I need to tell you my story, and why I was wandering around last night.'

'You don't have to.'

'I want to and I think I need to tell someone.'

I told him everything, about the factory, about Gideon, about Lance being beaten up. I wasn't shy about telling Barnaby what had happened in the brothel.

He fell back onto his chair and roared with laughter.

'Well, I didn't think it was funny.'

'Come on, it is funny, the prostitute thinking you had the hots for onions.'

'I guess it is.'

'Look, Mark, when you get to my age, you realise most casual sexual encounters are ridiculous. I think you should have told Gideon what happened.'

'Why?'

'I'm only judging from what little you told me, but he seems like a genuine friend, trying to make his best friend happy. I'm sure if you'd told him—'

'That he turns me on.'

'Well, don't quite put it that way. Just tell him nothing happened with the prostitute and you think you might prefer boys.'

'But I don't like boys, just him.'

Barnaby shook his head. 'God save me from closet queens.'

'What?'

'Look, Mark, you're young, a virgin. It's hard to come out. Believe me, I know, but stop lying to yourself.'

'I'm not lying.' I stood up. 'Look, if you're just going to accuse me of being a poof—'

Barnaby grabbed my arm. 'Stop being such a hissing idiot and sit down.'

I tried to pull my arm free, but Barnaby's grip was too strong.

'Look, I realise everything must seem so difficult, even impossible. But believe me, this time will pass, and when you get to my age, you probably won't even remember it. We always over-enthuse about the good times, and over-agonise about the bad. Don't get carried away in the moment. I can tell you now, you'll have far more distressing times than this.'

'That really doesn't help.'

'Look, you're young, healthy, good looking, in a little

boy lost kind of way, intelligent. You've got your whole life waiting to be lived. Lift your eyes and look up.'

'I have no job, no money. I'm terrified I'm a poof who's attracted to my best friend. And when I see him, I'll either have to pretend I feel nothing for him, or just stop seeing him and try to come up with some lie to explain.'

'For fuck's sake Mark. Just tell him the truth. He went to a Catholic boarding school. How straight can he be?'

'You haven't seen him chasing girls.'

'He'll probably be flattered. To be honest, he strikes me as a bit of a narcissist. He probably thinks the whole world wants to sleep with him. You've got two months to decide what you want to do. Plenty of time to think. And you can stay at mine for all those two months if it helps. Stop all this self-pity and moping and get on with it.'

I wanted to argue, but I knew he was right. I needed to pull myself together and sort things out.

Barnaby lifted his glass to his lips. 'Let's go back home. I'm knackered.'

15

Before I went to bed, I'd asked Barnaby to wake me early so I could make a prompt start with my job search. So when I woke and saw it was eleven, I went downstairs, determined to have it out with him. However, when I got into the kitchen, I found a note and a key.

IN LONDON. MAKE YOURSELF AT HOME

What was he doing? Working? Another concert? Visiting a lover? I was angry that he hadn't woken me up. Again I'd wasted a lot of time. But I was touched he trusted me to leave me alone in his mansion. I brewed a pot of tea and took it out to the gazebo. As I drank, I looked at the house. It had to be worth hundreds of thousands, maybe a million. It would be so easy to take something and use the proceeds to pay off my debts. Barnaby probably wouldn't even miss it.

I thought about his "closet queen" comment. Although I still objected to it, I was beginning to think maybe there was truth in it. After all, it wasn't only Gideon I'd been attracted to, there'd been Nick, and the boy at the Pond. All slim, golden-haired, impossibly beautiful boys. The big difference about what happened yesterday was the boy at the Pond wanted me too. That was surprising, as I'd never thought of myself as attractive, so to have someone as stunning as him wanting me was a shock. Even though Barnaby was probably right, the boy had been desperate for sex and I just happened to be there, to be lusted after by someone so stunning, was a confidence boost.

As I was looking at the house, I noticed there was a window on the ground floor, which I knew wasn't part of the lounge or the kitchen. I walked towards it. Held my hand over my eyes to shield them from the sun and peered inside. It was difficult to see much as the curtains were drawn. But through a gap, I saw a desk covered in documents, and on the wall was a framed gold disc. The sort I'd seen on television and in the papers being presented to pop stars who'd sold a million records.

Was Barnaby a pop star? I'd never heard of him. Perhaps he'd been big in the late fifties or early sixties, before The Beatles came along and made pop music good. A one-hit wonder? I went back into the house and shuffled down the corridor. When I got to the door, I paused to make sure Barnaby hadn't returned, then tried the handle. Locked. Which made me even more curious. I went outside and tried to open the window, but it too was locked. What could be in there? I knew none of the other rooms were locked. I'd even noticed Barnaby didn't lock his bedroom. So what was so special about this room? I also wondered where were all the people, the staff. Barnaby had mentioned a Mrs Carter, where was she? And someone must look after the garden. Where were they? It made me anxious. Especially as I had no idea when Barnaby would be back. What would happen if someone showed up? To them, I would be a thief. They'd probably call the police. I decided to get out of the house. Hopefully, when I got back, Barnaby would have returned.

I walked to Highgate Village and spent the afternoon wandering up and down the street. I asked for work in a pub and a cafe and was refused at both. At six, I bought some cod and chips and returned to the house. Still he wasn't back. I ate in the kitchen and spent the evening watching television with the curtains drawn and all the lights out. At midnight, with Barnaby still not returned, I went to bed.

When I got up the next morning, he still wasn't back. For a moment, I wondered if this was his house. Had he brought me to some stranger's place and abandoned me? Was I trespassing? Should I pack my rucksack and leave? I decided to go out for the day, come back in the evening, then if Barnaby still wasn't back, I'd leave.

I didn't want to get any more job rejections. So instead of looking for work, I decided to spend the day in the one place I could go where I knew I wouldn't have to spend any money: The Men's Pond.

I ambled along the lane from the house until I reached the grassy bank. I didn't want to go into the carcass-filled compound. It had been bad enough with Barnaby, but to go in there alone would be even harder. So I spread my towel on the grass, took off my T-shirt and lay down. I closed my eyes and listened to the chatter and the splashing. When I leaned on my side, I could just about see through the leaves to the pontoon. I longed to swim back there. Despite the two giggling queens and the freezing water, it had been relaxing. I could lie on the pontoon for hours soaking up the sun, worries floating away over the water. But the prospect of going through a jungle of leering eyes, and then having to swim through icy water, put me off.

The golden boy flashed by on his bike. I stared at him, my heart thumping and my breaths short. I was relieved and saddened to see he didn't stop at the Pond. But rode up the hill.

It was getting hot. Which made the water look more inviting. I was desperate to get onto the pontoon, but couldn't face the eyes in the compound. So I wrapped the towel around my waist and pulled my shorts and undies down. Then, with a few hip wiggles, I changed into my trunks. I strode down the bank and through the narrow path to the door of the compound. I pushed it open, then with my eyes fixed on the door opposite, I strode through without even a glance to either side.

There was a gentle breeze coming over the water. As I stood on the jetty, I took a long breath, then went over to the steps. This time when my foot touched the icy water, I was expecting it, so I didn't flinch. I eased into the pond and then swam towards the pontoon. Even though the water was a little less cold than before, I still shivered. I lifted myself onto the pontoon, then lay on my back with my legs dangling in the water. There were three other people doing the same as me, lying back, sunbathing. I closed my eyes. This was the best moment as the sun dried and warmed my cold skin, bringing my body back to life. The only things that existed were the sound of water lapping around me, the press of the pontoon against my back and the kisses of sunshine on my face. With all my troubles floating away, I fell asleep.

'You again.' A voice whispered. At first, I thought it was a dream. Until I felt something in my ear.

'Your prince has come to wake you.'

When I opened my eyes, I thought I was hallucinating: the golden boy was leaning over me, gazing at me, his little finger stroking my earlobe. His eyes matching the sky, his moist strawberry lips just inches from my mouth.

I pressed back into the pontoon. 'You... you were here the other day.'

'Correct.'

I rubbed my eyes.

'If you're still sleepy, I can wake you with a kiss.'

I gulped. 'That won't be necessary. I'm fully awake.'

'Pity.'

I lifted myself and moved away from him. 'Wouldn't it be illegal?'

'Very probably.' He held his hands in front of him with his wrists pressed together. 'So cuff me.'

I looked around and was relieved to see we were the only two left on the pontoon. 'What are you doing here?'

'I come here every day. So the real question is, what are *you* doing here?'

'Don't expect me to follow you into the toilet. I'm no pansy.'

The boy roared with laughter. 'Oh dear, is that the word your grandad uses? How very pre-war. In these post-neanderthal days, we prefer to use the more benign, gay.'

'A perfectly good English word stolen by you lot. Anyway, whatever you choose to call yourselves, I'm not one.'

'Really? Last time your tongue was hanging down to your knees.'

'No.'

'And here you are again, same time, same place.'

'You don't know why I'm here.'

'And without your sugar daddy.'

'He's not my sugar daddy. Just a friend who's helping me out.'

The boy looked sceptical; I tried to think how I could convince him.

He just smiled and with his face to the sun said, 'Good, glad to hear it. We all need help occasionally.'

I couldn't help gazing over his body. His oiled skin in the sunlight made him glisten like a brand-new statue. He had pert nipples on a muscular chest above a washboard stomach, down which drips of water were rolling like mercury. But it was his legs, smooth, muscular, with just the faintest ghosts of hair that excited me the most. I longed to press against him and feel the legs wrapped around me. I started to get aroused, so I lay on my stomach.

'You really are desperate for it aren't you?'

'Desperate for what?'

'Sex. I saw your little soldier standing to attention.'

'No, it's…it's—'

'There's nothing wrong with it. It happens to the best of us.' He nodded to his crotch.

Even though I knew I shouldn't look, I had to. He was not only hard but throbbing. I looked away.

'For fuck's sake man, just enjoy it. Clearly we're both desperate for it. We can go in there.' He nodded towards the toilet.

I imagined it was smelly, dirty with the ever-present danger of someone coming in and finding us. I couldn't imagine a worse place to have sex, and yet the boy was right, I was desperate to go in there and do …I had no idea what… all I knew was I needed to go in there and hold that godlike body.

'But there are people.'

'It's fine, happens all the time.'

I was about to say I know, I saw you before, but didn't want to show I'd been watching him. 'I've never done anything, it, you know…with a man.'

'Oh, you don't say?' The boy stretched his fingers over the pontoon so they touched the tips of mine. 'Let me lead you into the wonderful world of gay sex.'

'I…I don't know.'

'I promise we won't do anything heavy.'

'Heavy?'

'Anything anal.'

'Jesus!' That hadn't occurred to me, even as a possibility.

'It'll be as vanilla as vanilla ice cream, with vanilla frosting on a vanilla meringue pie. I promise I won't do anything you don't want to.' He nodded his head towards land and wrapped his fingers around my forefinger. 'Come on, you never know, you might even enjoy it.'

I looked towards the jetty. There weren't many people around. My dick was fully erect now and throbbing. It took all my willpower to stop from putting my arm around the boy's neck and kissing him.

'Come on.' He lowered himself into the water and swam towards the jetty.

I followed. I was worried about getting out of the water and people noticing I was aroused, but after a few seconds, the icy water meant the blood flowed from my cock, to what were, despite my longing for his body, still my more vital organs. By the time I reached the steps, I was flaccid.

He headed towards the toilet. I waited a few seconds before following. My legs were like jelly. I was sure everyone must be watching. They must all know what we were up to. I told myself I had a choice. I could go through the door into the concrete courtyard, climb the bank to my towel and leave, or I could follow.

But in reality, I knew I was kidding myself. There was no choice.

My dick hardened again. I shuffled along the path, looking at the leaves, the birds, studying the cracks in the flagstones, trying desperately to look like some casual walker out on his morning stroll. When I got to the entrance, the boy was standing at the latrine. I shuffled up beside him; I looked down and his dick was out, fully erect. He grabbed my hand and pulled me into a cubicle.

I gulped. I couldn't believe I was standing so close to such a god, breathing his breath, feeling his heat. A god who wanted me as much as I wanted him. My breathing became short and fast. He pulled my head and kissed me hard on the lips. At first, I kept my lips closed, but he nibbled until I parted them. Then it was as if my tongue was being sucked out of my head into him. His arms were a vice around me. When his tongue swirled around mine, I swirled mine too. Then his fingers slid into the back of my trunks. As he caressed his fingers to the front, the tingling made me tremble.

Oh God.

The moment he touched my dick, I knew I was going to shoot. I tried to stop, but the sensation was so intense, I couldn't. I wanted to groan, cry, scream, but I remembered where I was, so all I said was, 'Oh God, oh God, oh my God.'

I fell against him. My chest pressing against his smooth skin. When he caressed the back of my neck, I let out a sigh that had been waiting to be released all my life.

'I was just starting to enjoy that.'

I pulled myself away and whispered. 'Sorry...I—'

'That's okay. Kiss me.'

My desire of a few seconds before had almost evaporated. I looked towards the door.

'Don't worry, nobody will come. Kiss me.'

It was a struggle to kiss as fervently as before. As we

kissed, the boy pumped his dick. I just wanted him to shoot so I could get out before anyone came in. Thankfully, it was only a minute before he did.

He made no sound, just gave me one last kiss. 'Thanks.' He opened the door, stepped out, and washed his hands in the basin.

I had mixed emotions. I felt dirty. Now I noticed the toilet stank of piss and the floor was sticky. I was ashamed of what I'd done, but I was also elated. I wanted to talk, maybe go for a coffee or snack, and get to know each other. Kiss each other again, again and again. But it was obvious he wanted to get away. I was confused, only moments before I'd been the one person in his life, the only reason he wanted to live, but now it was as if I'd become the biggest irritant in his life and he wanted to get as far away from me as possible.

'So this is goodbye?' I said.

'See you around.' The boy nodded and left.

I cleaned myself, pulled on my trunks, and went outside. He ran along the jetty, then dived into the water. My whole body wanted to follow so we could swim together like dolphins. But I knew it would be the worst thing I could do. So I went to sit on the grass.

At last I knew what true sexual excitement meant, what I'd heard people, especially Gideon, obsess about for years. I'd never believed them, but now I knew it existed. I wanted it again. The ten or twenty per cent of doubt about whether I was gay was gone.

Shit!

I sighed. Is this what being gay meant, a lot of meaningless, dangerous, tremendous sex and then nothing? I wanted more than that. I needed more. I wanted dinner with wine. To lie in bed, kissing the whole night. Long talks and laughter.

For the first time since I'd left Amsterdam, I yearned for Gideon. His smile, the sound of his voice, his care and generosity. I remembered the long talks we'd had, the meals, the nights we'd shared a platonic bed. How wonderful those times had been. What had just happened made me realise how wonderful sex, the passionate touch of another human being could be. Now I'd tasted it. I wanted it again, but I wanted it with Gideon. I wanted to hold him, to kiss him, to make love to him. To become his lover, share his life and die with him.

    I lay on my front and sobbed. I'd always known Gideon was unattainable, but now I knew how wonderful sex, lovemaking could be, it made knowing it would never happen with the one person I wanted, unbearable.

16

When I was out of tears, I fell asleep. When I woke, the Pond was a rumpus of splashes. Many more guys were swimming, diving, and bombing into the water. I guessed they were workers who'd come for a dip, fumble, or both, before heading home. Sleep hadn't boosted my mood, on top of which lying in the heat had made me sticky and sweaty. I decided to go back to Barnaby's for a shower.

As I wandered along the lane, a mixture of thoughts beset me. I was elated because I'd experienced sex for the first time, but forlorn at the way the boy had wanted to get away as fast as he could. I was pleased all doubts about being gay had gone, but anxious about what that would mean for my life. I was relieved to finally admit I was attracted to Gideon, but heartbroken, no, devastated that it would never be reciprocated. Despite my overall sense of foreboding, I couldn't help smiling at the irony. I'd left Amsterdam to get away from Gideon so that with time and distance my feelings for him would die, but instead, after a couple of minutes with the golden boy, my desire for Gideon was stronger than ever. If that wasn't enough, I still had to find a job and if Barnaby wasn't back, somewhere to live.

What a bloody mess!

At least one problem disappeared. When I opened the front door to the house I saw Barnaby's linen jacket draped over one of the chairs in the hallway, and the sound of scraping metal was coming from the kitchen.

'Oh, you're back.' Barnaby momentarily disappeared behind a mushroom cloud of steam coming from a wok. 'Want some stir-fry?'

'No thanks. I bought these.' I held up a plastic bag.

'Ahh...back on the old sarnies? Where've you been?'

'I was at the Pond.'

Barnaby tossed some spice into the wok and then stared at me, his thick eyebrows like two furry black caterpillars colliding above the bridge of his nose. 'Oh really!'

'I had to get out of here in case anyone showed up.'

'Sorry about that. My note was a bit short. You needn't have worried. I gave Mrs Carter time off. Sorry for staying away so long.'

'Hey, you've nothing to be sorry for.'

Barnaby shook the wok, turning the noodles and vegetables over. 'Are you sure I can't interest you in this?'

'No, I'm fine. You want some tea?'

'Good God no! With dinner I always have wine.'

I switched on the kettle, put my sandwiches on a plate, and sat at the table. 'What were you doing in London?'

'I had some business which went on a bit long so I stayed at The Dorchester.' He turned and looked at me. 'And I thought you could do with some space.'

I knew what he meant by giving me space.

He emptied his food onto a plate and sat opposite me. 'So, did you take advantage?'

To avoid looking at him, I poured myself some tea.

'You did. You dirty bugger.'

'I didn't bring anyone here...I wouldn't.'

'So...' Barnaby cupped his chin in the palm of his hand, his eyes fluttering like some silent movie star. 'Tell me... everything.'

'It was nothing, really.'

'But it was something.'

I tapped my sandwiches nervously and then looked at him. 'Don't laugh, but it was the boy from the Pond.'

'Shit! Adam Adonis! I knew it, the way the two of you were staring at each other. Well done!' He jumped up and pulled a bottle from the wine rack and placed two glasses on the table. 'We need bloody Chardonnay for this.'

'I'm happy with tea.'

'I'm not happy with you being happy with tea. So drink and spill.'

I was anxious in case he was expecting something more exciting than what had actually happened. I would have embellished had I had the foggiest idea about what I could embellish with. 'Nothing happened, not really.'

He filled my glass. 'Drink that and answer me again. What happened?'

I gulped a mouthful. It was like eating apple, lemon and pineapple at the same time, tangy. 'I was resting on the pontoon, and he woke me by stroking my earlobe.'

'Bloody hell! He never struck me as the tactile type. And?'

'We spoke—'

'Cut the intro. What did you do?'

'We went into one of those filthy, stinky cubicles. I don't know how—'

Barnaby waved his hand. 'Yeah, what a vile place to make love. I know all this. Come on. Details Mark. Details. Did you?' He pushed his tongue into his cheek and pumped with his fist.

I wasn't sure exactly what he meant, but could guess. 'We kissed, we touched. We kissed again.'

Barnaby refilled my glass. 'Have another mouthful.'

'Oh, it was an amazing kiss, I've never—'

'Go on.'

'We touched, he squeezed me. Really tight. He has amazing arms.'

'I've seen his bloody arms. Now come on.'

'I became very excited and I..I…you know.'

'Jesus, you dropped your bombs before reaching the target.'

'Umm…yes… I guess.'

'Oh bloody hell! I bet he was livid.'
'Why?'
'Too quick my boy, too bloody quick.'
'I couldn't help it. Kissing him made me so excited.'

Barnaby drained his glass. 'Well, that was a bloody waste of bloody good wine.' He picked up a pair of chopsticks and piled noodles into his mouth. Whilst chewing, he mumbled. 'But did you enjoy it?'

It was the most intense, exciting experience of my life, but I couldn't detach it from what happened after. 'Yes, but afterwards—'

'He cut you dead?'

'How did you know?... Did I do something wrong? Was it because it was so quick?'

Barnaby sighed. 'I've had nights where we've shagged as if our lives depended on it, and then they've sodded off in the morning without even a goodbye.'

'Jesus!'

'That's the way of gay sex in the big wicked city. There's always a bigger dick around the corner. He's had you, done you. If he sees you in a bar, he knows you won't come over and frighten some potential shag away.'

'Is it always like that? Before, he treats you as if you're the most wonderful being on the planet but, after, your dogshit.'

'Not always.'

'That is so...I don't know...shallow. Do you do that?'

'When I was younger, now I'm too bloody knackered. Don't fret about it. The important thing is you've kissed another man. And you enjoyed it?'

I nodded. 'But we didn't—'

'Shag? It doesn't matter, go at your own pace. And my God! What an Adonis to start with...Let me tell you, they won't all be like that.'

'I don't know if I want it again.'

Barnaby laughed. 'Oh you will, mark my words, you will. We all have our moments of regret and resolve never to suck dick again. But then as sure as dicks are dicks and bums are bums, when the next boy smiles at us, or wiggles his tight little arse, we forget all that and bam...we're back on our knees.'

'You may be, not me.'

'We'll see. Don't beat yourself up about being quick. I'm sure he's done the same.' Barnaby poured some more wine. 'And what about Gideon?'

'What about Gideon?' I tried to sound as insouciant as possible, as if Gideon hadn't crossed my mind.

'Now you know you like it with a man. Will you pursue Gideon?'

I wanted to say I craved him more than ever, but knew if I did so, Barnaby would probably encourage me to pursue him. 'Nothing's changed.'

He reached across the table and squeezed my hand. 'You'll find everything has changed. When you see him again, you'll look at him more closely. Every smile, every touch, every kind word. You'll ask yourself, does he want me?'

'But he doesn't. I know he doesn't.'

'Oh Mark, I can hear with every word. You want him more than ever.'

'No, I don't.'

'Okay. Plan of Action. What you need to do is explore Gay London. Experiment. Have more fun. Meet more guys.'

'I don't know if I can take more rejection.'

'You'll get tougher. Eventually, you'll find someone to replace Gideon.'

I doubted that. 'But I need to find work.'

'Sod that! Stay here. Free bed and free food.'

'I don't like being a freeloader.'

'Don't worry about that. Look Mark, you're young. You need time to sort yourself out, find out what you want. Do that. Relax. And besides, I like having you here.'

'Really?'

'We can even go out together. And today you kept an eye on my place.'

'I didn't.'
'Did it burn down?'
'No.'
'Was I burgled?'
'No.'
'There you go. Here.' He pulled out two twenty-pound notes.

'No Barnaby.'
'Take it. And I'll give you a hundred every week.'
'No.'
'That's what you would've earned washing the onions, isn't it? You want more?'
'I don't want any.'
'If you stay, you'll cheer me up. We'll be doing each other a favour.'
'I don't know.'
'And just think how much studying you'll get done. Then come September, you can go back to Norwich, seduce Gideon, assuming you still want him by then. And make him forget all the silly girls he's slept with.'

I drained another glass of wine. The idea of staying and devoting my time to studying and perhaps meeting more men appealed. I looked at Barnaby's face. Was there a kinder man on the planet? I felt a warmth and security I'd never felt before. The wine had made me so lightheaded, I almost leant over and kissed him.

'And one day when you're rich and famous, maybe you'll do the same for another lost soul.'

Hearing the word famous reminded me of the gold disc I'd seen in the locked room.

'Barnaby, can I ask you something?'
'Go on.'
'When I was walking around the garden, I looked into the window of a locked room.'
'Spying on me—'
'No, I just. Sorry. I didn't mean…I saw a gold disc.'

'That's right.'

'Are you some secret pop star?'

For the first time, Barnaby's face darkened. He bit his lip as though stopping himself from exploding. 'Don't ask me about that again.'

I was jolted into sobriety and confused by his change of mood. 'Of course, sorry. I won't go anywhere near the room again.'

'Just mind you don't.' He picked up his plate and took it to the sink.

Why had he reacted like that to a simple question about a disc? Surely he should be proud of having been a pop star, even if he was only a one-hit-wonder. I punched my thigh for asking such a stupid question and watched as he stood by the sink; I wasn't sure, but I thought his shoulders were shaking as if he were crying.

17

The next morning Barnaby unsettled me by coming into my bedroom and dumping a leather jacket at the end of my bed. 'Wear this tonight.'

I sat up, still half asleep. 'What?'

'I'm not going to let you fester in Highgate. You're going to get a taste of Gay London.'

I was relieved he wasn't still angry after the night before. But I wasn't sure I wanted to go headlong into Gay London. The taste I'd got of it at the Pond, although wonderful and revelatory, the way it ended, had saddened me. I picked the jacket up off the bed. It was a lot heavier than I'd expected. 'It isn't my usual style.'

'I've worked that one out. So, put it on.'

It was a biker jacket, which made me wonder whether Barnaby was taking me to a convention of Gay Hell's Angels if there was such a thing. It wasn't new. The leather was creased and there was more than a hint of tobacco. It was so heavy when I put it on I had to consciously press my shoulders back to stop it from crushing me.

'Do you have a white T-shirt?'

I shook my head.

'I'll lend you one.' Barnaby stroked his chin as he scrutinised me. 'Confirms what I've always said. The only men who ever looked good in leather were Brando and Presley.'

'So why make me wear it?'

'If you don't. You'll look out of place. Give us a twirl.'

'Barnaby!'

'Go on.'

I rotated like a clumsy ballerina. When Barnaby stared at me, for a moment he seemed to be in another world. 'Barnaby…Barnaby.'

'Sorry, what?'

'It's bloody heavy.'

'You'll get used to it. Leave around eight?'

I could see from his eyes it was important to him. I couldn't understand why. Surely it was just some bar. I would rather have stayed in but considered a few hours of discomfort and awkwardness in a leather jacket was a small price to pay for what Barnaby had done for me. I hung the jacket over the back of a chair and went to sleep.

That evening, after I'd changed, I was surprised when I glanced in the mirror. The jacket made me look like a "hard nut", the name we gave boys at school who were always spoiling for a fight. The hem lay tight just above my buttocks, giving me something I'd never had before, a pronounced bum. And Barnaby's tight white T-shirt gave my chest some definition. As the weight forced me to hold my shoulders back, my chin was lifted out of my chest. I barely recognised the face in the mirror. There was none of my lifelong stooping fearfulness, and although I couldn't say the face was handsome, it was on the cusp of cuteness. Overall, with my new bum and prominent chest, the jacket made me look modestly sexy.

'Well! Cinderella *will* go to the ball.'

I was embarrassed at being caught admiring myself, my shoulders slumped. Barnaby was standing in the doorway, his arms folded in front of him.

'I suppose a Bargain Basement Brando is better than no Brando at all.'

'Oh, thanks.'

'Just kidding, see, what a transformation a little leather can make.' Barnaby walked up to me and stared into my eyes. 'No, I don't think so.'

'You don't think what?'

'I was thinking mascara.'

'With leather!'

'A killer combination. But in your case, I think your eyelashes are alluring enough.'

'Really?' I leaned towards the mirror. I'd never noticed my eyelashes before. When I looked at them up close, they looked a tad girly.

Barnaby was also in jeans and white T-shirt. His leather jacket was softer and much tighter: it emphasised his paunch. I couldn't understand why he was wearing it rather than mine.

He straightened the leather Breton cap on his head, then stood next to me. 'What a fine couple we make.'

I smiled as I remembered Gideon had said something similar when we were preparing to go to the brothel. 'Do you always go out dressed like this?'

'Not always.'

'What about on the Tube? Is it safe?'

'You get the odd faggy comment, but I just ignore them.'

'Wouldn't it be better to blend in?'

'No way! We've been bloody well blending in for centuries. Now is the time to stand out.' Barnaby looked into my eyes. 'Okay, I can see you're scared. We'll go by cab.'

'Do you think we should swap jackets?'

'No way…I could never wear this.' Barnaby stroked the lapels of my jacket.

'Then why buy it?'

He looked away. Then crouched to pull a pair of DMs from a cupboard. He sat on one of the armchairs, then put them on. When he'd finished, he said, 'Are ye ready boots? Start walking!' He grinned at me. 'Come on, let's find a cab.'

The cab dropped us opposite St Martin's Theatre, just off Trafalgar Square. I looked around for a pub, but all I could see apart from the theatre was the Coliseum Opera House.

'This way.' Barnaby led me down an alley running alongside the Coliseum to a door blocked by two heavy-set bouncers, who looked like they'd been thrown out of the Kray gang for being too brutal.

'Don't worry, it'll be fine.' Barnaby squeezed my forearm.

One bouncer nodded at Barnaby, then in a surprisingly high-pitched voice said. 'Long time no see Barnsy dear. Who've you been shagging?'

'Ooh… no one you'd know.'

'And who's this?'

'Just a friend.'

The bouncers nodded and winked at each other, then moved aside to let us through. The inside of the bar was so dark and the air so thick with smoke, I found it difficult to tell where the black walls ended and the customers began. If I'd been alone, I'd have run out. Barnaby grabbed my hand and dragged me through the blackness. Once my eyes began to adjust, I could make out some heads and faces. I felt like I'd stepped into a cave filled with leather-clad giants, who lived on beer, nicotine and probably the blood of boy virgins. They glowered at me like I was their next victim. I stared at Barnaby's back and followed.

Halfway down a staircase, two men were snogging. The rubbing of their leather jackets sounded like the squeaks of terrified mice.

Downstairs was even darker. Above the chatter, I heard the pleading sound of Marc Almond singing "Hold me, hold me, hold me".

When we battled our way to the bar, a topless barman in pink latex shorts smiled at Barnaby. 'Whatd'ye want sweetie?'

'Mark?' Barnaby shouted.

I wanted to leave. My lungs were clogging with smoke, sweat was trickling down my back and I was getting a headache.

'Lager?'

I nodded.

'Two Carlsbergs.'

The barman smiled. 'Cum…ing right up, sweetie.'

'Are you okay?' said Barnaby.

I nodded.

When the barman came back with the drinks, Barnaby said, 'This way.'

He pushed his way through the narrow bar towards a wall. Where there were three alcoves. In one a couple was snogging, in the next was another snogging couple except, they were accompanied by another man, who had his back to them, he was holding a pint in one hand whilst his other hand was rammed down the back of one of the snogger's leather trousers.

I thanked God the next alcove was empty.

Barnaby managed to edge himself into it, then pulled me inside. 'It'll be a bit less bumpy here.'

I took two long gulps of lager. Then coughed. 'What is this place called?'

'Nada To Vada.'

'What? Portuguese?'

Barnaby laughed. 'It's about as Portuguese as my cock. It's from *Nada to Vada in the Larder*.'

'What the hell does that mean?'

'It's Polari. Gay slang.'

I remembered the two guys on the pontoon when they were swooning over the golden boy. They'd used phrases I'd never come across.

'It used to be very popular before legalisation in '67.'

'So what does it mean?'

'*Nada* means nothing. *Vada* means see. *Nada to vada*, nothing to see. *Nada to vada in the larder,* nothing to see in the larder.'

'I don't understand. This isn't a restaurant.'

'It means not much, down there.' He pointed to my crotch.

'Oh, I see.' I shook my head. 'Why name a bar after something like that?'

'It's just fun, a bit of a laugh.'

The place was frenetic. There were staircases at both ends so there was a constant flow of guys going upstairs as others came down, like two lava slides of black leather rolling through the bar. I noticed not everyone was wearing leather. A few were in T-shirts or even blouses, younger ones mostly, some did look incredibly young, barely legal. Guys were mostly alone, some, like I assumed those in the alcoves were pairing off. I had to admit, although it was uncomfortable with the heat, the smoke and the noise, it was exciting. The thought that if I smiled at a guy or looked at him in the right way, we could be snogging, tantalised me. Especially when I remembered how I'd looked in the mirror. The jacket made me look kissable.

'If you stand here long enough, you'll see every gay in London go by.'

'Really?'

'Not quite, but not far off.'

'Where's the toilet?'

'Through there.' Barnaby pointed to the far wall.

I groaned. I felt safe in the alcove, but I needed to go.

'Want Mummy to hold your hand?'

I sneered at Barnaby. 'Very funny.'

I pushed my way through the bodies, trying as best I could to look like I was used to this and knew exactly what I was doing. All three urinals were occupied. I stared at the floor. After thirty seconds, nobody had finished. I looked up. The guy in the middle was stroking an enormous erection. He alternated between leaning to look at the guy on his right, and leaning to look at the guy on his left, both of whom were stroking their cocks. I was tempted to say. "Hurry up! Some of us bloody well need to pee!"

The door of the only cubicle opened. I moved towards it then stopped. The guy from the Pond came out. With the added allure of black leather and his skin glowing against a bright white T-shirt, he looked even more stunning.

'Oh, hello again.' My voice was almost a squeak. My body trembled as the desire for him returned. I hoped as I looked so kissable, he wouldn't be able to resist me. He'd grab me and suck my tongue into his mouth again.

He looked right through me.

'It's me, don't you remember?'

He brushed past me and headed to the door. A couple of seconds later, another guy came out of the cubicle. He was tucking his T-shirt into his leather trousers.

It hurt me. He could've just smiled or even nodded. Why behave as if nothing had ever happened? I felt worthless. One urinal became vacant, so I jumped in front of it. The guy in the middle looked over.

'Do you fucking mind?'

The guy snorted. 'Nada to vada anyway dear.' He zipped up and left.

When I'd finished, I pushed my way back to where Barnaby was standing. 'Can we go?'

'Why, what happened?'

'Nothing. I just need some fresh air.'

'Okay, let's drink outside.' Barnaby took my lager and led me upstairs, then outside.

As I leaned against the wall of the Coliseum, I took a long breath of nicotine-free air.

'Are you okay?'

'This place is disgusting.'

'Don't judge.'

'But it's full of people getting up to all sorts. You know, when I was trying to pee, some guy stared.'

Barnaby sniggered.

'It isn't funny. And when I complained you know what he said?

Barnaby shook his head.

'Nada to vada anyway dear.'

Barnaby almost spat his lager as he laughed. He managed to stop and said, not entirely convincingly. 'Oh, that wasn't very nice.'

'It was bloody rude. And I saw the guy from the Pond.'

'What did I tell you? Eventually, you see everyone here.'

'He blanked me. Fucking blanked me.'

'Sorry.' Barnaby squeezed my shoulder. 'But what did you expect?'

'A nod. A smile. It's just good manners. It was only a couple of days ago.'

'Manners! Oh Mark forget about bloody manners.' He shook his head. 'Sadly, that's how London gays operate.'

'I'd at least say hello.'

'You say that now. Come back to me in six months and we'll see.'

'Six months! I couldn't live like this. No wonder you lot get so much abuse.'

His eyes widened just like when I'd asked him about the gold disc. 'What do you mean by you lot?'

'Poofs. Queens. Fairies.'

'Just remember one of "you lot" has been taking care of you the last few days.'

I gasped. I'd stupidly let my anger get the better of me. 'Oh Barnaby, I'm so sorry, really sorry. You'd never behave like that.'

'Wouldn't I? Wouldn't you?'

'No, never.'

'Really. So if the boy from the Pond had been open to another snog, would you have refused?'

'No… I don't know. But I wouldn't stand next to him staring at his dick.'

'Okay yeah, that is pretty gross, but these guys are probably closeted.'

'But even so.'

'Perhaps I should've taken you somewhere less cruisy. But the truth is, many gay bars are pretty much like this, windows blacked out, heavy bouncers. Noisy, smokey places. With the throb of rampant lust all around.'

'I thought the Ponds was bad enough.'

'Think about it this way. If there had been laws illegalising straight sex, and if they faced the ever-present danger of being beaten up even for holding hands. Don't you think straights would meet in safe places like this?'

'I'd never thought of it like that.'

'And if the world was like that, and if straights had to meet in places like this, don't you think they'd behave in the same way?'

I nodded. 'I guess.'

'Barnsy...how are you?' A man who looked to be the same age as Barnaby, fatter, with bright red cheeks and too much makeup, ran up to us. He hugged Barnaby tightly.

'Hello Damien. How are you?'

'I'm fine, and who is this?' Damien looked at me. 'My God. My fucking God.' He leaned towards me and examined my face. 'That's fucking uncanny. It could almost be—.'

'Damien, this is Mark.' Barnaby pulled Damien away from my face. 'He's a brilliant student friend of mine. He's staying for a few days.'

'Of course he is.' Damien took my hand. 'I'm Damien, but my real friends all call me Dame.' His hand was soft and his shake weak, nervous.

'Pleased to meet you,' I said.

'Likewise. You going in?' Dame nodded towards the door.

'Already been and come out. Mark hated it.'

'I didn't say that.'

'Come on, you couldn't get out fast enough.'

'Oh, poor you...Barnsy can be such a cruel bitch. You could've at least taken him somewhere nice. He pinched my cheek. 'Amazing, absolutely amazing.'

'Damien, you really need to go.' Barnaby aimed a kick at Dame's backside, just stopping short of hitting it with the tip of his DMs.

'Okay Barnsy dearie, a lady always knows when she's not wanted.' Dame let go of my shoulder and then stepped away, his arse wiggling towards the door.

'Sorry about that. Damien can be over-familiar.'

'It's okay. What did he mean, uncanny?'

'God knows what he's thinking half the time.'

'You've known him long?'

'More than I like to admit to. He's okay once you get to know him and hasn't got half a brewery in his bloodstream.' Barnaby looked down the road towards Trafalgar Square. The crowds were pouring out of the theatre. 'Now, normally I'd go to Heaven—'

'Heaven?'

'A disco under Charing Cross. But I fancy you've had enough gayness for one night.'

'Don't let me stop you.'

Barnaby shook his head. 'I could do with an early one.'

I was relieved. It had been overwhelming. I was sweaty, smokey, just plain dirty. All I wanted was a shower, a gargle, half a tube of Colgate and bed.

18

When I woke the next morning, my mouth felt like I'd munched through a million cigarettes. I went into the kitchen and drank a glass of water, then gargled, then drank another glass. Everything about the night before had been terrible. The bar, the smoke, the noise, even the few sexy guys had had their allure obscured by a miasma of tawdry uncontrolled lust. The worst moment, of course, was when I was snubbed, cut dead. It made me feel like a piece of meat, bitten off, chewed, then spat out. And had transformed the time at the Pond, which had been one of the most, perhaps *the* most, exhilarating encounters of my life, into something deeply hurtful. Is that what gay life was? Quick snogs and shags in dirty bars and stinky toilets. Then being made to feel worthless? It made Gideon's many one-night stands look saintly.

I yearned to see him.

When I went to sit in the gazebo, I couldn't stop thinking about him. I wanted to talk to him. Even though I wouldn't be able to say much about what had happened, I missed being with him. His optimism, the way he embraced life, ran at it head-on and somehow always came out the other side unscathed. I had a crazy idea. If he'd returned to Norwich and I rang his house, he might answer. I wouldn't say anything, just listen. Enjoy the elation of hearing him saying "Hello". I dismissed it as ridiculous, a symptom of how wretched I was feeling. But later, when I went back into the house and passed through the hallway, I saw the phone and couldn't resist.

As I listened to the dial tone I smiled as I imagined him

striding down the corridor, probably in one of his silk dressing gowns, or if he was with a girl, in a quickly grabbed towel, wondering who could be calling him so early. I knew deep down, he wouldn't be there and I was wasting my time and should hang up, but every time I heard the dial tone I told myself, "Just one more ring, he may answer the next one." It made me feel closer to him. It was only when I heard the crunch of gravel on the driveway, looked out the window and saw a red Aston Martin convertible, swooping to a stop in front of the portico, that I put the receiver down.

As I opened the front door, Dame eased himself out of the car.

'Good morning Mark, is her majesty in residence?' He was in a cerise double-breasted jacket, red bow tie and dark green cords, which made him look like an overgrown Christmas elf. He looked up at Barnaby's window.

I shrugged. 'Still sleeping. I think.'

'Only think? Really?'

I knew what he was implying but decided not to dignify it with a denial.

'Best not disturb. You never know who he's got in there.'

'He's alone.'

'Old Barnsy must be getting tired in his dotage. Anyway, how are you honey?'

'I'm fine.'

'Survived last night?'

I nodded.

He stared at my face. 'Amazing.'

'What's amazing?'

'Nothing.' He leaned towards me. 'You really shouldn't be allowed out in this light. Soooo munchable.' He chomped just in front of my nose. 'You could get a girl in trouble. Anyway, aren't you going to invite me in?'

'I don't know if I can.'

'Oh, don't be silly, Barnsy and I go back before you were

a sperm in your daddy's willy.' He pushed the door open and brushed past me. 'Come on, Danny.'

'Danny?'

'No Mark, sorry.'

Dame headed straight for the kitchen and switched on the kettle. 'Cuppa?'

'I think I should give Barnaby a knock.'

Dame waved a hand. 'Don't bother dear, sit, sit.' He tapped one of the chairs. Then put three heaped teaspoons of Darjeeling into the pot. 'I take it Barnsy has taken you to the Pond?'

'Yes, it's lovely there.'

'Mmm...' He shook the teapot. 'Not my kind of place.' He looked down at his belly. 'Too much bloody fat.'

'There were a few chubbies there.'

Dame narrowed his eyes. 'Dearie, you need to learn your lines, when I say, "Too much bloody fat" and I'm looking down my front. Your line is. "Oh no, you're not at all fat."'

I panicked. But when I saw the grin on Dame's face and the twinkle in his eye, I relaxed.

'So, shall we try it again?' He raised an eyebrow.

I nodded.

'Not my kind of place.' Dame patted his belly. 'Too fucking fat.'

'Oh no! You're not fat.'

'Better dear, better.' The kettle boiled, and Dame poured steaming water into the teapot. 'Okay, Mark, so whilst we wait for it to brew. Tell me your story.'

'What do you mean?'

'It's a straightforward question. Who are you? Where are you from? And what do you want with my friend Barnsy?'

I wondered whether he'd come to see Barnaby at all or did he want to get me alone to probe me. Nevertheless, I told him about Holland, the factory, the onions, and about Barnaby rescuing me. I didn't feel comfortable enough to confide in him about Gideon or the brothel.

'I see.'

'Does Barnaby do that a lot?'

'Pick up young boys, you mean? Of course dear.'

'But he hasn't said anything about sex. Not once.'

He raised an eyebrow. 'Now that does shock me.'

'Why?'

'I'm amazed he hasn't touched you.'

'Why? I'm nothing special.'

'True.'

'Now who's not following a script?'

Dame leaned back and laughed. 'You're a quick learner. I suppose you have a certain rough beauty that Barnsy has always found irresistible.' He pursed his lips as if he was deciding to choose his words very carefully. 'And…and—'

'And what?'

'Nothing.' He took a sip and looked out the window. 'It should be a beautiful day. Going back to the Pond?'

'Come on. Don't change the subject. What are you implying?'

'Nothing.'

'Last night you gawped at me and said, "uncanny" and just now you called me Danny.'

'Just a mistake, dear.'

'And just then, you looked like you were about to say something.'

'Ignore me.'

The way he'd asked what I wanted with Barnaby, I was sure whatever it was had something to do with him. Was he jealous? An ex? His stare was unsettling, almost accusatory. But I could sense he was bursting to speak. I thought perhaps, with a little prompting, I could get him to blab.

'How do you know Barnaby?'

'Goodness, we've known each other for decades. We worked together in the fifties.'

'What line of work?'

'Music. Records.'

'So you must know about the disc in the locked room?'

He turned and stared at me. 'Barnaby has shown it to you?'

'No, I looked through the curtain. He got really angry.'

'No wonder, dear, in all the years I've known him, I've never been allowed inside. Don't think anyone has been since—'

'Since when?'

'Nothing.'

'No come on, since when?'

Dame finished his tea, picked up the teapot then sighed when he realised it was empty. He looked directly at me. 'Why are you here?'

'Because Barnaby invited me.'

'Stop being so bloody obtuse. Are you here to hurt him?'

'No, no of course not. Why would you say that?'

'Who sent you?'

'Nobody sent me. We met outside The Albert Hall and he invited me here.'

'So you expect me to believe you just happened to be outside The Albert Hall looking all gorgeous in your little boy lost way, when Barnaby was there too? All completely by accident.'

'That's exactly what happened.'

Dame shook his head. 'What do you want from him?'

'I don't want anything. Why are you saying these things? He offered me a place to stay. I was only going to stay one night. Then go.'

Dame bit his lip and shook his head. 'You make it sound like some innocent, bloody bedtime story.'

'Because it was innocent.'

'Why don't you go back to whatever filthy swamp you came from and leave Barnsy alone?'

His comment put a spark to the anger that had been building inside me since starting at the factory. The work, the onions, the attack on Lance, my unrequited feelings for Gideon, the snub, even being bloody knocked over the moment I arrived in London. It all exploded. I dived across the table grabbed his lapels and tightened them around his throat, just like Kenny had intimidated Jimmy.

'Barnaby fucking invited me. That's the fucking truth. You understand? You fucking nancy boy poofter!'

There was real fear in his eyes. He nodded. I let him go and looked at my hands, not able to believe what I'd done.

Dame coughed and loosened his bow tie.

'I'm really sorry. I've never—' I was even angry with myself now as I'd probably just confirmed that I was out to hurt Barnaby. 'I've never done anything like that.'

Dame drank a glass of water. 'You're either telling the truth or you're a fucking brilliant actor.'

'I can't act for toffee.'

'A good actor would say that.'

We stared at each other. I took a breath to calm myself. When he sat back down, it was as if we'd made an unspoken agreement to behave more calmly.

'Barnaby's been conned before. We all have. But what you're trying to do is of a completely different order.'

'But I'm not trying to do anything.'

'Oh, I think you are.'

I could feel anger welling up again. I took a slow breath. 'Please just explain what the hell you're going on about?'

Dame took a gold cigarette holder out of his jacket pocket. He lit a cigarette and took a long draw, then as he let out the smoke he said, 'You know that jacket you wore last night? It isn't brand new.'

'I bloody know that. Barnaby lent it to me.'

'And it wasn't Barnaby's, originally.'

'Was it yours?'

Dame leaned back and scoffed. 'The only time you'd see me in leather was if I died and one of my fucking enemies buried me in it as some cruel joke.' He took another draw. 'No, it belonged to Danny.'

'Danny? That's the—'

'Yes, I called you that by mistake. Danny as in Danny Blase. Heard of him?'

I shook my head.

'For a while in the late fifties, he was going to be the English answer to Elvis. Leather jacket, jeans, Tony Curtis hair, no pelvis, sadly. Even had a couple of hits.'

Remembering the disk in the locked room, I asked, 'Was Barnaby Danny Blase?'

'Good God no! Barnsy can't sing a note, dear. Besides, he never had "the look", few do. Danny did, my God, did he have the look—smouldering eyes, cheekbones as high as Big Ben. Girls adored him. Your mum probably fingered herself thinking of him.'

My fury of earlier came back, and I stood as if I was about to grab him.

He put up his hands. 'Sorry, sorry. Danny was... special.'

I sat back down. 'So where is he now?'

Dame went over to the sink and stubbed his cigarette in it. He stared out the window, sighed for a moment, then turned to look at me. 'Danny died sweetie. Danny died.'

'Oh.'

'When Barnsy first saw him, he was busking in Camden. For a time, they were the happiest, most devoted couple. And nobody knew...well, we all knew, but kept it quiet. Then one night Danny, the silly sod, went cottaging in Soho. Got caught. Sentenced to six months.'

'So his career was over.'

Dame's voice quivered. 'He never came out dear, never came out.'

'What?'

'Hanged himself in Wormwood Scrubs.'

'Shit!'

'Of course, everything was hushed up. Like it never happened. As if Danny Blase had never existed.'

'Poor Barnaby.'

'Yes, poor Barnsy.'

'But I don't understand. What has this got to do with me?'

He reached into his pocket and pulled out a small notebook. He slipped a picture from between the pages and lay it on the table. There were three people in the picture: Barnaby, Dame, and another guy.

'That is Danny Blase.' Dame tapped the guy in the middle.

I picked the photo up and squinted at it. 'Jesus Fucking Christ!'

19

Although the photo was small and monochrome, it was clear enough to see the boy in the picture could be my twin.

Dame tapped his finger on the photo. 'And that jacket was the one you wore last night.'

'Shit. But…but…I had no idea—'

'Really?'

'I've never heard of Danny Blase, let alone seen him.'

'I believe you, but whoever sent you must have known about him.'

'Nobody sent me.' I picked up the picture and looked at it closely. 'And last night, Barnaby made me dress like that.' I tossed the photo on the table and got off the chair.

'Where are you going?'

'I need to get away.'

'Because you've been rumbled?'

'No! No, because he's using me to reincarnate Danny.'

Dame grabbed my arm. 'You can't just leave.'

'Why not?'

'It'll kill him.'

'So I stay and he makes me sing? Fucks me?' I was scared. Maybe Barnaby had just been prepping me, biding his time. I shook myself out of Dame's grip.

'Please, Mark. At least let him explain.'

Even though I was desperate to leave, I did want an explanation and wanted to find out if Dame was telling the truth. 'I'll stay on one condition. That you stay and help me.'

'If he finds out I told you. He'll fucking kill me.'

I wanted Dame there, so most of Barnaby's fury would be directed at him rather than me. And he'd know how to calm him way better than I did. 'You go, I go.'

'I need whisky?' He went into the lounge and came back with a bottle of Scotch. 'Want some?'

I shook my head. 'How long were Barnaby and Danny together?'

'Just over two years. Danny had two hits. One night, they'd just finished recording his third single. Danny left the studio to "get some shuteye" whilst Barnsy stayed to finish the production. And that's when Danny got caught.'

When we heard Barnaby's footsteps on the stairs, we both turned and looked towards the door.

'Bloody hell, I should never have fucking come here.' Dame swigged a mouthful of whisky.

'That makes two of us,' I said.

Barnaby appeared in the doorway. Whereas when I saw him floating over the garden in his red dressing gown on the first morning, I thought he looked like an angel, this time I could only see a devil who'd deceived me with kindness. It made me want to cry.

'Damien! What are you doing here?'

'Just thought I'd pop in to make sure you got home safe and sound, sweetie.' He took another gulp of whisky.

Barnaby's eyes narrowed. 'In all the years I've known you, you've never done that.'

'First time for everything.' Dame looked at me as if he expected me to say something.

There was a long silence. I stared at Barnaby. He stared at me, then at Dame.

'Is everything okay? What's going on?'

'Nothing, nothing,' said Dame.

I could sense Dame was on the verge of making excuses and fleeing, so I glared at him.

'You two look like you've been planning to kill the Queen. What is it?'

I was angry with Barnaby for deceiving me, and I wanted to grab his shoulders and do what I'd done to Dame. But I could still see the kindness in his eyes. And I felt empathy. He'd had the love of his life taken away and I knew I was never going to be with the love of mine. What he'd done had been unbelievably creepy. But I didn't want to hurt him any more than he'd been hurt already.

'Come on? What are you two up to?'

I shut my eyes, then said, 'Why didn't you tell me about Danny?'

'Oh fuck,' said Dame. 'Just go right in there and beat that sodding bush, why don't you?'

'What?'

'Why didn't you say anything about Danny Blase?'

Barnaby looked at Dame, his eyes burning and tearful at the same time. 'Why couldn't you keep your poofy mouth shut?'

'I was worried about you, sweetie.'

'Don't call me sweetie.'

'I dragged it out of him,' I said.

'Oh, and I bet he put up the same fight he puts up when a Clone waves a big dick in front of his poofy lips.'

'Sorry Barnsy—'

'You've said enough. Get out! Get out now!'

'But...but.' Dame looked across at me.

It was clear his presence was making Barnaby angry, so I glanced towards the door. Dame got up and reached for Barnaby's arm, but he pulled it away before he could touch it.

'Goodbye Barnsy, sweetie.' Dame shuffled over the floor and disappeared.

Barnaby gripped a kitchen unit, his head bowed. He took long deep breaths, as if trying to quell the fire raging deep inside him. It wasn't until the crunching of Dame's car as it sped over the gravel had passed that he spoke.

'Mark, I'm really sorry.' He turned from the worktop, his eyes red, tears running down his cheeks.

'Barnaby, what's this all about? Why did you lie to me? And trick me? Why did you make me wear Danny's jacket and take me to that terrible place?'

'Come.'

'Explain to me here, now.'

'Please Mark, it'll be easier in the room.'

I began to wish Dame had stayed. Now I was alone with Barnaby, in his vast house and well out of earshot of anyone.

'Come on, please.' He smiled weakly, his voice shaking.

I followed him out of the kitchen, then down the corridor towards the locked room. He unlocked it. I didn't move.

'Please, you need to come in.' He disappeared for a second, then a faint light spread through the gloom. 'Come on Mark, please. Look, if you're scared, we'll keep the door open.'

I wasn't sure how that was supposed to reassure me, given we were alone.

'You need to see this.'

I peeked inside. All I could make out was a leather sofa, a desk and a chair. He pushed the door fully open. I crossed the threshold and stood a couple of feet inside the room. There was a musty smell, unlike in any of the other rooms, and a hint of tobacco, which puzzled me, as Barnaby didn't smoke.

'Please sit.' He pointed to the sofa.

As I sat, I looked up at the gold disk, trying to read any of the details, but it was too dark. When I looked directly ahead, I gasped. The wall opposite was covered in black and white photos and newspaper clippings. There were pictures of Danny alone, of him waving to crowds of fans, several of him receiving his gold disc. There were newspaper stories about him. Some colour magazine covers featuring his smiling face. It was like seeing dozens of pictures of my twin, of me.

'As Damien said, bloody uncanny,' said Barnaby.

I got off the chair and took a closer look. There were clippings with stories about Danny's success, his appearances, some letters from fans, a couple of pictures of him attending film premieres with a young actress, and speculation about an engagement. At the bottom of the display, there was one newspaper cutting, smaller than any of the others. It was a single paragraph with no picture. It had the headline, "Rock And Roller Found Dead".

After staring at the display for almost five minutes I noticed at one end of the room, there was a mannequin in jeans, a white T-shirt with the jacket I'd worn last night, draped over its shoulders. Now I understood where the smell of tobacco was coming from.

'Please, Mark, sit.' Barnaby pointed to the sofa. 'I wouldn't blame you if you wanted to run out of here as fast as you can. But please, just give me a few minutes to explain.'

I wasn't scared or nervous. Curiosity was my overriding feeling. So I lowered myself onto the sofa. I perched on the edge, my body erect, alert. Barnaby spun the chair under his desk around and sat opposite me.

'Can I get you anything to drink?'

'Just give me an explanation.'

Barnaby nodded. He kept his head bowed, staring at the desk. I wasn't sure if he was too embarrassed to look at me or mournful.

'I saw him on Camden High Street, busking outside Sainsbury's. The most beautiful boy I'd ever seen. Eighteen. Singing for pennies. I stared at him for what seemed like hours but was probably only minutes. When I dropped ten pounds into his cap, he said. "Hey, mister, that's too much". I smiled at him and said. I don't know how I dared to say this, but I said, "If I had a million in my pocket, I'd give you that. I'd give you everything I have." He replied, "That's a bit rum, sir." So polite, so courteous. All I wanted was to kiss him, and I was sure all he wanted was to punch me. But I didn't care if he did. So I said. "You come with me and I promise I'll make you a star."

'You really said that?'

'A cliche, but I knew I could make him a star.' He said, "Because my mum taught me to be polite to gentlemen, I won't tell you to bugger off, but please sir, leave me alone"'. Any sane person would have left. But at that moment, I wasn't sane, and I wasn't scared. I thought, I don't care if he kills me, because if he doesn't come with me, I'm dead anyway. "You're the most beautiful boy I've ever seen, and if you don't come with me, I'll never be happy, and nor will you."

'Jesus.'

'I expected him to batter me to death. I didn't care. He stared. And I stared back. I could tell from his eyes, he was seeing me for the first time. Maybe seeing himself for the first time too. I saw him gulp. "Who are you?" and I said 'I'm Barnaby, I make records, I'm a homosexual and I think, no, I know, I love you. And you, who are you?" And you know what he said? "I'm a nobody, I eat, I live, I sing. And you're the first person to ever say they love me." And we stood as the icy wind blew through Camden, and I said, "Then you better come with me."

'Wow!'

'And I kept my promise. I made him a star. And we loved each other until...' Barnaby looked up at me. 'I guess Damien told you what happened?'

I nodded. 'I'm sorry.'

Barnaby shook his head and sniffed. He looked up at the wall. 'Why did you do it? Wasn't I enough?'

I wasn't sure if he was addressing Danny or me, expecting me, because I looked like Danny to have an answer.

He held his head in his hands and, sobbing, said. 'I told him it was only six months. When he got out, we'd move, abroad if we had to. But...but...I couldn't help him in prison. And he was so bloody young. He couldn't take it. Every day I think if I'd left him on Camden High Street he'd still be alive.'

'You can't think like that.' I went across and put my arm around his shoulders.

'I can't help it.' He looked at me and tried to smile. 'Christ! What a fucking fool. I'm so sorry Mark.' He shook his head. 'When... when I saw you outside the Albert Hall, it was like... like Danny was back.'

'But—'

'I know you're not Danny. I'm not crazy. But I knew you needed help, just like my Danny.'

'But what was your plan? To keep me here?'

'No! You've been free to go whenever you wanted, you know that.'

'But why didn't you just say? Were you trying to get me to fall in love with you so you could pretend Danny was back?'

'No, of course not.'

'And why did you put me in his jacket?'

'I don't bloody know what I was doing. I'm so sorry.' He looked into my face and gave a sad, rueful smile. 'I loved him madly, completely loved him, and then he was taken away. So just to be reminded of him, to see his smile again, made the pain go away, just for a moment.'

'If Dame hadn't seen us, would you have kept lying to me?'

He shook his head. 'I don't know, maybe, but I would never have imprisoned you here. Please believe that.'

I did believe him. But I did wonder if all his kindness and generosity had been to make me dependent on him.

We sat in silence, apart from the sound of Barnaby's quiet sobs. As he cried, I patted his back like he was a puppy, taking its final breaths. Eventually, he stopped.

'Sorry.' He rubbed his red eyes and gave a fragile smile. He sniffed again. 'It's been more than twenty years and it still breaks me. Pathetic, isn't it?' He turned to me. 'I guess you want to leave. I'll give you anything you need and pay for somewhere for you to stay.'

I should have left, but I still liked him. Also, I was worried about him. And if I was completely honest, part of me admired him. He'd behaved so much more courageously with Danny than I had with Gideon. 'I can stay if you want me to.'

'Are you sure? After what I've done?'

'What you did was stupid, but I understand why you did it.'

'I promise I won't do anything so stupid again.'

I could tell by his eyes he meant what he said.

'I'll stay on one condition.'

Barnaby nodded, as if bracing himself to hear me make an impossible request.

'Never take me back to that bloody awful *Nada to Vada*.'

The relief made him shake with loud, barely controllable laughter. When he'd recovered, he said, 'The crazy thing is, Danny would've hated it too. He would've said "Too noisy, too crowded." And being Danny Blase, he would've attracted so much attention. He hated all that.' Barnaby gazed at the display on the wall.

'What?'

'Do you think that's why he went cottaging? Did he want to destroy himself? Destroy us?'

'Barnaby.' I squeezed his arm.

'I know.' Barnaby nodded. 'I need to stop thinking about it.' He poured himself a whisky and went over to the mannequin. He brushed some imaginary dust off the jacket, then gave a loud, deep sigh. Turned around and gave me a weak smile. 'Anyway, what did that old slapper say?'

'He was only trying to help.'

'What did he say?'

'He thought someone had found me and sent me to con you.'

'Always one for the melodramatic that one. Turning up here like that.'

'You should call him.'

'I'll let him stew for a few days.'

'Barnaby, do you mind if I go and lie down? It's been—'

'Of course. Of course.'

When I went up to my room, I lay on the bed, but after a couple of seconds, I went over to the door and locked it.

20

For the week after the Danny revelation, things between us were awkward. But after that, it got better; we ate together. We talked about concerts he'd been to, and I spoke about my studies. He never mentioned Danny.

Even though I spent a lot of my time studying, I went to the Pond most days. Of course, the golden boy was always there. At first, I looked towards him, waiting, probably hoping, for even the merest flicker of recognition. Perhaps part of me wanted another invitation to the cottage. I'm not sure what I would have done had I been invited. He always pretended not to see me. After a fortnight of gazing at him and no acknowledgement, when I saw him I just noted his presence and carried on with whatever I was doing. He went into the cottage with a different guy every day.

I ogled guys' bodies, and sometimes when I lay on the pontoon, especially at the weekends when it was busy, I let my leg touch the warm skin of another guy. And if he didn't move, my heart raced. I lay there motionless, not wanting the touching to end. I never spoke to them or hinted about going to the cottage. I just lay with my eyes shut, savouring the touch.

As the days got shorter, leaves turned gold then brown and when they died, they fell. The Pond became even colder. So cold, I couldn't even make it to the pontoon and had to turn back. There were fewer old men in the compound and some even wore bathers and vests to keep warm. The golden boy kept coming and no matter how cold the water was, he swam and he cruised. I noticed as the days grew colder, and there were fewer young fit guys around, at least guys who he hadn't already taken to the cottage, he went with older and fatter guys. That made me feel better.

My last visit to the Pond was the day there was a storm. It rained so hard I had to shelter in the compound alongside the naked old men. Some leered, some smiled. I stared at the darkened sky. When the storm passed and I stepped out of the compound. Branches were bare and the green bank was strewn with dead leaves.

'Summer's over,' I said and strode over the sodden grass.

One day, I was in the corridor at Barnaby's house and noticed the door to the locked room was open. I shuffled towards it and peered inside. The mannequin was lying on the floor; it had been stripped of the T-shirt, jeans and jacket. Barnaby was in the room, removing the pictures of Danny from the wall.

'I've decided I need to get this room sorted out.' He put a pile of cuttings on the desk. 'I'm going to put all this stuff in the attic.'

I stepped inside. 'Are you sure?'

'It's been too bloody long. Look at this room, like something out of a horror movie, creepy.'

'But it's his...it's Danny's room.'

Barnaby picked up a cardboard box. He had a more determined look than I'd ever seen him have before. 'No, this was never Danny's room. He barely came in here.' He put six framed pictures of Danny into the box.

'You know what I mean.'

Barnaby looked at me. 'You think I've gone crazy?'

I thought he was being hasty and might regret it, but thought it best not to say so.

'I know it looks like that. But having you here, and especially after that bloody stupid night when I took you to the Nada. When I didn't consider your feelings, not for one second. That's not me.'

That was true. Barnaby was the most generous and

thoughtful person I'd ever met. And that night had been an aberration.

'This craziness has gone on too long. Twenty years Mark. Twenty bloody years I've spent longing for that beautiful bastard to come back. And for what? Cutting myself off from anyone else, any new lover. Danny would never have wanted that.' Barnaby picked up the mannequin. He stared at it wistfully for a moment. 'This can go to the dump.' He put it in the corridor and came back. 'Maybe it was okay when the only person I was hurting was me, but then I dragged you into, my, well, my madness.'

'Not madness. And I survived. Don't torture yourself about it.'

'Even so, it was wrong. Maybe that night was what I needed, getting you to look so like Danny. It brought it home to me. He's never coming back. And this, all this.' He waved his arms around the room. 'Isn't real. Just shadows. I've got to live again before it's too late.' He went over to the gold disk and touched the frame. 'No, I'll keep that here. My greatest achievement, making Danny Blase a star.' He turned and smiled at me. 'And you, you need to start living too. You need to go back to Norwich.'

'Are you chucking me out?'

'No, you can stay as long as you want. But you need to go to Norwich and tell Gideon you love him.'

'I could never do that.'

'Why not? You do love him.'

'But he...he's straight.'

'So what? He's your friend, your best friend, tell him. And if he's scared off by it then perhaps he isn't such a good friend after all. And you never know, maybe he feels the same.'

'There's no bloody chance of that.'

'Look Mark.' He gripped my shoulders. 'You need to find out. What if in fifty years you're still best friends and he's lying on his deathbed—'

'Bloody morose!'

'And he tells you he always loved you, didn't love any of the girls, he always wanted you. What then?'

'Fantasyland Barnaby, fantasyland.'

'One day the person you thought was going to be around forever…' His voice started to shake.

'Barnaby.' I squeezed his arm.

'I'm fine. Because… one day you'll wake up and they won't be there.'

'But I don't want him to hate me.'

'He won't. I'm sure of it. He might even respect you.' Barnaby gave a wry smile. 'Don't go through life wondering if I'd said this or done that. So just tell him you love him and see what happens.'

I smiled and nodded. I was sure it would be a disaster, but maybe it would be better to tell Gideon the truth rather than torture myself. My time in London had proved I was attracted to men. I didn't want casual sex, one-night stands, or quickies in dirty toilets. I wanted a lover, a man who would love me completely and forever. I knew that was probably an impossible ideal. But Barnaby was right, I had to tell Gideon, not because Gideon might say he felt the same, but because I knew I'd never be able to find someone else until I heard Gideon say, "No Marky, I love you, but I cannot be your lover."

'I'll keep some pictures of Danny in here. I'm not banishing him from my life.'

The next day, I packed my rucksack and went downstairs. Barnaby was in the lounge doing *The Guardian* cryptic crossword.

'You off?'

I nodded. 'Gideon, I'll never be able to thank you enough.'

'Oh it was nothing.'

'You probably saved my life.'

'Don't exaggerate.'

'If you hadn't found me on that night, God knows what would have happened.'

He looked away in his usual wonderfully bashful way. 'And thank you too.'

'What for?'

'For making me see sense about Danny.'

I couldn't help hugging him.

'Of course, if you stay here, I promise I'll make you a star.'

I pushed him away. 'Barnaby!'

He had a huge grin. 'A couple of months ago, I couldn't have made a joke like that. I've ordered you a cab.'

'Thanks.'

'And any time you want to come here. Just give me a tinkle. Or even just turn up. Just promise me one thing. Tell Gideon how you feel, right?'

'I'll try.'

The sound of the cab grinding through the gravel cut into the lounge and we went out to the portico.

'Well, good luck.'

We shook hands. I rubbed a tear off my cheek.

'Onions?' he said.

'No, you.' I said and ran to hug him again. 'Thanks for everything. I hope you find your love.'

I slipped into the back seat of the cab. As it pulled away I looked through the back window. As I waved, I cried, as Barnaby waved...he smiled.

21

The day I arrived back in Norwich, I took my trunk to the room I'd been allocated. Once again it was in Waveney Terrace, but this time in a different corridor, or as Gideon would have probably said, "In a different carriage of the derailed train." Instead of orange, the carpet was pale blue, but the design was the same. So the first thing I did was squint at it, and once again hundreds of mini-Hitler silhouettes appeared. After I'd unpacked my trunk, I lay on the bed. I couldn't relax. I wanted to see Gideon. I needed to see him. But would he even speak to me? I knew I had to apologise and explain why I'd left him in Amsterdam, but all I wanted to do was say, "I love you".

I resisted for as long as I could, but In the end, the desire to see him was overwhelming. I caught the bus to Tombland. Previously, I'd always been so excited about seeing him and I'd bound down the Close. But this time my stomach was churning. I could feel blood throbbing in my temples. There was a force dragging me back, telling me I was making a terrible mistake. I sat on a bench outside the Cathedral cafe. I thought about catching the bus back to campus, I could say all I needed to say when we bumped into each other, rather than my turning up on his doorstep, with all the awkwardness that entailed. At least that way I could keep the hope he'd forgive me alive for longer. If I turned up and he slammed the door in my face, I didn't know how I'd survive. I sat on the bench for almost thirty minutes. In the end, I decided I wouldn't be able to sleep or study or do anything until I knew. I took long deep breaths to calm my nerves, then headed towards the house.

When I saw Gideon's front door, I calculated it was fifty-fifty that he'd slam it in my face. The evenly matched calculation, probably the triumph of hope and blind optimism over reality. After I rang the bell, I had the urge to run, and when I heard his footsteps, I thought I was going to vomit.

His deeply tanned skin made his eyes stand out even more than before, and achieved what I'd thought was impossible, making them more piercing, and sexier. I braced, my heart thumping against my chest as I waited for him to slam the door. After five seconds, it was still open. We stood, him staring into me; I avoided his eyes by looking beyond him into the hallway. I realised he wasn't going to say anything until I had, so I gave a half smile and said, 'Hello.'

'What the fuck happened to you?'

I shifted the weight from one foot to the other. I so wanted to say, "I bloody fell in love with you. That's what happened."

Gideon started to close the door.

I looked up. 'Please Gideon, I can explain.'

He folded his arms across his chest. 'I'm all ears.'

I looked into the next garden. Gideon's neighbour was weeding her lawn. 'Please, not here.'

Gideon let out a snort and stood aside. After I'd edged past him, instead of going straight into the lounge as usual, I stopped in the hallway.

'You know where the lounge is.' Gideon closed the front door.

'I wasn't sure—'

'Oh bloody hell, just go in!'

I stepped into the lounge and stood in the middle of the carpet, my hands clasped behind my back.

'Are you going to stand there like a prick in a convent?' He pointed at the sofa.

I perched on the edge of it. I crossed my arms but thought that looked too formal, so I let them hang down by my side, which made me feel like a chimp at a London Zoo tea party, so in the end I lay my hands on my knees. Gideon sat opposite me on a leather armchair, his fingertips tapping in front of his mouth, like a professor waiting to hear a student's excuses.

I wanted to tell him everything. Why I'd left Amsterdam. Why I hadn't said anything. I wanted to tell him all that had happened in London, about Barnaby, and the Pond, about the golden boy, and me discovering my sexuality, but most of all I wanted to tell him I loved him and had always done so. But I had no idea where to start.

'Come on, I haven't got all day.'

There was contempt in his eyes, something I'd never seen before.

'I'm sorry Gideon, I'm truly, truly sorry for leaving you like that. I should've said goodbye.'

'Is that it?'

'No, no.' I let out a deep breath. I looked down at the carpet, then directly at him. "Tell him you love him before it's too late". But there was so much anger in his eyes, there may even have been hate. Telling him I loved him would have been bloody difficult if he'd been in a good mood. If I said it now, I was sure he'd react with venomous homophobic hate.

'Everything in Amsterdam was all too much, the hotel, the brothel. Feather, I had to get away. When I woke up and saw your note. I couldn't stay.'

'But why didn't you just tell me? I would've listened.'

'Would you though?'

'Of course I bloody well would.' Gideon shook his head. 'No, no, this is all lies. You would've gone back to the factory. That's what bloody muggins here, assumed you'd done. When I saw you weren't there I was fucking furious. I was going to dump your precious books in a fucking onion barrel. But that bloody do-gooding commie bastard stopped me.'

'Oh Christ Gideon! I'm so sorry.'

'I did one more shift at that hellhole then scarpered. I didn't even hang around to collect my pay.'

'Where did you go?'

'Flew down to Lisbon for a couple of nights, then drove to the Algarve.'

He would normally have gone into great detail about what he'd done and the girls he'd shagged. Instead, he glared at me, waiting for more explanation.

'I couldn't take any of it. The twelve-hour shifts, the noise in the dorm. The onions. The food. I wasn't getting any revision done. I had to go.'

Gideon shook his head. 'You said nothing about any of that.'

'Then, after what happened to Lance. I panicked, I just, you know.'

'No I don't bloody know.' Gideon stood and poured himself a whisky. 'You're the most level-headed, calmest person on the planet. You wouldn't be so hasty. And besides, you wanted to find out who attacked Lance.'

'Please Gideon.'

'And the only reason we ended up in that sodding place was because you needed to earn enough to clear your debts. So why leave so early?'

I couldn't argue. He was right about all that. I couldn't come up with any more excuses and feared I would tell him the truth, so I changed the subject. 'What did you tell your dad?'

'I lied and told him I worked there for a month. I blamed you, saying you couldn't take it. Luckily, he was happy with that.'

'So it wasn't a complete waste of time.'

'No…no it wasn't.' He drank some more whisky. 'You know, Mark, I thought we could tell each other anything. If you had any problems, you could come to me, and I could do the same. But then you ran off without a word. Yes, abandoning me like that made me furious. But more than that, it bloody hurt me. Really bloody hurt me. And even now you're not telling me the truth.'

'If I could go back and change everything, I would.'

'It's too late Mark. Too bloody late.' He went upstairs.

Was that it? Did he expect me to leave? Without a goodbye? Was he giving me the same treatment I'd given him? After a minute, he came back carrying a box.

'Here.'

When I opened it, I almost collapsed. Inside were all the books I'd left at the factory. 'Jesus Gideon. I…I—'

'I know how important they are to you. I posted them here.'

'Thank you so much.' I felt even more wretched. But the gesture, as well as making me love him even more, made me remember the caring, thoughtful Gideon. And I remembered Barnaby saying if I told him the truth, he might even admit he loved me. And saving my books after I'd angered him so much, was surely a sign that that might not be such a ridiculous idea. So now was my chance, I continued. 'Gideon, I need to tell you—'

'It being Finals year, I guess you'll be too busy reading those to want to meet.'

He spoke with the monotone of a judge passing sentence. He was saying this is final.

'Yes, yes, I've got a lot of studying to do.' I tapped the box lid.

'You were about to say?'

'Nothing, just that. Study. Study. Study.'

'You don't want me distracting you.'

'No, no of course not.'

'And I'll be bloody studying too.'

'Yes, of course. Great.' I stared at the box, not wanting him to see the tears welling in my eyes. 'Oh, you'll be wanting this.' I reached into my pocket and took out the key to his house.

'Thanks.' He said with the same unfeeling monotone. 'Good luck with your studies, not that you'll need it.'

I nodded. And with my voice trembling said, 'Thanks.'

He led me into the hallway and held open the front door.

'Goodbye Gideon,'

'Take care Mark.'

As I walked away, I resisted the urge to turn to see if he was waiting. I stared straight ahead and told myself he waited for me to wave.

22

Socially, my final year was a repeat of my first. With no Gideon to drag me around bars and discos, I spent my time either studying in the library or my room. I never saw Gideon on campus, so assumed he must have been partying.

The last term was a blur. It started with four weeks of revision when I became almost robotic. I'd get up at six every day, go for a walk around the lake, then back in my room I'd have one bowl of cornflakes and two cups of tea. Then I'd go to the library and revise until seven. After dinner, I'd go back to my room where I'd revise until I went to sleep at nine. Those four weeks were followed by two and a half weeks of exams. After breakfast on exam days, I'd sit in The Square, just a few yards from the exam hall, obsessively flicking through my revision notes, inscribed on dozens of index cards, until we were called into the exam.

I didn't see Gideon until the day of my last exam. He sauntered into the hall wearing his preferred disco clothes, slate grey chinos and a bright red polo shirt. The clothes and the florid love bite on his neck made it obvious he'd come straight from his, or someone else's bed. He had an air of peeved insouciance as if irritated that his morning had been interrupted by this onerous obligation, an obligation he, therefore, treated with indifference bordering on contempt. When he saw me, he nodded and smiled. I was worried his presence would be a distraction, but as soon as I turned over the exam paper and read the questions, I forgot he was there.

After the exam was over, he came to me. 'Where are

you going to celebrate?'

'Celebrate?'

'Wasn't that your last exam?'

I was surprised he came over and also touched that he knew it was my final paper.

'I'm going to a Labour Party rally.'

'Bloody hell Mark! You should get pissed and get laid.'

Thatcher had called the General Election for 9 June. As soon as she did so, I'd been tempted to go back to the Socialist Workers to help with the campaign. But I didn't want to be distracted from my revision, so didn't go. However, I'd noticed that Michael Foot, the leader of the Labour Party, was due to address a rally in Norwich on 21 May, which was the day of my last exam. So I'd been counting the days until I could celebrate by attending the rally.

'I'll enjoy it.' I couldn't help smiling when I saw the incredulous look on Gideon's face.

'Bloody hell Marky, only you could go and celebrate finishing your degree by going to a sodding political rally.'

He called me Marky! I wasn't sure whether it had been a mistake, or whether it was a sign he was forgiving me.

'And Labour are going to be demolished.'

Gideon was right, all the polls were saying Thatcher was going to win easily. Even so, I wanted to attend the rally.

Talking to Gideon, I felt alive for the first time in months. It excited, but also alarmed me. I don't know whether it was my exuberance at having just finished my exams, or whether I was desperate to spend more time with him but I said, 'You should come, you might learn something.' I was sure he'd say no, bursting to get back to whichever girl's bed he'd fallen out of.

He looked into my eyes, then with a faint smile said, 'You know what Marky, I think I might just join you.'

'What?'

'Why not? I'll revel in mocking the opposition.'

'You really want to come?'

'Yes.'

Gideon would never have attended a Michael Foot speech by choice, so I hoped his agreeing to come with me was his roundabout way of saying, "Let's be friends again". I was elated. The last few months without him had been grim.

'It's in St Andrew's Hall at 3 pm.'

'Excellent. We can go to Jarrolds for lunch, then wander around in time to throw tomatoes at old Worzel Gummidge.'

'Are you sure? After what I did?'

'Amsterdam and all that?'

'Yes.'

'Marky, I've hated the last few months, not seeing you and not being able to go out with you. I've missed you.'

'Really?'

'And haven't got laid nearly as much.'

I pointed at the love bite. 'But you haven't been a eunuch.'

He touched his neck. 'I'm still bloody angry with you. But Marky, I think we're better together.'

I was so relieved, I wanted to hug him. Instead, I said, 'I promise I'll never do anything like it again.'

'You better not. So I'll go home, get clean, we can meet at Jarrolds, oneish?'

I nodded.

The restaurant was on the top floor. We were lucky to get a table by the window overlooking the market. After he'd sat down, Gideon gazed out over the multicoloured canvas roofs of the market stalls. 'I'm going to miss little old Norwich.'

'Me too. But I won't miss the Siberian winters.'

'We had a lot of fun here, didn't we?'

I nodded. I was happy Gideon said we. It showed he still remembered and had fond memories of the times we'd shared. 'A Fine City, as they say. You'll go back to London?'

'Yep. That little excursion to Holland was enough to show Daddy that I'm, "Not a complete time-wasting wanker" as he put it. I'm not sure what he wants me to do. Probably clean the bogs in one of his supermarkets. What about you?'

'No idea. I've been concentrating on my studies, I haven't looked beyond my exams. I guess I'll go back to Bristol to see the family then, I don't know.'

'But after you get your First, you'll have your pick.'

'Stop it Gideon.'

'Why? You're the brainiest, most hardworking person I've ever met.'

'You'll jinx it.'

'Jinx it! You know, for a Marxist you're remarkably superstitious. You're going to walk a First, bloody walk it. If you don't, I'll be asking questions.'

Gideon's belief touched me. 'If I fail, it'll be my own fault.'

'I wish you'd learn to believe in yourself.' He squeezed my hand.

I felt his power and for a moment I did believe in myself, but the touch of his skin also sent waves of desire through me, so I pulled my hand away. 'Can we stop talking about it until it happens?'

Gideon ran the tips of his thumb and forefinger across his lips.

When the waitress came over, I ordered a Full English breakfast.

'Breakfast Marky! How can you have wine with brekkie? Come on, choose something else. Be daring. You've just finished your exams.'

'I think I can manage wine with a Full English.'

Gideon grinned. 'Interesting combination. Fair enough.'

Gideon drank most of the wine. I had a few sips, which kept him happy. After we'd finished, we walked the short distance to St Andrew's Hall. We were the first to arrive. As we sat in seats near the back, a steward approached us.

'Can you do me a favour and sit near the front?'

'Why?' said Gideon.

'We're worried about a poor turnout and it looking bad on the news.'

I could see Gideon was about to say something like, "You expect me to help you Marxists." So I quickly said. 'Of course, come on Gideon.'

'If I get caught on camera here, that'll ruin my chances of ever becoming PM.'

I laughed.

'Why are you laughing?'

'You're serious?'

'Of course.'

The first time I'd ever seen Gideon, at the student council election, I assumed he'd stood for a laugh, to get a bit of attention or probably to get laid. His comment about becoming PM was the first time he'd said anything about entering politics, I was sure he was joking, but the look on his face suggested maybe not.

As it turned out the steward had panicked unnecessarily. The hall was packed. Every seat taken, every aisle filled. People even had to sit on the stage behind the podium. When Micheal Foot entered, his long white hair flowing, sunbeams burst through the windows. The sound of cheering and stamping was like thunder. He gave a speech so full of passion, as I was listening to it, I believed Labour could win. And as the crowd shuffled out of the hall, there were whispers of miracles and a knife-edge result. When we got to my bus stop I said, 'Wasn't that great?'

'It was a magnificent speech. There's no denying, but you're still going to lose.'

'How can you say that?'

Gideon looked at me. 'Come on Marky, unilateral nuclear disarmament, renationalisation, they're vote losers. You know that.'

I was surprised Gideon knew anything at all about the Labour Party manifesto. 'But they're all the right things to do.'

'You rabid Socialists have no idea about the British people.'

'What? Of course we do.'

'Do you think the granny pruning her roses, the miner drinking in the Dog and Duck, the farmer harvesting in Somerset, or the fisherman hauling his nets in the North Sea, are all going to wake up on June 9th and vote for revolution?'

'It's not revolution, it's fairness.'

'We Brits love our dogs, our gardens, our football and our kids. Usually in that order. Not revolution.'

I'd never heard Gideon speak so passionately about anything other than sex. He'd always been a Maggie fanatic, but that was uncharacteristically eloquent. Had he been inspired by Michael Foot's oratory or was it something he'd thought about for a long time but only now voiced? Seeing this side of him unsettled me, but also worryingly, made him even more attractive. Deep down, I knew he was right. There just wasn't enough desire for revolution, but I'd never heard anyone put the lack of political fervour in Britain so vividly as he just had.

'Do you want to come to Ritzy's tonight?'

Aaah...I was relieved to see the old Gideon back. I would've loved to go with him, but feared I might get carried away, and drink too much and tell him I loved him. 'No thanks, I...I—'

'Come on Marky, you don't have any studying to do.'

'I know, I know. But I'm going canvassing.' I was sure Gideon could tell I was lying, but fortunately my bus arrived. I jumped aboard and shouted from the doorway. 'Thanks for coming with me. And good luck with the rest of your exams.'

Gideon nodded. He looked disappointed. 'I'd wish you luck too, but you don't need it.'

The next two weeks were agony. Waiting for the results both of the election and my exams. I tried to forget about my results by concentrating on the election, but when it was clear, the Tories were still way ahead in the polls; I tried to take my mind off the election by thinking about my results. Then when that made me so anxious I felt sick, I thought about the election again. And so it went on, a vicious circle of worry. I knew the one person I should call to break me out of this circle was Gideon. But I refused to succumb.

The exam results were due to come out the day after the election. Helga and Bryony invited me to their squat to watch the election results. I didn't want to go but thought it would take my mind off my exams, so I went. Helga had bought a small black-and-white TV from a car boot sale. And one comrade who'd been a TV engineer had rigged a makeshift aerial.

We sat on bean bags that stank of nicotine and sipped lukewarm Barleycup. Most of the comrades smoked weed. I was tempted but, despite my anxieties, I resisted. The TV reception was fuzzy and snowy and the sound crackly, but it wasn't bad enough to hide the truth - Labour was heading for a huge defeat. Helga, Bryony and the other SWP comrades got more depressed as, one by one, their candidates barely registered more than a couple of hundred votes. I'd intended to spend the whole night at the squat, but when the early results were so bad for Labour, and Helga and friends became drunker and more stoned, I snuck away.

Before I went back to my room, I sat by the lake. I feared the election result was a bad omen for my results. With Maggie in power for another term, things were only going to get worse. More unemployment, more cuts. It filled me with gloom. Who was going to employ anyone with a Third Class degree in Philosophy, especially one with a Sociology minor?

As I was heading back to my room, I saw three shadowy figures. I walked towards them. Two were drinking, the other was digging. My mind was so preoccupied with exams, my first assumption was they must have kidnapped a marker to torture them into giving good grades, then accidentally killed him and were now burying the body.

One of them noticed me. 'Andy, stop digging!' he shouted.

'What are you doing?'

'None of your fucking business.' The students giggled.

'Hey Guy, no need to be rude, he's just asking. We're burying a biscuit tin.'

'A what?'

'We're going to come back in ten years and dig it up.'

'We've put momentoes and letters inside.'

'Like on Blue Peter.'

'Bloody idiots.' I turned away. There was less chance of the tin surviving than their friendship. And with Maggie and Reagan in charge, the chances were everything was going to be blown up anyway.

I spent the night tossing and turning. The results were due to be pinned to the noticeboard outside The Registry at 11 am, which seemed an aeon away. At seven, I filled a bowl with cornflakes, took one mouthful, then dumped the rest. I switched on the radio, but when I heard Maggie saying how grateful she was to the British people, I switched it off. The newspapers would be full of Tory Triumphalism. So I lay on my bunk, wishing the time away.

I prepared for the worst by planning what I'd do when I got a Third. I'd go back to London and get some dreary job. I knew Barnaby would let me stay if I needed to. That was something. Perhaps I'd become a Dilly boy. Wear leather trousers, after all, there must be a market for an escort with a cute leather-clad arse, even if the owner of said arse only had a Third Class Philosophy degree with a Sociology minor.

I slotted *War* into the cassette player. As Bono sang "Sunday Bloody Sunday" I strode up and down the narrow space between my bed and my desk. The pleasure I got from stamping on hundreds of Hitler silhouettes distracted me for a couple of minutes.

I needed to get out of my room. So I went and sat on the concrete steps around The Square. I found a shady spot; I leaned back on my hands and watched people go by.

I couldn't believe three years had passed. I looked across to the Student's Union building, where I'd bumped into

Gideon. How different my time at UEA would have been had I not bumped into him. Duller certainly. When I looked back, that had been the most significant moment. He'd shown me a different lifestyle. A wealthy lifestyle, one I realised I deplored and yet envied at the same time. If it hadn't been for him, would I have realised I was gay? Probably not, maybe I would've done later. I wondered if I could go back, knowing what I now knew. Would I have avoided bumping into him that night? As I was thinking of the answer, I heard a familiar voice.

'Marky, you look like a bloody corpse.'

Gideon was wearing a white linen suit and pink tie as if he were a British Ambassador who was about to soft soap the corrupt movers and shakers in some tropical banana republic.

'I'm so bloody nervous.'

'Why, for God's sake?' Gideon lowered himself next to me. 'You'll get a First, no problem.'

'Please Gideon, don't jinx it.'

He laughed and squeezed my shoulder. 'You're such a worrier.'

I took a deep breath and looked at my watch. Thirty minutes to go. 'Why this outfit?'

Gideon shrugged. 'I might as well make an impression, my grade won't. Well, only in a bad way.'

'You don't know that.'

'Oh, I do. I should never have been here. I only got in because Daddy funded some bursary.'

'Really? You kept that quiet.'

'Some PhD in Development Studies or some time-wasting crap like that.'

As we sat, more people gathered. There was a mood of tense, nervous excitement.

'They should open the bar early. They'd make a fortune,' said Gideon.

'I couldn't drink anything.' I looked at my watch.

Gideon jabbed me in the ribs. 'It's time.'

'It's early. Jesus. I can't go.'

'Yes, you can.'

'I don't want to know. I think I should just go home to Bristol.'

Gideon crouched in front of me and gripped my shoulders. 'Marky, calm down. You're going to do brilliantly.'

For a moment, I wanted to harangue him for making me waste my second year by dragging me out partying. But I stopped myself. 'Can you go and look for me? And if it's bad, just kill me.'

'Don't be silly. All you need to do is look at some noticeboard.'

'Honestly Gideon, I don't think I can even walk. Please, go for me.'

'Okay Marky. But you're being unnecessarily bloody pessimistic.'

As I watched him saunter along the concrete walkway to The Registry, I wished I'd never applied to university. I should have got a job straight from school. If I'd done that I'd have three years of experience, not to mention salary, maybe even been promoted. I wouldn't have wasted three years of my life.

After five minutes, I saw him. He was moving more quickly, almost skipping. Must be a good sign, but perhaps he was happy about his own result.

'Please don't tell me. I don't want to know.'

'Shut up Marky, you got a bloody First.'

I looked into his eyes, trying to see the twinkle, the sparkle he had when he was pulling someone's leg. 'You're kidding.'

'I wouldn't joke about something like this. You got a bloody First Marky, a bloody First! You creep.'

'No...no...no.'

'Go and look for yourself.'

'If you're playing with me.'

'Look, if you don't go, I'll drag you there by your bloody bollocks.'

I shuffled along the walkway. Gideon followed a step

behind. I was sure even if he wasn't joking, he must have read the notice incorrectly, seen someone else's result, and thought it was mine. There was a gaggle in front of the noticeboard. As I approached, my stomach was spinning. At first, it was difficult to see, as so many heads were in the way. There were gasps and sighs as people found their results, some tears. When I got to the front, I saw my name, Mark Ludgrove, under the list of First Class Honours. I stood transfixed.

'You see. You clever wanker,' said Gideon.

I turned and saw him smiling. Before I knew it, he'd wrapped his arms around my waist and lifted me off the ground. As I looked down at him grinning and looking so happy, his lips so inviting, I leaned forward and kissed them. Only for a second, then pulled away.

'Sorry Gideon, I don't know what the fuck happened.'

Gideon looked shocked, but not angry. 'That's okay. You're excited, I get it.' He lowered me to the ground.

I'd got a First. A bloody First. All that work had paid off. But even though I was ecstatic about the result, the memory of the touch of his lips meant I could still feel them. I wanted to kiss him again. But knew I never would, or could. Then I realised I had no idea what grade Gideon had got.

'Sorry Gideon. What did you get?'

'A Third of course.'

'Shit. I'm sorry.'

'Hey, I didn't work. I didn't deserve anything better. Don't let it spoil your day.'

'But...but—'

'The important thing is my little Marky has got a bloody First. Tonight we're going to get plastered. I've ordered extra champagne.'

'Champagne? But you got a Third.'

'I knew you'd get a First. And now the important thing is you can do whatever you sodding well want.'

He was right. The result gave me so many more options. My life suddenly had so many possibilities. But at that moment, all I wanted to do was kiss him again.

23

We went back to The Square; the bar had opened, so we bought some beers and we drank them sprawled on the concrete. My embarrassment mounting as Gideon told anyone who came within range, "This is Mark, my best mate, he got a bloody First". My attempts to stop him were fruitless, so I decided to go to my room. On the way I checked the noticeboard to make sure I hadn't misread it. It was the same. Confirmed. I'd got a First.

I went to a phone booth.

'Hello Mum.'

'Sweetheart, how are you?'

'I'm great, just great. We got our results today.'

'Oh goodness, let me sit down.'

'I got a First!'

'Is that good?'

I laughed. 'Yes it is Mum. I couldn't have done any better.'

'Oh, that's wonderful. Wonderful. HE GOT A FIRST.'

I could hear my dad in the background. 'And what's that when it's at home?'

'HE SAYS HE COULDN'T HAVE DONE ANY BETTER.'

'WELL DONE SON.'

'When are you coming home?'

'Soon Mum, soon.'

When I hung up, I leaned against the side of the booth and blinked as tears formed in my eyes. I smiled at how little they knew about university degrees. I changed my mind about going to my room and went back to The Square. Gideon was still there, chatting to a couple of girls.

'Here he is, Mark, the philosophy genius.'

'Gideon!' I smiled as the girls glanced at me before they turned their gaze back to Gideon.

'Anyway, girls, me and the Plato of Norwich are going to celebrate. So see you around.' Gideon finished his beer and then put his arm around my shoulder. And whispered. 'We won't, of course. We'll be gone soon.'

'Don't you want to have fun with them?' I said as we strode away.

'Nah! Not today. Today is just you, me and Monsieur Bollinger.'

The effects of the beer, and only having eaten a mouthful of cornflakes, were making me woozy. 'I don't think I could manage champagne.'

'Come on Marky, for once in your life forget you're a bloody Marxist and let your hair down.'

'I'm hungry.'

He frowned as if my words had reminded him he had a stomach. 'Actually, I'm pretty bloody starving, the champers came in the hamper we can—'

He must have noticed my unenthusiastic look, because he continued,

'No, better idea. Fish and chips, hamper and champagne.'

That sounded much better, so I nodded.

After we'd bought the fish and chips, we sat eating in his kitchen.

'Are you sure you don't want some bubbly?'

'Maybe later.'

I poured a glass of water and sat opposite him. I didn't need champagne. It had been a wonderful day. My incredible exam results then spending the day with Gideon. After what had happened in the summer, I would never have dared dream the day could be like this. I was joyful just being with him and knowing we were friends. I'd even kissed him! And though I was sad it would be the only time I did so. At least I could treasure that moment.

'Marky, you know what we should do tonight?'

'Sleep?'

'Don't be sodding silly. Ritzy's...find us a couple of pert secretaries.'

Of course, a black cloud had to roll into the blue sky. I didn't want to be surrounded by Oranjeboom-drinking girls in cheap make-up. And I definitely didn't want to be Gideon's wingman.

'It's been a tiring day.'

'We'll have a snooze, then go. Come on, put what you learnt in Amsterdam to good use.'

Now there was thunder. The one thing I'd learnt in Amsterdam was I wanted to sleep with him. I certainly didn't want to feign interest in a girl. 'But my clothes are filthy.'

'I can find you something upstairs. Come on, we must celebrate your result.'

'This is celebration enough.'

'Don't be silly. Don't we owe it to the Norwich girls to give them a last chance to get the benefit of our gorgeous bodies?'

'You go and reward them. I'll stay here.'

'Marky, no! You've been in your room all year.'

I nodded. 'I had to study.'

'And you got the result you richly deserved, but now's the time to let your hair down, before you forget all you learnt in Amsterdam.'

'Another time.'

'No, no. Come on.' He grabbed my shoulder and tried to pull me out of the chair.

'I'm bloody tired.'

'You were tired when we went to the brothel, look what happened there.' He grinned.

The combination of the frustration at not being able to have him, and my the arising because he was ignoring what I was saying, erupted. I pushed his hand away and jumped out of the chair. 'Shut the fuck up about the bloody brothel.'

He staggered back against the stove and frowned, mystified by my reaction. 'But It was just a visit to a bloody brothel.'

As well as being angry at him, I was angry with myself for reacting the way I had. It would only make him curious.

'What's the matter Marky? I've never seen you like this.'

'I'm fine.'

'You're acting like you crapped your degree. Is it because I kept boasting about your result?'

I shook my head and murmured, 'Nothing happened.'

'What did you say?'

I looked up at him. 'In the brothel, nothing happened.'

'What do you mean, nothing happened?'

'I didn't do anything, with Feather.'

'No Marky. No way.' He squinted as if he was trying to recall. 'No, no, I remember you said—'

'I didn't say anything, you assumed.'

'Shit! You're kidding?'

I shook my head. 'Nothing bloody happened with Feather.'

'But…but…' He sat back in the chair and stared at the table for a few seconds. He looked up at me. 'Shit, is that why you left?'

I shrugged.

'Why didn't you tell me?'

'I was too embarrassed.'

'But..but……don't you like black girls? I could've got you a white one.'

'Skin colour has nothing to do with it.'

'But she was stunning.'

'Yep, she was, and very patient. She tried everything.'

'Jesus Marky! It must have been first-time nerves.'

'I guess.'

He finished the champagne in his glass, then poured himself another. When he'd drunk half of it, he nodded firmly. 'So that settles it, we have to go to Ritzy's.'

'No, Gideon!'

'You have to lose your cherry tonight.'

The prospect of going to Ritzy's and having to pretend to be interested in some secretary, whilst Gideon egged me on was hellish. 'No.'

'We'll rest, get cleaned up, then go. Oh wow! First class degree and first shag. A double First. Get it?'

It was obvious he wasn't going to give up. The thought of faking it in Ritzy's with him beside me, when all I wanted to do was take him into a dark corner and snog him, made me nauseous. I just wanted him to bloody listen to me for once. So I thumped the table. 'Fucking hell Gideon! Why don't you fucking listen? I'm not going to fucking Ritzy's.'

He looked like he'd just seen Maggie Thatcher streaking around Red Square, holding the Soviet flag. 'Marky!'

I sat back down, closed my eyes, and took a long breath. 'I…I'm not a virgin.'

'But you just said—'

'Life happens without you.'

'Yes, sorry.'

'I lost my cherry this summer in London.'

He smiled. 'Marky! That's great.'

He looked as if he was going to come over and hug me.

'Shut up! And bloody listen. I lost my cherry…' I closed my eyes again. 'To…to a man.'

I was expecting him to tell me to get out, instead; he was silent. When I opened my eyes. He was staring at me, his jaw dropped as if Maggie was now shagging Brezhnev.

He nodded and bit his lips. 'Of course, of course, bloody hell.'

'I'm sorry. I swear I didn't know myself until…'

Gideon frowned. 'I knew it…I knew it when you didn't seem bothered about girls, maybe in the back of my mind—'

'You're not disgusted?'

'Good God. Why should I be? I'm just so bloody sorry for dragging you around Ritzy's all those nights. And shit, the brothel. That must've been bloody torture.' He gave his chin an upper cut. 'Gideon, you bloody idiot.'

'I did keep it well hidden.'

'That's why you left Amsterdam, of course.'

I was happy for him to carry on thinking that.

'Are you…dating him? Boyfriends?'

'No, no, oh no.'

'Just a quickie?'

I nodded. I yearned to hug him for being so understanding, but knew I couldn't.

'Bloody well done Marky, I hope the lucky guy was really sexy.'

'An Adonis.'

'Wow! And treated you well.'

'A real gent.'

'Excellent. Now you have to have champagne?'

'Why?'

'To celebrate of course. Bloody hell, what a day.'

He handed me a glass. 'To my brilliant, handsome, loyal, gay, and no longer virginal friend.'

I wanted to laugh and sob at the same time. But instead knocked back the champagne.

His eyes widened. 'Hey Marky, you know what we should do?'

'What?'

'Go to a gay bar.'

'No Gideon.'

'Yes, yes. Tonight we'll find strapping young farm boy for you.'

'I don't even know if there's a gay bar here.'

'Even little old Norwich must have one.'

'No Gideon.'

'Look, you've come with me to so many straight places,

now it's my turn to return the favour.'

'But there's bound to be people we know.'

'Who bloody cares?'

I feared in the dark and lustful atmosphere I'd be overcome and kiss him again. I'd gotten away with it when I kissed him earlier. I wouldn't be so lucky the next time. And the way he was being so supportive made me adore him even more. Part of me wished he'd been a bigot. It would've made it easier to hate him. But the idea of going to a gay bar and have people look at us and think we were a couple excited me.

'So let's get clean and introduce you to the fine boys of this fine city.'

We rested, showered, then changed. Gideon lent me a bright pink polo shirt.

'That's the sort of thing gays wear, isn't it?'

I shrugged.

As we walked through Tombland, we passed the queue to Ritzy's. I thought it would be safer to go somewhere familiar rather than go into the gay unknown with Gideon. 'Let's go there.'

'No way Marky. Tonight is your night.'

'But we don't even know where to go.'

'Leave that to me.' Gideon hailed a taxi. 'Hello my friend, twenty pounds if you take us to the nearest gay pub.'

'Fuck off you poofters.' The driver sped away.

'Come on, let's forget about this.'

'Patience Marky, someone'll help.'

There were two more abusive taxi drivers, then the next one smiled. 'Jump in lads, it isn't far.'

It took less than a minute to reach The Caribbean. When Gideon handed him the fare, the driver said. 'No charge. You lads have a good night, yeah?'

'Oh we will won't we Marky?' Gideon put his arm around my shoulders and led me to the door. 'You see, not everyone in the world's a bigot.'

'Are you sure you want to do this?'

'Absolutely.' He grabbed my hand and pulled me inside.

Every head turned. Gideon wasn't put off in any way, even though this time, most of the looks were from middle-aged balding men rather than the young women he was used to impressing. I wanted to disappear.

He strode to the bar. 'A Babycham for Martha and I'll have Guinness.'

'Gideon!'

'Trisha, babe it's Trisha.'

I leaned towards him and whispered, 'What the hell are you doing?'

'Just having a bit of fun.' He winked at an overweight guy clad in double denim. 'You must be a sugar beet farmer.'

The man turned away and talked to his friend. I took Gideon's elbow and pulled him over to a table.

'Do you have to be so over the top? Just act normal.'

'I'm trying to put these old guys off. Did you see how they stared at us?'

'That's because we're new. Let's go. This was a mistake.'

Gideon closed his eyes briefly. 'Sorry, I'll behave. I just don't want any of these creeps pawing you.' He looked around. 'Now where's that strapping Norfolk farm boy?'

I realised more than ever I didn't want to spend the night with a farmer or any strapping young man; no matter how sexy. I wanted to be alone with Gideon.

'Anyway, I need the bog.' Gideon stood, twirled, then minced over to the toilet. I shook my head.

A few seconds later, someone came over to me.

'Sorry, I'm not interested,' I said.

'You've got tickets on yourself. I'm not interested either.'

He had brown hair and spoke with a posher accent than I'd expected.

He leaned towards me and whispered. 'How well do you know that guy?'

'None of your business.'

'He's a fucking bastard.'
'You don't even know him.'
'He's Gideon Grieve.'

I'd never seen the guy on campus. And was pretty sure he wasn't a friend of Gideon's. But somehow he knew Gideon's name. 'Oh, I see, sorry.'

'We were at school together.'

'Oh wow! You should say hello.'

'No fucking way! And you should be careful.' He picked up a beer mat, took out a pen and wrote a number on it. 'If you want to find out what he's really like, give me a call.' He handed me the mat and then headed to the exit, followed by his friends.

I was going to throw the mat away. No doubt the guy harboured some petty grudge from school. And was trying to get revenge by undermining what he assumed was my relationship with Gideon. But I was so curious to find out what Gideon had been like at school; he never talked much about it, so I slid the beer mat into my pocket. A couple of minutes later, Gideon returned.

'Any joy?' he said.

24

I wondered if I should say something to Gideon, something like, "The strangest thing, whilst you were away someone came over and said he knew you." Or more provocatively, "Someone just told me you're a fucking bastard." I decided not to say anything. It was too late in the evening to get into anything heavy, and I needed to think.

'Can we go?' I said.

'But we've only just got here.'

'It's not great.'

Gideon looked around, his face a series of over-the-top horrified looks as his gaze passed from one customer to another. 'Looking at this lot, I'm bloody grateful I'm straight.'

'Gideon!'

'Sorry, but look at them. Fat, greasy, old. There's no one good enough for you here. How and where did you meet the Adonis in London?'

I didn't want to admit I'd met him at the Pond and then had sex in a dirty toilet. I was sure he wouldn't mock me, but I suppose as exhilarating as that moment had been, I was ashamed. 'It was at a party.'

'Party! Unlike you.'

'The guy I was staying with threw one, and I just happened to be there.' I hated lying to him, so said, 'Gideon, I appreciate you coming here with me, but let's go. It's been one hell of a day.'

He nodded. 'You're bloody right about that.'

'I keep thinking someone's going to tap me on the

shoulder and say, "Sorry, we made a mistake."'

Gideon leaned towards me. 'Shut up. Stop talking like that. You worked for it, you bloody deserve it. Nobody's going to take it away from you.'

I smiled. The guy who gave me the number had to be wrong. There was no way Gideon was a bastard. 'Let's get out of here.'

We walked up Prince of Wales Road towards Tombland. Taxis were pulling up outside Ritzy's and ferrying young men and women away. There was a group of girls sitting on the steps between the statues of Samson and Hercules. When they saw us, one of them shouted, 'Hello boys!'

'It isn't too late to pick up a girl,' I said.

'Not tonight.'

'Are you sure?'

Gideon nodded. 'You know what Marky. This is the end of my Norwich life. Part of me wants to go over there, give a bit of chat, and splash some cash. And I know in a few minutes, I'd be snogging at least one of those girls.' He put his arm around my shoulder. 'But, you know, all the girls I've shagged, there must have been dozens—'

'Hundreds more like.'

'And where are they now? None of them are here with me, unlike you. You've always been here.'

'Apart from when I abandoned you in Holland.'

'Yes, apart from that. So I think for my last night here, it should be just the two of us.' He squeezed my shoulder. 'So sod those silly girls. Let's go home.'

We carried on past Ritzy's, through the Erpingham Gate and into the Cathedral Close. The Close was a different world, quiet, the air stiller, colder. The cathedral spire was lit, shining against the blue-black of the night sky. There was nobody about.

As we walked side by side, I felt Gideon's fingers brush against mine. Thinking I'd veered too close to him, I moved away. He moved closer and touched them again. I pressed my hand against my leg so my fingers no longer touched his. He touched me again. Was it just an accident? Was he unsteady because he'd drunk so much throughout the day? But we'd walked side-by-side hundreds of times before, and there had been times when he'd been more drunk than this, never had anything like this happened. I held my arm rigid, not wanting to lose touch with his fingers. As we went under an arch, Gideon's hand wrapped around my middle and forefingers. He pushed me against the wall and pressed his lips against mine.

I pulled away. 'Hey, what are you doing?'

'I'm kissing you. What do you think I'm bloody doing?'

'But..but—'

'Shut up.' Gideon locked his arms around me, then kissed me again. This time, I opened my mouth and let his tongue probe into me. I wrapped my arms around his neck, swirled my tongue around his, and moaned as his body pressed into me. I got hard. Not wanting to repeat what happened at the Pond, I pulled away.

'Hey, what's the matter?'

'I'm about to shoot in my pants.'

He laughed. 'Wow! I must be even sexier than I thought.'

He grabbed my hand and dragged me to his house. As soon as we got inside, we started kissing again. He pulled my shirt off, then undid my belt. I thought I should be doing more, but I didn't want to do anything that might make him stop, so I just let him carry on. When I was naked, I thought he would strip too, but he dragged me to the sofa, turned me around, put his hand on my neck, then pushed me forward. He spat onto my arsehole, then unzipped his trousers. Two seconds later, I gasped as I felt the most excruciating pain as his dick pressed into me.

'Owww!'

I gripped the sofa. The pain was so intense, like a fiery sword deep inside me, I wanted him to stop. But I also wanted him to stab deeper. I waited to hear the same sounds and groans I'd heard through the wall in the brothel. But he was silent, concentrating, thrusting. Beads of sweat fell on my back. I started to play with my dick as he thrust faster and deeper.

He let out a loud 'Yeees! Thank fuck'. He withdrew immediately.

I reached back, yearning to touch him, but he strode into the kitchen. I fell forward onto the sofa, still hard, desperate to touch him. When he came back into the lounge, I wanted him to kiss and stroke me.

He said, 'You should wash.'

I stopped stroking. 'Yes, of course.' And went upstairs for a shower.

When I came back, he was asleep on the sofa. I found two blankets. I lay one over him, the other I wrapped around myself, then lay on the mat.

When I woke, the first thing I noticed was the throbbing pain in my arsehole. Although it was excruciating, I loved it: it was proof it hadn't been a dream. Gideon had been inside me.

Why had he done it? I rated the explanations in order from the least likely. One, he'd realised he wanted me more than any girl. After all, he'd said, "You're the only one who's always been there". Two. He'd known all along that I wanted him and decided to reward me, to give me the perfect end to a perfect day. Three. He'd been so pissed, he hadn't known what he was doing. But there had been other nights like that, nights when we'd shared a bed, but nothing like it had happened. Four, and sadly, I feared the most likely explanation. He needed release, and I was the nearest human orifice. He'd probably done the same countless times at boarding school. After all, there had been no groans of pleasure like at the brothel, just frowning silence until the triumphant yell at the end, like a soldier impaling an enemy, rather than a lover climaxing inside his beloved.

It should have saddened me. But the sensation, shock and sheer joy of being the only person in the world for him for those few seconds. Made me happy. Gideon was dead to the world. I wanted to climb onto the sofa and hold him. To kiss him. But instead, I stared at his body, his sleeping, breathing wonderful body and stretched my trembling fingertips towards it. Just before I touched his silky skin I pulled my hand away.

What would happen when he woke? Would we pretend it never happened? Talk about it. Laugh and say it was just one crazy mistake. I was sure Gideon would never want to do it again. So as I sat and looked at the muscles on his washboard stomach flex as he breathed, I knew when he woke, he wouldn't let me touch him, or ask me to lie with him. He wouldn't kiss me, he might even despise me. I couldn't take that. I didn't want to see his shame and be the object of his contempt. I wanted my last memories to be of him sleeping as he was now, and of him inside me. I picked my clothes up off the floor. After I dressed, I wrote a note. There was so much I could have written, but in the end, all I wrote was

'Thanks for everything. And I mean everything.'

I took one last look at him and smiled as tears formed in my eyes. As I walked towards the front door, I felt something in my pocket. At first, I didn't know what it was. When I saw it was the beer mat with the phone number, I was about to rip it up and throw it away, but I slid it back into my pocket and pulled open the door.

25

The next morning, I got up early. Whilst eating breakfast in the canteen, I stared at the spot on The Square where Gideon and I had sat waiting for the results. If there was ever a day I wanted to relive, it would be yesterday. From being convinced I was going to fail, to getting a First, then to end the day kissing and shagging Gideon. If Gideon had been affectionate, it would have been perfect.

He was due to move to London today; I assumed he'd be too busy to contact me even if he wanted to, but just in case he came to my room before he left, I decided to spend the day in the library. Although so much of me yearned to see him, I knew if we met, he'd say last night had been a terrible mistake. I couldn't bear to hear that. I wanted to always tell myself he'd wanted it as much as I did.

Instead of going to the Philosophy section, I went upstairs to Literature, picked a copy of *War and Peace* from the shelves then found a desk as far from the stairs as possible: one which was also hidden behind shelves. I settled down as comfortably as I could, given the twinge in my arse, and read until lunchtime. For lunch, I got a baguette from the canteen and ate it by the lake. Then went back to the library and stayed there until it closed.

When I got to my room, the first thing I did was look at the Adolf Hitler patterned carpet, searching for a note. Even though a meeting with Gideon would have been awkward and probably heartbreaking, I'd spent the day harbouring the tiniest hope he'd bang on my door and beg me to run away with him. So

I was disappointed not to find anything on the floor. I couldn't help thinking Gideon was probably back in London, looking for girls to expunge the memory of what he'd done with me.

The next morning, the sky was big and grey, and the air filled with the sort of drizzle I knew would last for days. I fell back onto my bed. There was nothing to get up for, no lectures, no seminars, no essays, no exams, and, of course, no Gideon. I sighed and picked *War and Peace* up off the floor, but only read half a page before putting it back down. It took until noon for me to drag myself out of bed.

Without thinking, I caught the bus into the city. As I walked past Jarrolds, I sighed as I remembered going there with Gideon; I did the same when I passed St Andrew's Hall. I knew where I was heading, and I knew I shouldn't, but there seemed little point in doing anything else. I shuffled down the shiny wet cobbles of Elm Hill, the soft drizzle spattering against my face. When I reached Tombland, I looked up. A haze of drizzle obscured the spire of the cathedral. Before I went through the Erpingham Gate, I stopped and asked myself, "What am I doing?"

I didn't know. I just knew there was nothing else to do. I crossed into The Close, then headed towards Gideon's house. I remembered how nervous I'd been the first time I'd visited. Today I was the same. I didn't know why, as I knew he wouldn't be there. The house looked the same, the door, the windows, the blue roses, but there was an aura that told me Gideon wasn't there. I opened the gate and walked the short path to the front door. I leaned towards it. I couldn't hear anything. I reached for the bell and gave it a feeble pull. Silence. I bit my lip and pulled again. Longer this time. Silence. That was it, confirmation. He'd gone.

I retraced my steps and caught the bus back to campus.

I lay on my bed, reflecting on that pointless yet vital journey. I was empty and without purpose. My studies were over and Gideon had gone. The man I loved would never love me, and no other man could ever match him. Was I gay or was I just

Giddy? A good word to describe my love for that one ineffable man.

I sighed. For the first time in my life, I had to decide my future. Where was I going to live? What was I going to do? Was I ever going to love again? Until now, academically everything had been decided, school then university. Now I had to look for a job, but I had no idea what I wanted to do. I never had. That was why I'd chosen philosophy rather than something vocational like law or economics. But the last three years had given me neither direction nor inspiration, if anything, I was more perplexed than ever. Should I do what I'd done last summer and live like Kenny and the guys at the factory, travel around Europe going from one menial job to another, living a hand-to-mouth, directionless life? Maybe. Or should I move to the anonymity of London and explore gay life? But my experiences of that life had ultimately turned out to be disappointing. And no man would, or could, ever compete with Gideon. Gideon, being unattainable, made everything else meaningless.

In the end, I decided to go to Bristol, where I could be morose and still get pampered and made to feel important.

Before heading home, I went for one last look in the pigeonhole in the Philosophy Department, in case Gideon had left me a note.

As I was rifling through, Professor Scott-Martin came out of his office.

'Mark, good to see you. Congratulations.'

'Thank you, Russell.'

'Not a surprise, surely.'

I gave a wry smile as I remembered the state I'd been in before I got my results. 'I was so nervous, I had to send a friend to look at the noticeboard.'

'Really? Have you got a moment?' Russell beckoned me. 'Please, come into my office. Tea or coffee?' He switched on his kettle.

'Coffee please.'

He picked up two mugs and put a spoonful of coffee in

each. Then lifted a pile of manila folders off a chair. 'Please, take a seat.'

'Thank you.' I looked at the shelves crammed with books and periodicals. On the top shelf were small busts of Descartes, Leibniz and Spinoza.

'Aaah…admiring my collection of miniature Rationalists?'

'Yes.'

'Dainty little pieces, aren't they? Milk?'

'Yes, and one sugar.'

'Coming up.'

When the kettle had boiled, he poured water into the mugs, then gave them both a vigorous stir. He handed one mug to me and then sat behind his desk. He lifted the glasses hanging around his neck to his eyes and then peered at me. 'So, what are your plans?'

'Plans?'

'About your future.'

I gave another wry smile.

'Why the smile?'

'This morning I was asking myself the same question.'

'And what was your conclusion?'

'Onions and grapes look the most likely.'

'I don't understand.'

'I was thinking about drifting around Europe cleaning onions and picking grapes.'

'Ahh…summer jobs.'

'Only I was thinking of stretching it beyond the summer. Indefinitely actually.'

'Oh dear. Feelings of post-degree angst?'

'I guess. I'd never thought beyond my exams. And now —'

'You're at a bit of a loss.'

I nodded. He didn't know half the story of why I felt so empty. 'The worry I was going to mess up my degree gave me purpose. I didn't want to fail.'

Russell put his coffee on his desk and leaned forward. 'Damn it Mark! There was never any chance of that. You sailed through.'

'Really?'

'Your set of papers was one of the finest I've come across in all my time here. Clear, lucid, and thought-provoking. Excellent. That's why I wanted to speak to you.'

'Okay.'

'Spend the summer doing whatever you do with onions and grapes, but next year come back here and do your Masters.'

Although I'd always known there was a possibility of further study, I'd never allowed myself to think about it seriously. Firstly, because I wasn't sure I was suitable and secondly, I didn't want to jinx my exams.

'I'll bend over backwards to keep you here.'

'I hadn't —'

'If money is an issue, we can sort out the funding, even get you to assist in some seminars.'

Although accepting the offer wouldn't solve my big problem, doing a Masters would mean I could throw myself into studying again. When I was immersed in study was the only time I didn't think about Gideon. And perhaps it would get rid of the emptiness I'd been feeling all day, and the despondency I knew would only get worse. I wasn't sure how living in Norwich and staying at the university would be. There were so many places where I had memories of Gideon. But maybe it would be easier and less painful to relive them here, where they'd happened, rather than in some soulless, distant office.

'Wouldn't staying here be better than slaving for some company or joining the Civil Service?'

'Yes, yes, of course.'

'If you need more time—'

'I don't need time. Thank you Russell. I accept.'

'Excellent. We'll sort out the details later.' He reached across his desk. 'Welcome aboard.'

26

After spending a curative summer in Bristol, I returned to Norwich. I found a bedsit on the Unthank Road, a twenty-minute walk from the university. On my first evening back, I caught the smell of chocolate and couldn't resist going into the city. The closer I got to the centre, the stronger the aroma of melted chocolate became. So when I reached Chapelfield Gardens, I sat on a bench and savoured the sweet air for thirty minutes. After that, I carried on through the market, down Elm Hill, and into Tombland. Samson and Hercules looked even sterner and more disapproving than ever. I hesitated before going through The Erpingham Gate. I knew where I was heading. Was it a good idea? Even to just look at Gideon's empty house? Over the summer, I'd barely thought of him. Did I want to revisit where I'd had some wonderful but also distressing times, and risk becoming obsessed with him again? Despite the danger, I was impelled to go.

The curtains were drawn, the letterbox jammed with flyers, a corner of the house's flint facade was damp, the result of heavy rain and a blocked gutter. The garden, without its blue blaze of summer roses, looked dull, commonplace. The roses' once vibrant blue petals were scattered over the lawn, decaying. I stood, waiting to see if my yearning for Gideon returned. I remembered the times we'd shared and took a sharp intake of breath as I recalled that last night. I still couldn't believe what had happened. Why had he done that? It wasn't because he loved me or even desired me. I knew that. I would only find out if I spoke to him. Which I had no intention of doing. Ultimately, that night had left me brokenhearted, but the summer of repose had helped me recover. Now I was merely confused and bitter. I did feel nostalgic for those times, but the yearning? That didn't return. When I noticed a neighbour's curtain twitch, I left before they called the police.

The Caribbean wasn't far away, and I presumed would be open. I decided to go and have a look. After all; I was going to be in Norwich for at least another year. I should give the pub a longer test than I had on that night with Gideon.

I ordered a beer and sat in the darkest corner. "Who's That Girl?" was playing on the jukebox. Every time Annie Lennox sang the chorus, a group of four guys in jeans and floral-patterned shirts shrieked along with her and pointed at each other. I shook my head. This still wasn't me, sitting in a noisy smoke-filled bar surrounded by camp gays. I resolved that during Freshers' Week, I would join Gaysoc. They, at least, were students. I'd have more in common with them. I shook my head as I remembered how I used to think they were pretending to be gay in order to get sex, because they were too skinny and ugly to attract a girl. How stupid and nasty I'd been back then.

The door opened and someone who looked familiar came in. It took me a few seconds to recognise the guy who'd given me the beer mat.

'Shit.'

I pressed my back against the wall, hoping the darkness would hide me. I didn't want to explain why I hadn't called him. But I was also curious to find out what he knew about Gideon, so didn't leave either. He was alone and after he'd bought a drink; he looked around the bar, then sat at a table close to mine. When our eyes met, we looked at each other for a few seconds. At first, I wasn't sure whether he'd recognised me, but then a panicked look crossed his face.

'Where is he?'
'Who?'
'Grieve.'
'He's in London. I think so anyway.'

He looked relieved. 'Not hell? Pity.'

'Wow! What made you hate him?'

'May I?' He pointed at one of the stools around my table.

When I'd first seen him on that night, I'd guessed we were about the same age. Now I thought he was at least two years younger than me. When he looked around, his eyes were like that of a cornered dog, both fearful and vicious.

'Are you sure he's not here?'

He gulped down half his pint, then slammed the glass on the table so hard he spilt most of what remained of his beer. He stared into the mid-distance, lost in thought, almost as if he'd forgotten I was there, his legs pressed together and his skinny torso hunched forward.

'Are you okay?'

'Yes, yes.' He bowed his head.

I watched the top of it as it bobbed in front of me. His hands were shaking, and I thought I could hear sniffs. I wanted to make my excuses and go; I didn't want to get mixed up in whatever petty drama he was involved in. 'You just seem—'

He lifted his head, looked from side to side, then whispered. 'He raped me, fucking raped me.'

I remembered what had happened on my last night with Gideon, how he'd been rough and cold. It could have been regarded as rape by someone who didn't know Gideon and hadn't been yearning to go to bed with him for years. 'Are you sure?'

'Of course I'm fucking sure.'

'He likes rough sex.'

He looked up, his eyes full of contempt. 'I was twelve years old.'

'Jesus!'

'When I saw him here that night, I wanted to kill him.'

If the guy had been twelve, then Gideon must have been fifteen or sixteen. I found it hard to believe Gideon could do that. He liked sex; I knew that, but to rape someone, no, he could never do that. But the guy was clearly distressed. He gazed at the spilt beer and absentmindedly trailed a forefinger through it. Then, in a barely audible whisper, he said, 'Can we go outside?'

'I guess.'

We went and sat in a bus shelter. Going outside turned out to be a mistake. Once away from prying eyes, he burst into tears. I'd never had an adult sob so helplessly, even Barnaby didn't cry as much when he remembered Danny. I had no idea how to react. In the end, I tentatively squeezed his forearm.

'You don't have to tell me about it if you don't want to.' I said, hoping it would make him stop talking and sobbing.

'I've never told anyone about it.'

My first thought was, "Then why tell me?" I didn't want to have to handle this. But I was also curious to find out what Gideon had done.

He looked up and rubbed tears from his cheek. 'When I was twelve, the school put on a play. Me and my friend Vincent were chosen to play girls because we were young and "pretty". We had to wear tennis whites, you know, like women at Wimbledon, short skirts and blouses.'

I nodded.

'I loved it. I was always a bit of a sissy and enjoyed wearing a skirt. Poor Vincent hated it. On the last night...' He sniffed. 'On the last night, we were told there was going to be a cast party in one of the older boys' dorms. "Come in your costumes".

His voice shook. He closed his eyes and took two quick breaths. 'So we did, but...but as soon as we stepped inside, we knew there was something wrong. There were four older boys, none of them had been in the play.'

'Gideon?'

He nodded. 'They offered us beer. Vincent wanted to leave, but Grieve said, "Stay and have drinks with us". They were all much bigger. They...they...pushed me...I'm sorry I...I can't.' His body started shaking as he sobbed again. After thirty seconds, he got control of himself. 'They all took their turn.'

'Shit.'

'Before that night, I didn't even know about sex.'

'Why didn't you say anything?'

'They took pictures and told us if we blabbed, the photos would be passed around.'

'But Gideon likes girls.'

'He's a sex addict and doesn't care who he fucks.'

That last night, Gideon had stripped me and fucked me. And then ignored me. But I'd wanted it more than anything. It wasn't rape, but if Gideon was desperate, would he rape someone?

'They ordered us to go back whenever they wanted—'

'And you went?'

He nodded. 'They had the pictures.'

'Jesus. Why didn't you tell the teachers?'

'It was boarding school. The teachers turn a blind eye.'

I shook my head. The Gideon I knew had never done anything like that. None of the girls had ever complained. But I knew he had a huge sexual appetite. Then I remembered the programme I'd seen in Gideon's house. 'Shit!'

'What?'

'What was Vincent's surname?'

'DuBoise.'

'Bloody hell.'

'He killed himself in Lisbon.'

'Jesus!'

The guy fell forward, sobbing. I leaned towards him and held him as affectionately as I could, his body trembling in my arms.

I tried to reconcile what I'd just heard with the friend who'd looked after me, supported me when I came out. Who'd come with me to Holland and worked in a foul onion factory. The friend who chased girls like a truffle hunting terrier. I couldn't reconcile any of it.

'I don't know what to say.'

'Now you know what your friend is like.'

'I still find it...I'm sorry, I'm not questioning what you're saying, I just find it so hard to believe.'

'Did he ever... do it to you?'

'No. Never. Not like that.'

'You were lucky.'

'Did you ever go to the police?'

'Too scared. I wanted to forget about it. And I had until... until I saw him here. I should've killed the fucking bastard.'

I was relieved I could say something to help. 'Don't worry about seeing him again, he won't come back here.'

We sat for another five minutes in silence until the air became too cold.

'I must go,' he said.

'Will you be okay?'

'No, I don't think I ever will be.'

The only things I could think of to say was, 'I'm so sorry.' And, 'What's your name?'

'Chris,' he said.

As I watched him walk away, I wondered if Gideon appeared in front of me now, smiled, kissed me, and dragged me to bed. Would I ask him if what Chris said was true? I told myself I would. But would I? When he smiled and gazed at me with those penetrating eyes? Would I still question him then? I feared I wouldn't. I didn't want to put that to the test, ever. He was in London. I was in Norwich. He moved in circles far richer than I was ever likely to move in. If I stayed in Norwich and studied and found someone to love here, I was sure my memories of him would fade. A luxury Chris would never enjoy.

27

After my Masters, Professor Scott-Martin offered me a chance to do a PhD. I was tempted, but after sixteen years of studying, I wanted to do something else. I'd had a few articles published in *Tribune*, the Socialist newspaper, and found I enjoyed writing short pieces more than long Philosophical dissertations. I got a job at the *Eastern Daily Press*. At first, I didn't mind having to cover mundane events like flower shows and the weddings of wealthy farmers, writing about tangible events rather than abstract and abstruse Philosophical ideas was refreshing. But by 1986, I found it impossible to write engagingly about yet another church fete.

I'd balanced the tedium of the work by having fun with guys I met at The Caribbean, but I'd grown tired of seeing the same old faces. So I'd taken to travelling to London for weekends. I went to the Nada to Vada once, but only stayed for five minutes. I found the bars around Earl's Court, more to my liking. One Saturday I went to The Pond. I was amazed to see the golden boy was there, behaving exactly as he had four years earlier. As I was lying on the pontoon, he smiled at me. But I could tell by the lustful look in his eyes it wasn't because he remembered me, but because he wanted a shag. I didn't oblige.

Once, when I was on the train back to Norwich, I had a sense of dread at the prospect of going back to work. I also realised I spent most of my free time alone. In Norwich, there was nowhere like The Pond. Somewhere I could relax, sunbathe, ogle. A place that held the promise of casual, no-strings sex. I needed a new challenge and a new city. I decided to look for a job in London. So when I saw an advert for a reporter's job at the *Daily Mirror*, I applied for it and got it.

I did worry about bumping into Gideon, but we still moved in very different circles and even if our paths did cross, it had been five years. A lot of used condoms had swirled around my toilet bowl since that night. I was no longer the virginal ingénue and was sure I could resist his charms. Especially after what Chris had told me.

I moved just in time to cover the 1987 general election. I spent much of the campaign travelling around London and the South East, covering the constituencies the senior reporters didn't want to cover. I loved every second. Not only did I find the work stimulating, but U2 had released *The Joshua Tree*, I played it on my Walkman or in my car the whole time I was travelling.

Although Thatcher was re-elected, I was much happier than I'd been after the '83 election. This time the Labour Party campaign was much stronger, and whereas in '83, I'd wondered whether there would ever be another Labour Government, in '87 there was a glimmer of hope.

Two days after the election, I went to see U2 at Wembley Stadium. It was the first time I'd seen them live since the night I'd clashed heads with Gideon. Although I loved the concert, I was so far from the stage, I couldn't help wishing I was once again close enough to touch the hem of Bono's jeans. And as much as I tried not to, I wondered if Gideon was somewhere in the vast crowd. I recalled that night and remembered what had followed. I was angry at myself, especially during "With or Without You" for thinking the words could apply to me. None of my relationships had lasted more than two months. I always told my partners my job made it difficult for me to sustain a relationship. I maintained that attitude even when I was covering earth-shattering events such as the Wymondham Flower Show or The Cathedral of St John the Baptist Christmas Fayre. But I knew if someone came along who affected me the way Gideon had, I would've done anything to ensure the relationship survived. Nobody had come within a million light years of matching him.

Then, in the summer of '88, Gideon came back into my life.

I was working in the office when I saw a press release.

Gideon Grieve selected as Conservative Party candidate in the Chiswick by-election

I had to read the press notice three times. Gideon standing for Parliament! I went to find out about the constituency. It was a safe Tory seat. So bloody hell! Gideon was going to be an MP. Before he was thirty! I could only conclude "Daddy's" money must have had something to do with his selection. I remembered what he'd said at the Michael Foot rally, about not wanting to be caught on camera, in case it harmed his chances of becoming Prime Minister. At the time I'd thought he was joking, but had politics been his plan, even then? Perhaps I should've guessed from the passionate argument he made about Britain being conservative. But still. Bloody hell!

The next day I was called into Dennis, my editor's office.

'A little turd told me you're bosom buddies with Gideon Grieve.'

'That's an exaggeration. We were at university together. I haven't spoken to him in five almost six years.'

'But you were close?'

I knew where this was heading. He wanted me to write a background piece, perhaps offer some juicy gossip, but I didn't want to have to think about Gideon. Even though I was confident he wouldn't affect me as he used to, he'd always been lurking like a phantom in the depths of my mind. I didn't want that phantom to loom to the front.

'He was doing drama, and I was doing philosophy, so we had no cause to meet.'

Dennis, ever the hard-bitten hack, could tell I was

lying, and gave the telltale sign he did whenever he knew he was being lied to. He raised his left eyebrow. 'But you were there together?'

'Yes.'

'That makes you fucking soul mates compared to the wankers out there.' He waved his half-smoked cigarette towards the news floor. 'I want you to cover the by-election.'

Shit! That was even worse than a one-off article. If I had to follow Gideon around Chiswick, I'd be expected to ask questions, perhaps even interview him. 'But—'

'No buts. You'll be able to give insight during what is going to be a bloody tedious campaign.'

'But wouldn't it be better if someone more experienced covered it?'

'Sonny, I'm giving you an opportunity here.'

'I appreciate that.'

'Look, unless Grieve goes to the middle of Chiswick High Street, and has a shit in Margaret Thatcher's handbag, he's going to romp home. It's a fucking foregone conclusion, but we have to cover it. I want your insights so our readers don't drop dead from sheer fucking boredom.'

'If it's so boring, why are we covering it?'

'Are you trying to do my fucking job, son?'

'No, of course not.'

I knew if I didn't do as he said, Dennis would fire me or make my life so hellish I'd resign. So I had to accept.

At Gideon's first press conference, most of the Fleet Street and local London papers were there, so I hid in the back row. He'd put on weight, his cheekbones once so prominent were now hidden by flesh and his jawline was not as pronounced. His hair was shorter, held in place by gel. But the eyes were still as intense and penetrating as ever. There was a moment when he saw me. He stared at me for a second, no flicker or hint of a smile, before his gaze moved. I was angry with myself that even after five years I was hurt by his indifference, and because my heart started thumping and my breaths became short.

I didn't ask any questions. I just made notes and wrote my article.

'Fucking waste of paper!' said Dennis. 'I could've got more from Who's fucking Who. Did you ask a question?'

'No, sir.'

'Why not?'

'I...I—'

'Look, I can't print this. Get some interesting copy or get out.'

'Yes, sir.'

At the next press conference, fewer reporters turned up. I sat in the second row. When Gideon saw me, I saw a flicker of a smile cross his lips, followed by a look of near panic. I assumed he was remembering all the embarrassing incidents I could ask about. I kept raising my hand, but it was obvious he was avoiding letting me pose a question. At the end of the press conference, as Gideon and his minder were leaving, I stood up.

'Excuse me, I have a question—'

Gideon tried to leave, but his minder said, 'Yes, please go ahead.'

'Thank you.' I couldn't help noticing the flicker of panic in Gideon's eyes. There were so many questions I could ask.

Have any of the many girls you seduced got pregnant?

Do you still frequent Amsterdam brothels?

Do you still rape twelve-year-old boys?

I paused, enjoying the look of anxiety on Gideon's face. But when he stared at me, I lost my nerve. I was back where I'd been years earlier, yearning for him, desperate to kiss him. The other reporters were getting impatient, waiting for me to speak. Gideon's stare became more intense, with just a hint of a smile. I lost my nerve so in the end the only question I could come up with was, 'Can you explain, why you, a young and untested candidate who has no connections to Chiswick, has been parachuted in to fight this by-election?'

There was a look of relief on Gideon's face. No doubt a question he was ready and prepared for. 'Even though I was the youngest candidate, the selection committee could also tell I was the ablest. And if I'm fortunate to win, I fully intend to devote all my attention to the constituents of Chiswick.' Gideon gave the same grin he had whenever he'd left a disco with a girl.

I was angry. He'd won, yet again.

At the start of the last week of the campaign, Dennis called me into his office.

'Son, when I gave you this assignment I hoped for gossip about Grieve. Sultry nights of drugs and debauchery, stories from brokenhearted, deflowered young virgins. But there's been nothing.'

The only brokenhearted, deflowered young virgin's story I could tell was mine.

'You must have some fucking juicy gossip of your time as students.'

'Not really. He slept with more girls than most. He went to Amsterdam once, but other than that.'

'Drugs? Cheating? He's as thick as two short planks. How did he get his fucking degree?'

'He didn't care enough to cheat. I really didn't know him that well.'

This time I got two raised eyebrows. Two raised eyebrows meant, I know you're lying and I'm going to fire you. 'I'm fucking disappointed.'

The next day, I got a phone call.

'Is that Mark Ludgrove?'

'Yes, who is this?'

'I have a story about Gideon Grieve.'

I'd received similar calls during the campaign, but I'd ignored them as they were usually from cranks or rival campaigns offering lies. I was about to hang up when the caller said,

'Do you recognise my voice?'

I paused for a few seconds. 'No, sorry, who are you?'

'Please, can we meet?'

The caller wanted to meet at Haggerston Park in

Hackney. Which I thought was an unusual place to meet. Most contacts usually chose pubs. I had nothing to lose and needed a decent story to save my job, so agreed to meet.

After I'd wandered around Haggerston Park tennis courts six times, I decided, as the caller was over half an hour late, he wasn't coming. As I was walking to the gate, I heard,

'Hello Mark.'

I turned around and saw a black man on a bench. I walked towards him. He was hunched and wrapped in a long coat and scarf, which was odd as it was a warm evening. His face was wizened like that of an alcoholic sixty-year-old street sleeper. I wracked my brain trying to remember who it could be, but couldn't think of any contacts who looked like that. My picture had never been printed in the paper so I couldn't understand how he knew me.

'You don't remember me, do you?'

'Sorry, no, in my job I meet a lot of people.'

'I'm Lance.'

I stared at him. The only Lance I knew was from the factory, but he would still be in his twenties, so it couldn't be the old guy sitting on the bench. 'Sorry, I still—'

'From Holland.'

Then I recognised the nervous grin and the shy eyes. 'Lance, shit!. Sorry, of course. How are you?' I could've bitten my tongue off. Of course he wasn't well.

'I've been better.' He leaned over and sniffed his armpit. 'Finally managed to get rid of the stink of onions.'

I laughed, a nervous, embarrassed laugh.

Lance tapped the bench. 'Come. Sit.'

I sat next to him. 'Jesus Lance, it's great to see you. After what?'

'Six years.'

'That's right, six years.' The only question I wanted to ask was, "What happened to you?" but I didn't want to upset him by making it obvious I'd noticed how sick he looked.

'The answer to your question is AIDS. I have AIDS.'

'Fucking hell, Lance. I'm so—'

'Sorry? I know. Everyone is.'

Not wanting to stare at him, I looked over at the tennis courts. I was trying to work out why he'd asked to meet. He couldn't know anything about Gideon, so he must want a favour or money. I was both angry with him for doing so and ashamed because I wanted to get away from him as quickly as I could.

'I saw your name in the *Mirror*, you're doing very well.'

'Yes, I like it.' I thought about telling him I was going to lose my job, hoping it would dissuade him from asking for money. But how desperate must he be to have to ask for help from someone he'd met only briefly six years before? Perhaps I could spare a tenner.

'I've been thinking of calling you for weeks.'

'You should've done. If you need help, I can... I have contacts—'

'What do you think I am? I don't want your help.'

'But—.'

'I have a story about Gideon Grieve.'

I was dubious. What could he say about Gideon? At the factory, he and Gideon had barely spoken to each other.

'You remember I was attacked?'

'How could I ever forget? Did that Jimmy guy get punished?'

'I don't know. I never went back.'

'Oh Christ, yes. I always regretted leaving you in the lurch. It was terrible what happened to you, terrible. I hope Kenny got that Nazi.'

Lance lifted his head and looked straight at me. 'Mark, it wasn't Jimmy who attacked me.'

'What? But I remember he was calling you, that, that word. He hated blacks.'

'I know, but it wasn't him.'

'Then who was it?'

He bit his lower lip with the only two teeth left in his upper jaw.

'It was your pal, Gideon.'

'What? No! Not Gideon. Never.'

Lance nodded.

I leaned back on the bench, trying to recall that night. I'd been in the canteen, Gideon had been in his bunk, hadn't he? 'But I remember you said you didn't know who'd attacked you because it was too dark.'

'I lied.'

'What? Why?'

'If I said anything, it would only have caused more trouble. I just wanted to go home. I've regretted it every day since.'

'But I don't understand why would Gideon want to beat you up. I know he's a bloody Tory, but he isn't a racist. Not like that.'

'He tried to..to …you know—'

'He tried to what?'

'He tried to fuck me.'

'What? No way. He loves pussy.' I don't know why I said that, almost as if it was my instinct to defend him even after what Chris had told me, and what Gideon had done to me.

'I knew you wouldn't believe me.' Lance's eyes moistened. 'That night I couldn't sleep so I went for a walk. I don't know if he followed me or if he was waiting, but by the barrels…he jumped on me and…and…I fought him, but he was much bigger. He punched me and kicked me.'

I could see from the intense pain in Lance's eyes he wasn't making this up. He'd experienced it, every single punch, every single kick.

'I managed to get away from him. I wanted to run away, instead I hid until I knew he'd gone back.'

'Then you came into the canteen.'

'At first I thought he'd sent you to get me.'

'Jesus Lance, I would never—'

'I know, I know. You helped me. I was terrified, so when Dutch John offered to take me to the hospital, I was so happy. If he hadn't taken me, I would've gone to the ferry.'

'Jesus, Lance I'm so sorry. Did Gideon give you…you know—'

'AIDS? You can say it, it won't kill you. No, he never got that far.'

'I just wish you'd said something at the time.'

'What would you have done?'

What would I have done? I could tell myself I would have dropped Gideon, never spoken to him again, and taken Lance to the police. But would I? Back then? Would I have believed Gideon or a black boy I barely knew?

My thoughts turned to the present. Now I knew of two victims. With Lance and Chris's stories, they'd be corroborating each other. I was sure I still had Chris's number somewhere. I could research the DuBoise boy's suicide. I'd have a killer story for Dennis just before the vote. It would help Lance, save my job, and in destroying Gideon, end my obsession with him.

'So what are you going to do about it?'

'I'll tell your story just as you've told it.'

'Really?'

'Oh yes! My editor has been desperate to get dirt on Gideon. This'll destroy him.'

Lance gave a rasping cough, then smiled. 'Thank you Mark.' He reached out and touched my hand. I wanted to pull it away but managed to stop myself. 'I always knew you were one of the good guys.' He got up from the bench. 'I'm so tired. Thank you for coming.'

'Can I give you a lift somewhere?'

'No, I'm only down the road in the Mildmay Hospital. Goodbye Mark, and thank you.'

I watched as he shuffled along the path. Once he'd disappeared, I wrote most of the article as I sat on the bench. The factory, the onions, the unemployed boys who went there every summer. I wrote about Gideon being there and what he'd done to Lance. I didn't say I'd been at the factory too. All I needed was to speak to Chris, get his quotes, and do some research into Vincent

DuBoise. Then voilà! I'd saved my job.

'This is more like it son, juicy, juicy gossip. Grieve, a pedo bum-boy rapist. Wow! Who'd have fucking guessed? In the ranking of sexually deviant behaviour, that's pretty much a full house.' Dennis's cigarette flickered up and down as he read my piece, scattering ash over the paper.

'So you're going to publish it today, before the election?'

He leaned back in his chair, my story in his hand. 'No, sorry, son.'

'But after today it'll be too late.'

'Sorry, we can't publish it, today, tomorrow, not next fucking century.'

'But it's a great story. And I have two sources. It'll…it'll —.'

'You're right, it's a fucking brilliant story.'

'So why?'

'We have two victims. One is, actually, they probably both are, fucking bumboys. One also happens to be black and oh, just for good measure, is fucking dying of AIDS.'

'All the more reason—'

'We're a family paper, not fucking *Gay Times*.'

'But the other boy, the one who killed himself.'

'Corpses can't speak.'

'So we're just going to let Grieve get away with it and after tomorrow he'll be an MP.'

'Yep. He may go on to be fucking Prime Minister, but there's no way I'm running this story.' He scrunched my copy and tossed it across the desk. 'But good work, fucking good work.'

I left his office and, for a few seconds; I wanted to walk out, resign, and take my story somewhere else. But I knew it would be a waste of time and if I did, it would kill my Fleet Street career. So I sat at my desk. Fuming and feeling like shit. Gideon was winning and getting away with it again. I picked up the phone dozens of times, intending to call Lance to tell him and apologise, but every time I chickened out.

That night I got pissed. The next day I rang in sick. There was no way I wanted to cover Gideon's triumph. Dennis was surprisingly understanding. 'Have a rest son, you've earned it.' Perhaps it was his guilt.

The day after the result was declared, I managed to summon up the courage to call the Mildmay. I asked to speak to Lance.

'I'm very sorry, sir, but Lance passed away last night.'

I held the receiver, tears of anger, regret and self-loathing streaming down my cheeks.

Later, when I switched on the TV, the news was covering Gideon's arrival at the Houses of Parliament. I was about to switch off, but as he was shown being welcomed by Margaret Thatcher, for a moment the camera caught them so it looked like Gideon was caressing Margaret Thatcher's left breast.

It was funny, but I couldn't laugh.

Gideon had dominated my life from the moment I saw him struggling with the Margaret Thatcher cut-out. Even when I wasn't with him, he affected me. And there he was, a rapist being welcomed into Parliament by the Prime Minister. She looked like the proud headmistress awarding a prize to her brilliant new head boy. As she flicked dandruff off the shoulder of his sky-blue suit, he grinned; every bit the handsome, clean-cut, up-and-coming young Tory politician.

He stared into the camera. I remembered when I first looked into his eyes, I thought they were kind. Had I chosen to see them like that, or had Gideon made me see them that way? Probably the former, because even through the screen and knowing what I now knew about him, they still looked kind. I feared if he stepped out of the screen, smiled, winked and held out his hand, despite knowing the pain he'd caused, and the people he'd destroyed, I'd take it, and follow him wherever he went, and do whatever he wanted.

How had I let anyone, least of all Gideon dominate me? As I took off my jacket, the article dropped to the floor. I picked it up and was about to rip it to pieces. I stopped, smoothed the paper, then slid it into a folder. I had to hope that one day I'd be able to show the world what Gideon was really like, and maybe then I'd be able to break free from his control.

Without that hope, I was nothing but his plaything.

BOOKS BY THIS AUTHOR

Come Back I Love You

Philip moved to Bangkok for a new start. To help him forget the past, he wanted as much sex and fun with as many guys as possible. Chai's a student who is also running away. Will they find and save each other? Or will Philip heed the fortune teller's warning and leave Bangkok?

Set against the backdrop of one of Thailand's most tumultuous periods, this gay love story explores the power of human connection and the strength of the human spirit to overcome adversity. With themes of love, loss, and sacrifice, this novel will keep readers on the edge until the end.

The Gala Gala's Glare

The first time Oliver saw a gala-gala, the blue-headed lizard common in Southern Africa, he was terrified. It was perched in a tree, staring at him as if it knew all his secrets or maybe even his future. The first time he saw Yianni he was waving at him from his desk, smiling, and begging the headmistress to put Oliver on the empty desk next to him. Oliver and Yianni became best friends, soul mates. Susan's arrival would change everything.

Printed in Great Britain
by Amazon

47660880R00139